GW00995222

Demon Unleashed is a work of fiction. Names, characters, places, and incidents are the products of the author's imagination and are used fictitiously. Any resemblance to actual events, locales, or persons, living or dead, is entirely coincidental.

Published in the United States

Cover design: Damonza
Author Photo: © Marti Corn Photography

Printed in the United States of America

Books by Tina Folsom

Samson's Lovely Mortal (Scanguards Vampires, Book 1)
Amaury's Hellion (Scanguards Vampires, Book 2)
Gabriel's Mate (Scanguards Vampires, Book 3)
Yvette's Haven (Scanguards Vampires, Book 4)
Zane's Redemption (Scanguards Vampires, Book 5)
Quinn's Undying Rose (Scanguards Vampires, Book 6)
Oliver's Hunger (Scanguards Vampires, Book 7)
Thomas's Choice (Scanguards Vampires, Book 8)
Silent Bite (Scanguards Vampires, Book 8 1/2)
Cain's Identity (Scanguards Vampires, Book 9)
Luther's Return (Scanguards Vampires, Book 10)
Blake's Pursuit (Scanguards Vampires, Book 11)
Fateful Reunion (Scanguards Vampires, Book 11 1/2)
John's Yearning (Scanguards Vampires, Book 12)

Lover Uncloaked (Stealth Guardians, Book 1)
Master Unchained (Stealth Guardians, Book 2)
Warrior Unraveled (Stealth Guardians, Book 3)
Guardian Undone (Stealth Guardians, Book 4)
Immortal Unveiled (Stealth Guardians, Book 5)
Protector Unmatched (Stealth Guardians, Book 6)
Demon Unleashed (Stealth Guardians, Book 7)

A Touch of Greek (Out of Olympus, Book 1)
A Scent of Greek (Out of Olympus, Book 2)
A Taste of Greek (Out of Olympus, Book 3)
A Hush of Greek (Out of Olympus, Book 4)

Teasing (The Hamptons Bachelor Club, Book 1)
Enticing (The Hamptons Bachelor Club, Book 2)
Beguiling (The Hamptons Bachelor Club, Book 3)
Scorching (The Hamptons Bachelor Club, Book 4)
Alluring (The Hamptons Bachelor Club, Book 5)
Sizzling (The Hamptons Bachelor Club, Book 6)

DEMON UNLEASHED

STEALTH GUARDIANS #7

TINA FOLSOM

1

Enya drew from the straw and savored the feeling of the refreshing cocktail cooling her heated body, until the glass was empty but for the ice cubes that hadn't had a chance to melt. She'd needed this. Lately, life at the compound she shared with her fellow Stealth Guardians wasn't the same. All five males were now bonded to their respective mates, and physical affection was being displayed everywhere and at all hours. It was positively sickening—particularly since she had nobody.

Not that she wanted anybody. She did fine on her own. Perfectly fine. She didn't want a mate, didn't want to be shackled to an overbearing man who would probably curtail her freedom under the guise of wanting to protect her. Bullshit! No way was she going to tie herself to anybody. Sure, she occasionally had an itch to scratch, but that was what one-night stands were for. And bars such as the one she was currently visiting. The bartender, Drew, knew her, though she'd never divulged more than her first name and her preferred drink—a Pimm's with ginger ale.

"How about another one?"

The question didn't come from Drew behind the bar, but from somebody who'd taken a seat on one of the barstools close to her. Enya turned her head a few inches to the right and scrutinized the man. It took her only ten seconds to assess him. By the looks of it, the guy spent way too much time on his physical appearance. His hair was sleek, his clothes Euro-trash fashionable, his fingernails better manicured than her own. And judging by the glassy look in his eyes, he was inebriated. Most likely, he wouldn't even be able to get it up. And she was in no mood to coax a wilting cock into action.

"I'll get my own, thanks," she said, and turned her head back to the bartender. "Drew?" She pointed to her glass, and he nodded.

"Hey, come on, lady," the pretty boy continued. He motioned to the other customers sitting at the tables. "It's not like there's anybody else here who's even remotely in your league."

She cast him a sideways look. "If that's meant to be a compliment, you're not doing it right."

"Huh?"

Enya glanced at Drew, who was busy mixing her drink.

"Come on, you know what kind of bar this is. No woman comes in here to drink by herself." He motioned to her outfit. "Particularly not in that kind of getup."

Enya felt annoyance crawl up her spine. She knew she was wearing provocative clothing: a black bustier, a short leather skirt of the same color, and high heels. Her leather jacket hung on a hook underneath the bar. "Maybe I'm waiting for someone."

"You've found him." Pretty boy grinned and made a welcoming gesture with his arms.

"Trust me, you look nothing like him." The kind of man she was looking for tonight was somebody a little less polished, a little more rugged, and way less civilized. She was in the mood for wild sex and not the tepid action this half-drunk would provide.

From the corner of her eye, she saw Drew reach for her empty glass and at the same time set the new drink in front of her. She turned back to him, a *thank you* already on her lips, when the guy next to her put his hand on her forearm. She whirled her face to him, ready to slap him. She didn't get the chance.

"Take your hand off my girlfriend's arm, or I'll break your wrist." The deep, menacing voice coming from behind her sent a tantalizing shiver down her spine, and fear into the drunk's eyes. As if burned, he withdrew his hand.

"Maybe you should leave," her rescuer added.

The drunk fumbled for something in his pocket—his wallet, as it turned out—and tossed a few bills on the bar. Even faster, he jumped off the barstool and hurried toward the door. Slowly, Enya started to turn toward the man whose voice had sent that delicious sensation through her body. If a voice could make her come, it was this one. But she didn't want to get her hopes up. She'd heard many a radio DJ's voice and imagined him to be a hot hunk, only to be disappointed when she saw a picture.

"Thank you, though it wasn't necessary. I could have handled him myself," she said automatically when she was fully turned toward him—and stared at his chest. She had to tilt her head back to see his face, because her rescuer didn't only have a deep voice, he was also much taller than she'd expected.

"I'm sure you could have."

Enya barely heard his reply, her eyes drinking in the man's features. Hunk didn't exactly describe him. No, he was more than that. He was Jason Momoa, Cary Grant, and Jensen Ackles rolled into one. One perfect male specimen with olive skin, brown eyes, dark hair, and a goatee surrounding his full lips, behind which white teeth gleamed invitingly. His shoulders were broad, and the business suit he wore couldn't disguise his muscular build. The top button of his shirt was open, hinting at the dark hair on his broad chest.

Enya swallowed, suddenly parched.

"Well, he's gone now. Enjoy your drink." He motioned to her glass and took a seat a few places farther down the long wooden bar, leaving three empty barstools between them. Stunned, she watched the bartender approach him. Quickly, she glanced at her rescuer's fingers. No wedding ring. So why had he not taken the seat next to hers after so gallantly rescuing her?

"What's your poison?" Drew asked.

"Scotch, neat, please."

"Coming right up."

As Drew turned to pull an expensive bottle off one of the upper shelves, Enya called out to him, "Drew, put the scotch on my tab."

Drew looked over his shoulder. "You sure?"

"Chivalry should be rewarded." She turned back to the stranger, who now looked at her, a hesitant smile on his face.

"I only did what any guy would have done. No need to buy me a drink, ma'am."

At the formal salutation, she cringed. She didn't want to be called *ma'am*. It sounded like she was a shriveled-up spinster. "My name's Enya."

She hopped off her barstool and took a seat on the empty place next to him. He appeared surprised.

"Eric, Eric Vaughn," he said. "I had the impression earlier that you weren't looking for company. Please don't feel obligated to talk to me just because I made that ass leave."

Drew slid her glass in front of her and placed a scotch in front of Eric. "Cheers."

Eric nodded.

"Don't worry, I never do anything I don't want to do," Enya replied. "But if you'd rather enjoy your drink by yourself, I'll move back to my original seat."

He lifted his glass. "Please don't. I would enjoy a good conversation tonight that doesn't involve investment strategies or risk assessment."

"Stockbroker?"

He shook his head. "Investment manager. Private equity. Boring as hell."

Enya took her glass and clinked it to his. "Then how about we don't talk about investments tonight?"

"That's a great idea." Eric took a sip from his scotch.

"I have lots of great ideas." One of them was to rip Eric's clothes off and jump his bones. But, of course, she couldn't do this right here. Instead, she let her gaze linger on his hands and imagined what they would feel like on her skin. Was he the kind of guy who talked dirty during sex? With a voice like his, he wouldn't have to do much else to bring her to an earth-shattering orgasm.

"Enya?"

She ripped her gaze from his hands. "Yes?"

"I asked if you live in Baltimore or whether you're just here for business."

"I live here." She tried to make her response sound smooth, when in reality she was flustered and behaving like a ditsy blonde. A ditsy blonde who'd unexpectedly been handed the keys to a Maserati. And she wouldn't return this car before she'd taken it for a spin.

2

Zoltan looked at Enya's plump lips while she replied to his question, imagining what they would feel like around his cock. But he had to be careful and play his cards right. If he came on too strong, she would most likely reject him like she'd done with the previous guy who'd made a move on her. The slightly inebriated man had looked well off and handsome enough, but he hadn't read Enya right. She wanted to be in charge of picking whom to go home with tonight. She had to feel that it was her choice, and hers alone.

He would play along, because a woman like Enya needed a challenge. Besides, if he was too insistent, she would probably smell a rat. He couldn't afford for his plan to go up in smoke, because she became suspicious of him. But if she believed that she held the reins, then he had a chance to lure her into his net. Patience was what he needed now, even though his cock was already throbbing with the need to thrust into her and make her his.

"I live here too," he said casually. "Walking distance, actually, but I don't go out much. It's my first time at this bar. Seems like a decent enough place." He shrugged. "Apart from the occasional nitwit who thinks just because a woman is on her own, she's fair game."

Enya took a sip from her cocktail. "Can't avoid those. But I've learned to deal with them."

He chuckled. "How? With a kick in the balls?"

"Something like that." Enya winked at him, and her blue eyes seemed to sparkle with mischief.

"Sorry I got in the way. It's a reflex. I grew up with a younger sister and had to play the protective older brother for so long that I guess it's ingrained now." Of course, that was a total lie. He had no siblings, and growing up in the Underworld, a place where only meanness, brutality, and reprehensible deeds were rewarded, had meant looking out for only himself. His childhood hadn't exactly been a walk in the park. Survival of the fittest had been the motto. Still was.

"Don't apologize." She put her hand on his forearm, and even through the suit jacket and the shirt beneath, he could feel her warm touch. "It's a good reflex to have."

To his disappointment, Enya quickly removed her hand from his arm, but the mere fact that she'd touched him gave him hope that he was on the right track.

"And you? Any siblings?"

"Three younger brothers."

"Guess that means you had nobody to look out for you. No wonder you're a tough cookie."

She laughed softly, and the sound trickled down his spine like a sensual caress. Yes, she would make the perfect sex slave—once, he'd annihilated her race.

"What makes you think that I'm tough?" she asked.

He'd seen her fight, seen her make mincemeat out of his demons. He knew she was a ferocious warrior, a woman tough as nails. But, of course, he couldn't reveal what he knew about her. "You strike me as tough. You know, the way you talked to that guy, with such a calm and determined voice, I could sense that you're strong. Guess that drunk imbecile didn't see that, or he would have never tried to come on to you."

"So why interfere when you thought I was tough enough to deal with him myself?" Her eyes scrutinized him.

"As I said, it's a reflex. And when a man puts his hands on a woman uninvited, I see red."

"Mmm." She dropped her lashes a little, suddenly looking like a shy doe. "I guess I'm not used to a man fighting my battles for me. I'm sorry if I was ungrateful." She lifted her eyes to meet his. "I'll make it up to you."

At the obvious offer, Zoltan swallowed away the lust that bubbled up.

Down, boy! Let's not surrender too easily. Remember, she wants a challenge.

He lifted his glass. "You've already bought me a drink. But I guess I won't say no to a second one if you insist. Though I have to warn you: the more I drink, the less civilized I get." As if he needed any alcohol to unleash his true self.

Enya raised her eyebrows while she waved to the bartender for another round. "I'm curious to see what it looks like when you're less civilized."

"Are you trying to get me drunk?"

"Not drunk. What would be the point of that? But maybe another drink will loosen you up a bit."

He leaned toward her and lowered his voice. "You don't know what you're unleashing."

Before Enya could say anything else, the bartender placed their drinks in front of them. "I'm closing out your tab, Enya. Anything else for tonight?"

Enya directed her gaze to the bartender. "No, thanks, Drew. I've got everything I need." She looked back at Zoltan.

He recognized that look. She wanted him, and she was waiting for him to make the suggestion to go somewhere else, somewhere more private. It was his turn now, but he would play it his way, forcing Enya to make the first move.

"A shame it's closing time," Zoltan said, and took a big gulp from his second drink. "I had a really nice time talking to you. Would you... I mean, perhaps we could... Would you give me your phone number so I can call you sometime?"

Surprise flashed in Enya's eyes, just like he'd expected. For a few seconds, she remained silent, then she leaned closer. "How about you give me your number instead?"

Now it was his turn to be surprised. Was she not going to ask him to spend the night with her? Fine, if that was how she wanted to play it, he had no choice but to play along. He pulled a card from his inside jacket pocket and handed it to her. "That's my cell." In fact, it was the cell phone number he used only for his dealings in the human world, a burner he would get rid of the moment he believed it compromised. None of his demons had this number. Nobody could trace it.

Enya took the card, looked at it, then pulled out her phone and typed the number in. "Thank you. It was a pleasure meeting you."

It was his cue. "Thanks for the drinks." He stood up. "Can I call you a taxi?"

"No, thank you. It's not far." She smiled.

"Well, then, have a good night."

"Same to you," she replied, and turned to the bartender to settle her bill.

Zoltan walked to the door and exited. Outside, he took a deep breath. Maybe he'd played it wrong. Maybe she was pissed because he hadn't responded to her inuendoes. Maybe she thought he was too arrogant, too aloof. Fuck!

His phone rang. "What now?" he grumbled to himself as he started walking in the direction of his condo building. He pulled the phone from his pocket and stared at the display. *Unknown caller*, it said. He pressed *answer*. "This is Eric."

"Hi, it's Enya."

The words made him rock to a halt. "Enya."

"Yes, remember? We just met and you gave me your phone number."

He chuckled. "I have a vague memory of a beautiful blonde in a bar who wouldn't give me her number."

"That's just because that blonde doesn't like to wait for a guy to call her."

"Mmm-hmm." He heard a door closing and realized that Enya had just left the bar. She was only half a block behind him, but he didn't turn around. "Any chance that blonde would like a nightcap?"

"I've had enough to drink. But there's something else."

The sound of footsteps came closer.

"Anything I can provide?"

"I think so." Her words came from directly behind him.

Zoltan disconnected the call and shoved the phone into his pocket.

"It's not polite to hang up on a woman," Enya said from behind him.

"Nor is it polite to tease a man until he loses his cool." Slowly, Zoltan pivoted to face Enya. She wore a leather jacket over her outfit now, but she'd left it open in the front. "I would have called you if you'd given me your number."

Enya took a step closer, bringing her within a foot of him. She looked up at him, and it made him aware of how petite she was. "Why even ask for my number?"

"Because I didn't want to presume that you would accept an invitation to my bed after just meeting me. I figured maybe I'd take you out for dinner first, wine and dine you, before I seduce you."

"I'd rather skip the wining and dining." She licked her lips, and the action sent a jolt of energy into his cock.

He put his arm around her waist and pulled her to him. "Aren't you afraid of going home with a stranger? A stranger who might not be very civilized." Because right now he felt anything but. Enya was a tease, and she'd brought out his animal instincts.

"Who says I want civilized?" She put her hand on his nape.

"A woman after my own heart." He dipped his head to hers and captured her lips.

Ever since he'd first laid eyes on Enya, he'd known that the moment he had her in his bed, there would be fireworks. However, he hadn't expected that simply feeling her lips pressed against his would turn his insides into molten lava and unleash a lust that he'd never felt for any other woman, human, demon, or otherwise.

Enya tasted of sin, of pure, unadulterated sin that an ordinary demon couldn't match. But then, he wasn't an ordinary demon. He was Zoltan, the Great One, the ruler of the Underworld. And what Enya promised with her kiss was unmistakable: a coupling without restraints, without limits, without taboos.

Her lips were soft yet demanding, her breath sweet and addictive, her tongue assertive and delicious. She made no secret of her desire, didn't even attempt to play coy, didn't pretend that this was the first time she'd picked up a stranger. No, for all he knew, she was a pro at this and it was a frequent occurrence for her, one she made no excuses for. She was a hot-blooded woman who knew what she needed. And tonight, she needed him, or at least his cock. And he was more than willing to oblige. But first things first.

Zoltan ripped his lips from hers and took a deep breath. It did nothing to calm his thundering heart or his throbbing erection.

"I live close by. Five minutes' walk."

She met his eyes. "How long if we run?"

He would have chuckled at her eagerness were he not just as keen on getting her into his bed. Without answering, he took her hand, and together, they started running. It still seemed like an eternity until they reached his condo building. He opened the door with his fob, then called for the elevator. Inside the cab, he stopped himself from touching Enya. If he did so before they reached his place, he would fuck her right here in the elevator, and it would be over too soon. No, he had to make it into his condo.

When the elevator finally stopped on his floor, he took Enya's hand and almost dragged her with him. He unlocked his apartment door and ushered her inside, then shut the door behind him.

The under-the-cabinet lights in the open-plan kitchen were burning, shining into the small foyer that connected to it. Beyond the kitchen, and only separated by a bar, lay the living and dining room, which sported wall-to-ceiling windows affording a panoramic view over the city.

But Enya didn't seem interested in the view. Instead, she pivoted to face him. Light shone onto her face and spotlighted her eyes, their blue now more saturated, more vibrant. He was drawn to them like a fly to honey. But it was Enya who made the first move. She snatched the lapels of his suit and pulled him to her, making him aware of her physical strength. Had a demon female grabbed him like that, he would have tossed her on her ass, because *he* decided when, where, and how. He was the one who took charge. To be confronted with a strong woman like Enya, a woman who wasn't intimidated by him, was a refreshing change. So he let it happen and allowed her to take the reins.

3

Enya took a deep breath to inhale Eric's male scent. She had always been able to sense when a man desired her, and this man was no different. Only a few inches separated them, but she could feel his body heat, his need, his arousal. She pushed the jacket over his shoulders, and he helped her and freed himself from it. When he reached for her jacket to help her out of it, she let him, but when he tried the same with her bustier, she pushed him back. Instead, she was already unbuttoning his shirt.

"Take it off," she demanded, and he undid the remaining buttons.

While he slipped out of it, she reached for his belt, unhooked it. His chest bare now and dusted with dark hair, Eric brought his hands to the hooks of her bustier. He managed to open the top two before she stopped him. She had rules for one-night stands, rules she adhered to. She never undressed fully, never let her guard down. No man would make her lie on her back and spread her legs, put her at his mercy. What she needed was a quick, hard fuck, and the kitchen island at her back would be perfect. Beds were dangerous places where people let their guard down, where they got soft, where they started trusting others. Where they confessed secrets, secrets that could never be revealed.

"No," she said, gripping his hands and putting them down next to his sides. Then she unzipped his pants and shoved them down.

Stunned, he stared at her. "I wanna touch your breasts." His words were close to a growl, the sound making her shiver. A moment later, he was tugging at her bustier and managed to pull it down sufficiently so her breasts popped over the top.

"Fuck!" she hissed. She was too self-conscious about her breasts. They were too small, which was the reason why she wore a bustier: to make them appear larger. But now that Eric had freed them, she felt exposed, naked. Vulnerable.

"Gorgeous," Eric murmured, and dipped his head to her bosom. Before she could stop him, he'd already captured one nipple and was sucking on it, while he massaged both breasts with his palms. He let one nipple pop from his mouth, then blew a cool breath against it. She shivered at the tantalizing sensation. "Perfect." He moaned, then put his lips around the other nipple and drew it into his mouth.

"Oh God!" She couldn't allow this to continue. If he sucked her breasts like this, she would lose control. She had to be in charge. *He* was supposed to lose control.

Determined not to succumb to his ministrations, she gripped the seam of his boxer briefs and pulled them down to mid-thigh. A second later, she reached for his cock and wrapped her hand around it. He was big, his girth too much for one hand to handle, his length impressive. She took him in both hands and slid them from tip to root.

Eric groaned and his head shot up. A ragged breath exploded from his lips. "Fuck, Enya!"

Seeing that he was suddenly losing control, she smiled. "Yeah, I think that's the point. To fuck." She let go of his cock and pushed her leather skirt higher then reached underneath to free herself from her panties.

"Right here?" Eric watched her as she tossed the G-string on the floor.

Again, she took his cock into her hands. "I want you to fuck me here. On the kitchen island."

He grabbed her by the hips. "You're not gonna let me see all of you, are you?" He lifted her up on the marble island, then raised her legs so she could bring her heels to rest on his shoulders, while she lay back on the cool surface.

His gaze dipped lower, and his nostrils flared. When he pulled her ass to line up with the edge of the island, she closed her eyes and waited for the moment when she would feel his cock penetrate her in one quick thrust. But instead, she felt his head between her legs, his stubble tickling her inner thighs, and his warm tongue on her slit.

Shock jolted her to sit up and sever the connection. "What the—"

Eric grabbed her thighs roughly, pulled them apart farther, and pressed his mouth to her pussy again. A shudder charged through her body, and for a moment, she couldn't think or act. This wasn't what happened during one-night stands. No such intimacies were allowed. Only quick, hard fucks. That was the rule. Her rule. A rule that she'd put in place so she'd never get attached to anybody. A rule so she would never fall in love.

"Fuck," she murmured again. Perhaps, just this once, she could allow a man to pleasure her in a different way. Just for a moment, and then she would make him stop before he went too far.

Relentlessly his tongue teased her clit, stroked it, caressed it as if she'd taught him how. Her arousal was spiking, her body tensing like it always did just before she came. She had to stop him now, force him to take his mouth off her. She had to demand it.

"Eric… please…" But even to her ears, her command didn't sound right. It wasn't a command at all; it was a woman begging for release.

And Eric was acting on it. He pulled her clit between his lips and pressed down. Her body erupted. Spasms raced through her and exploded outward. Her body was on fire, and perspiration collected underneath her clothes. And just as she thought her orgasm was subsiding, she felt Eric's cock plunge deep into her, his hands on her hips so the impact wouldn't make her slide away.

"Now I'll fuck you," he said between gritted teeth. "Because now you're ready for my cock."

His deep voice sent shivers down her spine and bolts of heat to her nipples and clit. Thrusting deep and fast, Eric bent over her and sucked her nipples again.

"You have perfect tits," he murmured against her heated flesh.

"No, I don't," she protested. All men lied during sex. "And you don't have to pretend they are."

Eric lifted his head. "I guess I'm gonna have to pound the truth into you." He doubled the speed with which he thrust into her, his thick cock stretching her to capacity, its tip reaching farther than she'd ever felt any man.

Involuntary moans tumbled from her lips. She wanted to hold them back, wanted to hide what he did to her, but she didn't have the strength. Didn't have the will. All she wanted was to let go, to give herself over to this feeling of being desired, of letting another person take care of her, despite the dangers, despite the risk to her heart.

"You feel that, don't you, Enya?" he challenged, staring at her, while he moved his hips and thrust his cock. "Tell me you feel my cock. Tell me you love my cock."

Heat shot through her. But his voice was beseeching, his words tempting. "Yes, I love your cock."

He let go of one hip and grabbed her breasts, squeezed them. "And I love your tits. Because they're perfect. Say it." He let go of her breasts and snatched her hand, guided it to one breast. "Touch yourself." He motioned to her other hand. "With both hands. Take your tits. Now answer me." His gaze burned into her, the gaze of a man used to his orders being followed.

At first hesitantly, she cupped her breasts, then averted her eyes.

"Look at me!"

She snapped her eyes back at him, meeting his insistent look. Then she began to massage her breasts and squeeze them, and finally, she took her nipples between her fingers and rolled them.

She couldn't help but notice that Eric's movements became even more frantic. His cock inside her seemed to expand and his breath turned ragged.

"My tits are perfect," she murmured. "Lick them."

"Fuck!" He gripped her thighs now, thrusting hard. Eric bent over her, and she fed him one nipple after the other.

Then she felt him spasm inside her, felt the warmth of his semen shoot into her, fill her. Suddenly her channel contracted and another orgasm slammed into her. She moaned while her pussy spasmed around Eric's cock as if her body tried to suck his semen deep into her. She'd never felt anything this intense.

When she could finally think again, Eric had already pulled out of her and lowered her legs, so she could sit up.

"Wow," he said on a deep breath. "That was... Well, that was something."

Enya jumped off the kitchen island, her legs unsteady. With shaking hands, she pulled down her skirt then looked for her panties, when she felt Eric's hand on her arm. She turned to face him.

"You're getting dressed already?"

"I've gotta go." For so many reasons.

"Stay a little longer."

"I can't." She saw her panties on the floor and bent down to grab them. Quickly she put them on. Then she righted her bustier to cover her breasts again.

"Then at least give me your number."

She looked at him and hesitated. Her womb clenched and her clit throbbed, asking for a repeat of what Eric had done tonight. But this time, her head won out. "I have a complicated life."

Eric put a finger under her chin and made her tilt her head back. "I love complicated women. The others are, frankly, not worth the time." He brushed a kiss to her lips. "And there's so much more you and I could explore. Tonight was just an amuse-bouche. My appetite is much bigger."

She didn't doubt that. But rules were rules. If she spent the night, she would get too comfortable. Not just with Eric, but with the whole idea of being with somebody. Relying on somebody, when she knew that in the end she could rely only on herself.

"I had a nice time," she said. "Thank you."

Eric shook his head. "I can give you an even nicer time. Tell me you want to see me again."

She sighed.

"Was that a yes?" He dipped his head to look deep into her eyes. Something made her hold his gaze instead of evading it.

"I don't know," she said.

"Maybe this will help." He pressed his lips to hers and kissed her. Their first kiss had been urgent, passionate, demanding. This one was different. More tender, yet at the same time insistent. As if Eric wanted to show her that he was a man who didn't give up easily. Who fought for what he desired.

Cool air blew against her lips, and she realized he'd already severed the kiss.

"I need an answer," he pressed with that deep voice that made her want to surrender.

"I... uh... maybe... maybe I'll call you," she said finally, and picked up her leather jacket, ready to flee. When she touched the door handle, his voice stopped her.

"Enya..."

Against her better judgment, she looked over her shoulder. He stood there in the hallway, half-naked, the light from the kitchen shining onto his cock. She'd never seen such a virile man, such a perfect human specimen.

"Next time," he said, and took his cock into his hand, "you'll take the reins and do with me as you please. I'll be at your mercy."

She swallowed the sudden surge of lust that pulsed through her core. Did Eric understand her need for control because he, too, had that need? Were they maybe not that different from each other?

"I can't make promises, but…" She didn't finish her sentence, didn't know how to.

"But you'll consider it. That's good enough for me."

She nodded and left the apartment. When the door snapped in behind her, she leaned against it and closed her eyes for a moment. For the first time in a long time, she felt… happy.

4

Zoltan entered the cave and closed the door behind him. He'd made many changes in the Underworld in the last few months, and one of them was this meeting room, a cave that had only one entrance and lay somewhat separate from the main areas where his demons congregated, drawing as little attention as possible to the meetings held here. The seven demons who had been invited to this meeting were already assembled and consisted of men and women Zoltan considered either particularly loyal to him or particularly talented in a specific area of expertise. Some were both.

The previous Great One, who Zoltan had dispatched by killing him, had ruled with an iron fist and been hated and feared in equal measure, and while Zoltan was just as feared—and possibly hated for the cruelty he inflicted on demons that crossed him—he'd learned to seek counsel and delegate tasks to his underlings. His frequent absences had made it necessary, though he would never admit to any of them why their ruler wasn't always reachable. If they knew that the crushing migraine attacks he'd had for a long time forced him to hide out in the human world so he could recover, his underlings would rise up in arms against him and kill him. Nobody wanted a weak ruler. Least of all the demons. Why his attacks became more painful from one time to the next and didn't respond to any kind of medication or drug, he didn't know. And, of course, there was nobody he could ask. Doing so would mean he had to admit that he was weak. It would literally be his death.

Everybody was assembled around the stone table, a natural formation like so many in the underground system of tunnels and caves the demons called their own. Zoltan took his seat at the head of the table, and the conversations stopped.

"Oh Great One," they said in unison, the voices of five men and two women bouncing off the stone walls, sounding like the deep rumbling of a locomotive as it raced through a dark tunnel.

Zoltan nodded. "We have much to do. Let's get started."

He motioned to Vintoq, his right hand, a demon with above average intelligence, who'd earned his place here through loyalty. So far, Vintoq had never disappointed Zoltan—however, while Zoltan liked the fact that Vintoq was intelligent enough to immediately grasp whatever plan Zoltan laid out, that same intelligence could prove to be a liability one day. What if Vintoq was too smart to remain in his current position? What if he was ambitious and wanted to become the leader?

"All your orders have been executed," Vintoq said, and pointed to the others in the group. "I believe we're making great progress in all areas, strengthening our hold on humans under our influence and widening our network of spies."

"What about recruitment?" Zoltan asked.

"I'll let Quentin and Tamara speak for themselves," Vintoq said, and pointed to the two demons in question.

Tamara looked straight at Zoltan. "May I?"

She was beautiful, and her beauty made her an excellent demon. She knew how to seduce a human to do bad things, to do evil things, things that would eventually turn the human into a demon. She used her sexuality to achieve her goal, and Zoltan could attest personally that her skills when it came to sex were superior. He'd quite enjoyed sex with her, but he wasn't blind. Tamara was ambitious and had hoped to become his queen. However, while she'd pleased him in a carnal way, he felt nothing for her. So instead, he'd put her—and his loyal subject Quentin—in charge of recruitment, softening the sting of rejecting her. She'd taken it well and thrown herself into her new responsibilities.

"Go ahead, Tamara," Zoltan said.

"I've made headway recruiting several influential leaders of industry. We'll soon have an in with the software sector and the rare earth mineral sector."

"Rare earth minerals? Explain," Zoltan interrupted.

"Rare earth minerals are elements needed for virtually every electronic gadget on the market these days. Controlling this sector means controlling the production and availability of communications and computer networks. We'll be controlling the market and pitting countries against each other. And together with new recruits immersed in the software industry, we'll soon be able to upgrade our outdated systems and outsmart our enemies."

"How close are you?"

She gave him a sly smile. "Very close. Another month or so, and they'll both be mine."

"Well done," he praised, then looked at Quentin. "And what have you got to report, Quentin?"

Quentin had impressed Zoltan a few years earlier, when he'd insisted that he sensed a disturbance in the Underworld, which turned out to be an intrusion by a Stealth Guardian. Quentin's vigilance had led to a chase of the Stealth Guardian and her companion, but due to the dog handler's incompetence, that chase had ended unsuccessfully. Klaus, the dog handler in charge back then, had paid for it with his life.

"Also very good news," Quentin said quickly. "I'm working on several top-level politicians—leaders of their respective countries, in fact."

"Which countries?"

"Russia, North Korea, and the U.S."

Zoltan chuckled. "That's hardly an effort on your part. Those leaders are pretty much a shoo-in, don't you think?"

Quentin lowered his lids. "I don't disagree, oh Great One. But if I may say, despite the fact that these three leaders will fall into my hands like ripe fruit from a tree, nobody has ever attempted it before. As if it had been overlooked."

Zoltan nodded. "You have a point. Nobody before you suggested getting them to join us. Let me suggest you add the leaders of Saudi Arabia, Turkey, Syria, and Venezuela to your workload, and I'll overlook the fact that you're going for easy pickings."

"Excellent suggestion," Quentin said eagerly.

Of course it was an excellent suggestion. Zoltan didn't need Quentin to tell him that. He looked at Wilson.

The short, stocky demon sat up straighter in his chair. "Oh Great One."

"Anything notable in the weaponry department?" Zoltan asked.

"I'm afraid we're limited when it comes to acquiring new weapons. Well, of course they're not new. If they were, we wouldn't be able to use them. I mean old weapons," Wilson said, flustered as always.

If he hadn't turned out to be so loyal, Zoltan would have replaced Wilson long ago. But Wilson knew when to grovel. Besides, he knew his weapons. He could tell a dagger forged in the Dark Days from any imitation. And only weapons forged in the Dark Days were of use to them when it came to destroying the Stealth Guardians. They couldn't be killed with any other weapon. The same was true for demons.

Zoltan was already turning away from Wilson when the stout demon said, "But I might have a new source. A man who's worked on numerous archeological digs. I'm supposed to meet him later this week to look at photographs he's taken."

"Good." Zoltan pointed to Silvana. "How are the dogs?"

"Hungry." Silvana's Eastern European accent was as hard and grating as her demeanor. The job of dog handler was tailor-made for her. "Next time a Stealth Guardian tries to infiltrate here, they'll sniff out the bastard in no time. No matter how much they'll try to disguise their scent, they won't be able to get past the dogs. I promise."

Zoltan had confidence in her. Well-trained dogs were essential. Since Stealth Guardians could make themselves invisible, the demons needed a defense mechanism, so that their enemies couldn't sneak up on them.

"See that you keep that promise," Zoltan said rather than praising her. In many of his demons, praise seemed to have a negative effect: they became complacent. And complacency was the death of his quest for world domination.

"Yannick," he said to the demon who had a particularly sensitive job. Yannick was responsible for keeping track of the comings and goings of all demons. "Have you figured out a way of shutting down any of our vortex circles in case of a breach?"

Yanick bowed his head for a moment, then looked straight at Zoltan. "I'm afraid not yet, oh Great One. The mystical origin of the vortex circles seems like a finely tuned machine to which we've lost the instruction manuals. What I'm trying to say is that unless we can figure out how they were created in the first place, we won't know what it'll take to shut them down temporarily, which I believe is what you're asking, rather than permanently."

"What are you saying?"

"Well, shutting down the vortex circles permanently is one thing; shutting them down for a limited time is another, because it would involve knowing how to restart them."

"Are you saying there's a way of shutting down the vortex circles permanently, and trapping all demons in the Underworld?" Zoltan leaned forward, eager to hear the reply.

Yannick nodded. "While I can't confirm it with one hundred percent certainty, I believe flooding the vortex circles with lava would strip away their mystical powers and make them unusable."

Everyone in the cave gasped.

"Who knows about this?"

Yannick looked to the assembled demons. "I've never before mentioned it to anyone outside this group. And as I said, it's only an educated guess. And it defeats the purpose."

"Yes, yes," Zoltan said impatiently. "But if you're right, then it's even more important to learn how we can create new vortex circles. In fact, to control the human world once we've defeated the Stealth Guardians, we'll have much more traffic going through the existing vortex circles. We'll need additional ones to send more demons up top."

Demons used vortexes as a means to teleport from one place to another. Once in the human world, demons could cast their vortexes anywhere they had a visual, but to leave or enter the Underworld, they needed to cast a vortex in one of the vortex circles, of which they only had three. Clearly, his predecessor hadn't thought of logistics. It was up to Zoltan to plan for the future, because soon, the Stealth Guardians would be gone, and nothing would stand between the demons and the human population.

"I understand," Yannick said. "I have my best men working on this. Mathematicians, scientists, occultists."

"Then get me results," Zoltan thundered.

"I will, oh Great One."

Finally, he turned to Ulric, the demon responsible for intelligence. "Any new reports from your network of spies, Ulric?"

"They're keeping their eyes and ears open. Nothing will escape them."

Zoltan knew what that meant. "So you've got nothing!"

"I wouldn't say that, oh Great—"

Zoltan pounded his fist on the table. "Then how would you say it?"

Ulric did well to bow his head in shame. "My apologies."

Zoltan grunted. "Just as well that I myself am working on a direct lead to the Stealth Guardians."

All eyes landed on him.

"If you need any assistance," Quentin said, "perhaps I can—"

"I'll help with whatever you need," Vintoq interrupted.

"I can't risk any of you screwing this up. I'll fill you in when I'm ready to execute my plan." And when Zoltan could be sure that none of the assembled demons was a traitor. For quite some time now, he suspected that somebody was vying for his throne—and using any means possible to attain it, even resorting to assassination attempts. But so far, Zoltan hadn't been able to nail the culprit. "In the meantime, I'll have to spend more time up top to lay the groundwork. Baltimore is off-limits to any demon until then. Do I make myself clear?"

"Yes, oh Great One," they said in unison, sounding like the marionettes he'd trained them to be.

5

"Something's up," Enya said, and looked at her colleagues, who were all assembled in the great room, which sported a huge sectional with seating for at least ten, an oversized TV mounted on the wall, and was adjacent to the kitchen, where her colleagues' mates were chatting and preparing the evening meal. "I can feel it in my gut." She paced back and forth.

"Can't you just enjoy the calm for a while?" Hamish asked. "It doesn't happen every week that we don't have to rush to a demon sighting and kick their butts."

Enya tossed him an annoyed look. "Doesn't that worry you?" She looked at Logan, who was flicking through the channels. "Logan? Anybody?"

Logan stopped his channel surfing for a moment and looked at her. "What do you want, Enya? Don't you need a break from time to time? I sure do. So, enjoy the fact that the demons have been quiet this week. Relax. Recharge." He glanced at Winter, a psychic, who instantly met his look. "Do something fun."

"Pfff!" Enya scoffed. Easy for Logan to say. The way he looked at his wife right now, it wasn't hard to guess what he meant by fun. She ripped her gaze from him, sick of the lovey-dovey exchange she had to witness. Instead, she walked up to Manus, who was lounging in one of the large armchairs, and slapped him on the shoulder.

Manus whipped his head to her. "What?"

"Have you been listening at all?" she asked.

He motioned to the TV. "What now? Come on, Enya, I just wanna watch the boxing match if Logan can find the damn channel." He cast his friend an impatient look.

"I'm on it," Logan said, and continued flicking through the channels.

"There are more important things than boxing matches on TV," Enya scolded him. "Aren't you worried that the demons are planning something big, and that's why we haven't gotten a glimpse of them in the last week?"

"Like Hamish said, enjoy the fact that it's quiet," Manus said calmly. "Why are you so antsy? Haven't you kicked enough demon ass in the last few months?"

"Give her a break, Manus," Aiden interrupted.

Surprised that at least one of her colleagues seemed to be taking her side, Enya looked at Aiden. He'd changed a lot over the last few years. Now a father of six-year-old twins, he showed a lot more patience with his colleagues, and had lost a lot of his hotheadedness. His mate Leila had a lot to do with it. She was human and had been a scientist who'd discovered a drug to reverse Alzheimer's. Aiden had been assigned to protect her after it had become clear that the demons wanted the drug because it made humans more susceptible to their influence. The drug had to be destroyed and Leila had to go into hiding so the demons couldn't capture her and force her to recreate the drug for them. It had all worked out in the end—because Aiden had fallen in love with his charge, and she was now living in the Stealth Guardians' secret (and invisible) compound in Baltimore.

"Listen, Enya," Aiden continued, "if there's really something big brewing, then there would be reports from other compounds too, and so far, we haven't heard anything unusual, have we, Pearce?"

Pearce, their resident IT genius responsible for communications, nodded. "All other compounds report the usual level of demon activity. Nothing less, nothing more. I filed our weekly report this morning."

"And?" Enya asked eagerly.

He shrugged. "Neither the Council of Nine nor any of the other compounds contacted me to ask questions. Nobody is concerned that we've had a quiet week for a change."

"Yeah, but what if they're wrong? What if something is up?" Enya asked. She'd always trusted her gut, and her gut was telling her that the absence of demons in Baltimore was a bad omen. "After Zoltan's last defeat, do you really think he's sitting on his hands, doing nothing?"

"Of course not," Pearce said tersely. "I'm sure having lost possession of the source dagger must have stung. Can't have helped him prove to his demons that he's the right leader." He cast a look at Daphne, his mate, who'd been instrumental in snatching the valuable dagger from Zoltan's claws. "And getting his ass kicked by a woman with his demons watching... Well, I'm sure he's still doing damage control in the Underworld."

Hamish nodded. "Pearce is right. There've been persistent rumors from the Underworld that Zoltan's reign is anything but cemented. He's got other things to worry about than terrorizing Baltimore."

Enya braced her hands at her hips. "Let's assume you're right. Let's assume Zoltan is indeed in the middle of a power struggle or fighting off other demons vying for his throne. Well, put yourselves in his shoes. What would you do to accomplish that?" She let her gaze wander over her colleagues. "Anybody?"

There was silence, then Aiden spoke up. "We're not in Zoltan's shoes. Demons aren't like us. They think differently. Their actions often make no sense. They're irrational, impulsive, uncoordinated. That's why we've been able to defeat them so far."

"The grunts, maybe," Enya admitted. "But not Zoltan. He thinks like us. He's outsmarted us plenty of times. Take the source dagger, for example. He found it when it had been lost for centuries. It took him less than six months from the day he found out about its significance until he blew up the safe it had been in. Don't underestimate him. He was able to do something that our entire race was incapable of: finding the source dagger."

"Yes, he found the dagger, but we are in possession of it now," Pearce said. "Thanks to Daphne."

From the kitchen, Daphne called out, "What are you thanking me for?"

"For saving my life with the source dagger."

Enya tried to shake off the memory of what had happened only months earlier, when Pearce had been mortally wounded during a fight with the demons in which each side had tried to gain possession of the source dagger, the ancient artefact that made it possible to create portals the Stealth Guardians used to teleport from one location to another. But the source dagger also possessed another power—to reverse a mortal wound and save a person's life. Daphne's swift and brave action to snatch the dagger from the demons and use it on Pearce had saved his life.

Daphne came closer and winked at Pearce. "I believe you already thanked me plenty for it." She put her hand over her slightly rounded stomach. Her bump was barely visible, but everybody at the compound knew of Daphne's pregnancy. Pearce had been unable to keep the news to himself and announced it shortly after a pregnancy test had confirmed it. And she wasn't the only one at the compound who was pregnant. Winter was also expecting her first child with her mate Logan. It was as if the condition was contagious.

"So what's all the talk about the source dagger?" Daphne asked.

Pearce pointed to Enya. "Enya is concerned about the lack of demon activity this week. She thinks Zoltan is planning something."

"Of course he's planning something," Daphne said, to Enya's surprise. "He's always planning his next move."

"See," Enya said, glowering at her colleagues. "Even Daphne thinks so. And she isn't a warrior."

"No, she isn't," Logan said. "We are, and we've been doing this for a long time. You don't seem to remember that there've always been times when the demons were quiet. It's natural."

Enya grunted. "You're just getting complacent. You don't wanna see the threat. Fine! I'll deal with it myself if I have to. I'll go on patrol."

Aiden shook his head. "Don't, Enya." He sighed heavily. "I'll talk to my father. He's visiting this weekend anyway to see the twins. If he agrees, we'll send out an alert to the other compounds to be on the lookout for anything unusual. Maybe Zoltan pulled some demons off Baltimore because he needs them somewhere else."

Enya felt her pulse settle. "That's what I'm worried about."

With some luck, Barclay, Aiden's father, the head of the Council of Nine, would validate her concerns. He was experienced and wise, while her Baltimore colleagues were only seeing the upside of decreased demon activity: they could spend more time with their mates.

She wondered if she would feel the same way if she had a mate. She quickly dismissed the thought. First and foremost, she was a warrior. Nothing else mattered. However, it seemed that having mated had shifted her brethren's priorities.

Enya looked at the women in the kitchen. Now that every warrior in the compound except herself was mated, evenings like this one had become more frequent. Like a large family, they ate together whenever there was an occasion. Tessa, Hamish's mate, and Kim, Manus's mate, were already setting the table, and Leila was pulling a roast out of the oven. Winter was tossing the salad, and Daphne scooped the roasted potatoes into a large bowl. All the while, the women chatted and laughed. They'd become friends, accepting each other and their oddities and quirks.

For so many decades, Enya had been the only woman in the compound, but now, everything was different. Things had gotten more domestic. Suddenly, Enya was the odd one out, the only one without a partner. It had never bothered her before. She liked being different, liked not being like anybody else. She liked her freedom, her independence. And while she loved her brethren and their wives and children, she suddenly realized what she had turned into: the outsider. The person looking in through a window, watching happy couples live their lives.

The door opened and the two young vampire hybrids entered. Grayson and Ryder were on loan from Scanguards, the Stealth Guardians' vampire allies in San Francisco, and had become an integral part of the group. Both in their twenties, they were single, and while neither was in a relationship, they were regularly sowing their wild oats with any woman who tickled their fancy, be it human, vampire, witch, or otherwise. She glanced at the handsome youngsters. They were outsiders, too, but it didn't seem to bother them. For them, living at the compound and fighting demons together with the Stealth Guardians was an adventure. One day, they would return to San Francisco and make lives for themselves there. For Enya, this was her life.

"Dinner is ready, guys," Leila announced.

The men rose from their seats and trotted to the large dining table, where they joined their mates. The twins suddenly appeared as if out of thin air, giggling.

"There you are, finally!" Aiden scolded them softly.

Ever since Xander and Julia had mastered the skill of making themselves invisible, their game of hide and seek had taken on new dimensions. Watching over them and making sure they were safe couldn't be easy for their parents.

Enya caught Pearce and Daphne share a loving look as they smiled at the twins, and though she didn't know what Pearce whispered into Daphne's ear, Enya knew it had to do with the child they were expecting. A tightness suddenly clamped around Enya's chest. Damn it, she couldn't stand being here right now. This display of affection was making her physically sick.

Enya slipped out of the room and stepped into the quiet corridor. She could still hear their voices, their chatter and laughter, but nobody had noticed her leaving. Nobody would miss her. Nobody would look for her. As she walked to her quarters on one of the upper floors of the vast, castlelike building, she pulled out her phone and scrolled to her recent calls. She found the number—it had been over a week since she'd used it. So far she'd resisted giving in to the temptation to call, though she'd come close to it several times in the last few days.

But why resist any longer? Where was it written that she couldn't sleep with the same man twice? It was her own rule, which meant she could change it. It was a silly rule anyway. An arbitrary one. Maybe she would change it. Maybe she would allow herself to amend the rule to three times. Yes, she could do that. But no more than three times. She had to be firm on that.

Her heart beating an excited tattoo against her ribcage, she pressed the number and let it ring.

6

Zoltan put the lid on the casserole dish and slid it into the warm oven. He assured himself that the champagne was chilling in the fridge. The seafood cocktail was already plated and ready to eat. Glancing around the kitchen, he made sure that it looked sufficiently messy. His guest would believe he'd gone through the trouble of cooking a meal from scratch, when all he'd done was make a call to the most expensive restaurant in town.

Enya had called him the night before, telling him she wanted to get together, and he'd immediately suggested dinner at his condo, claiming he would love to cook for her. She'd accepted, and he'd prepared for her visit.

Right after their first encounter, he'd removed everything from his condo that could hint at him being a demon. He couldn't take any chances, because if Enya was as smart as he believed her to be, she would appear invisibly to check him out. He'd donned fresh contact lenses a couple of hours earlier. They would last for about eight hours and hide his green demon eyes. Judging by their first sexual encounter, there was no chance that she'd spend the entire night. He'd be lucky to coax her into his bed. Yet he was prepared to take her on any hard surface that presented itself.

He wasn't quite sure why she let him fuck her like that. Most women preferred a soft mattress to lie on, and a slow seduction to get them there. But Enya had been all business. Tonight, he would try to change that. He had to get under her skin, gain her confidence, her trust, no matter how long it took.

With the stage in the kitchen and dining room set, an hour before the agreed time, he walked into his bedroom and got undressed. He tossed his clothes into the hamper, then sauntered into the en suite bathroom and switched on the light. The massive shower was glass-enclosed and had room for a whole army. He reached inside and turned on the faucet, then waited for mist to accumulate. He didn't turn on the fan that would suck the moisture from the bathroom. Tonight, he needed the steam from the shower to let him know of the arrival of his visitor, who was sure to show up very soon.

Satisfied with the dense fog building in his luxurious bathroom, he stepped into the shower and began to soap up. He washed his hair, took his time washing his torso and limbs, his cock, and every inch of his body. When he was done, he rinsed himself off and began again, his body angled toward the door to the bedroom.

There was no sound in the apartment other than the running of the water. No creaking floors or doors that would alert him to a Stealth Guardian's presence. But he knew she would come. And she would see him naked in the shower.

Zoltan put his hand around his cock and began to tug. It took only a few seconds and the memory of Enya's tight pussy for his cock to stiffen. While the water ran down his back, he stroked his cock, but he wouldn't let himself come. No, this particular action wasn't for him. It was for Enya. For her viewing pleasure.

From the corner of his eye, he saw a sudden movement of the mist just outside the shower. Only a body could have displaced the fog like it did, an invisible body. She was here. Showtime.

Zoltan turned a little more to the side, so Enya got an eyeful of his rampant cock, and began to move his hand faster up and down. He braced himself against the glass and let out a loud moan. The fog didn't move any more. Enya had halted in front of the shower. Most likely she was facing him, staring right at him, at his cock, at him pleasuring himself.

Good. He could implement part two of his plan now. He closed his eyes and threw his head back, pumping his cock harder, bringing himself ever closer to a climax. It wasn't hard to do. Knowing that Enya was watching him, feasting her eyes on him, made him randier than he'd ever been.

He moaned again, but this time he allowed a word to roll over his lips. "Enya."

Did he hear a soft gasp? He couldn't be sure, not with the water at his back, drowning out most sounds. But he allowed himself to imagine that she was surprised—and pleased. It made him bolder.

Another moan, another lusty grunt, and more words burst from him. "Fuck, Enya!" He pumped harder and faster, sensing the birth of his orgasm. He wouldn't be able to hold it back much longer. "I'm gonna fuck you, damn it, Enya. I'm gonna fuck you all night. And I'm gonna lick your gorgeous tits. I want it all."

Hot semen shot from the tip of his cock, raining over his hand and squirting against the glass enclosure. His chest heaved from the powerful orgasm. Air rushed from his lungs, and his knees seemed to quiver.

"Fuck!" he cursed, and pressed his forehead against the glass, his eyes cast down, his breathing ragged.

His eyes caught the movement immediately. An invisible hand touching the glass where his cock stood still semi-erect. An invisible hand that left a print on the outside of the glass. A moment later, the hand withdrew.

Mission accomplished. Enya now knew that he masturbated thinking of her, and what woman wouldn't like to know that she was a man's fantasy? No woman was left cold by that knowledge. Particularly not a woman who'd just spied on said man and become witness to his desire for her.

~ ~ ~

Enya couldn't tear her eyes away from Eric's gorgeous body. Fuck, she'd watched him masturbate and utter her name while doing so. She could have reached through the glass and touched him, had wanted it so badly. She'd never seen anything hotter, anything more arousing. She'd creamed her panties watching him. Her clit throbbed with desperate need. And her nipples were hard little buds, aching to be touched.

She still stood there, paralyzed, when Eric suddenly turned his back to her and stepped under the spray of the water. She let her eyes trail over his muscular back down to his firm ass. There was an oddly shaped birthmark on his left cheek, but even that couldn't take away from his perfection. She dropped her gaze to his strong thighs, down to his calves, his feet. He was perfect in every way.

She'd never expected to become witness to Eric masturbating in the shower. All she'd wanted to do was check him out, to make sure he was genuine. It was a security measure. She'd arrived fifteen minutes earlier by walking invisibly through the entrance door. After looking through drawers and cupboards in the living room and kitchen and examining the mail that lay on a sideboard, she'd found nothing of concern and made her way into the bedroom. There, too, nothing had been out of place. She'd heard the shower, knew he was in there, and hadn't been able to resist coming closer. She'd been rewarded for her boldness, rewarded with something more than any porn movie could ever give her: the man she desired pleasuring himself while he fantasized about her.

Her heart beating excitedly, she rushed out of the bathroom and left his apartment. In the hallway outside his condo, she made certain that nobody was around and made herself visible again. Even though it was half an hour before the time they'd arranged to meet, she rang the doorbell. So what if he found it odd that she arrived early rather than late? Whatever he thought, he would forget about it the moment she was inside his place and on her knees in front of him.

The door opened. Eric, a towel wrapped around this lower half, his torso still wet, stared at her. "Enya? Sorry,

I…" He made a motion. "Time must have gotten away from me."

She ran her eyes over his chest. "I'm early." But she wasn't going to apologize for it. "Aren't you gonna invite me in?"

He stepped aside. "Of course. Come in." She walked into the foyer, while Eric shut the door behind her. "I'll just dry off and get dressed."

Enya stopped in the kitchen when Eric caught up with her. "Why don't you help yourself to a drink?" he said. "There's chilled champagne in the fridge, or harder stuff in the liquor cabinet in the dining room."

"Harder stuff?" she asked, and bridged the distance between them with two steps. She put her hand on his chest. "I wouldn't mind something hard." Slowly she lowered her hand until her fingers brushed up against the towel.

Eric sucked in a breath. "I promised myself I'd buy you dinner first this time. Like civilized people." The smoldering look in his eyes betrayed his polite words.

"And I promised myself to taste your cock this time. Like uncivilized people."

She took off her leather jacket, revealing the azure dress she wore underneath. While it wasn't as short as the leather skirt she'd worn when she'd met Eric, it was way less restrictive. The fabric was thin, though not see-through. Rather, it hugged her body like a second skin.

"Fuck, Enya, you're making mincemeat out of my good intentions."

"Good intentions are overrated." She pulled on the towel, loosened it, and dropped it to the floor, then wrapped her fingers around his cock. Eric sucked in a ragged breath. At the same time, his shaft began to fill with blood. "Mmm, looks like your cock and I are in agreement. Dinner can wait."

Eric laid his hand on her nape and pulled her face to him. "You little vixen. After our first night, I thought you couldn't wear anything more seductive than what you wore that night, but I was wrong." He placed a hand on her waist. "I'm surprised you made it to my place in one piece, dressed like you are." If only he knew that nobody had seen her dressed like this. Not even her compound mates. She'd snuck out of the compound invisibly and remained so until a few minutes ago.

"How am I dressed?" she murmured, her mouth only an inch away from his.

"Like a woman who wants to get on her knees and suck my cock."

She let her lips curl into a sinful smile. "Guess I chose the right dress."

Eric's lips were finally on hers, and he kissed her with a hunger she welcomed. She responded with the same passion and suddenly felt like floating, until she realized that Eric had lifted her off her feet and was carrying her to the living room. When he severed the kiss, they stood before a large armchair. He released her from his hold and sat down in the chair, his legs wide, his feet firmly planted on the carpet. His cock was pointing upward now, hard and heavy.

He looked up at her, pinning her with his gaze. She felt her nipples harden and press through the thin fabric of her dress. When his eyes moved lower and a satisfied smile appeared on his lips, she knew that he'd noticed her reaction.

"Put your hands on the armrests," she ordered him.

He complied without complaint, and she kneeled between his thighs. Eric sat at the edge of the armchair, giving her full access to his cock and balls, making it evident that he had assumed this position many times before.

Slowly, Enya put her hands on his knees and stroked up, her fingers pointing downward along his inner thighs until they could go no farther. Casting a glance up at Eric's face, she noticed him holding his breath in anticipation. But she wanted him to want it even more. To crave it. To crave her.

"How do you want it?" she asked, and wrapped her hand around his impressive girth. He was rock hard, even though he'd climaxed only ten minutes earlier.

"I take whatever you wanna give me."

"I like a man who appreciates certain things."

"Oh, don't you worry, Enya—I don't take this or you for granted." His cock twitched in her hand, and she rubbed her finger over the mushroom head, spreading his pre-cum. "Fuck, babe, are you trying to torture me?"

"Yes, but I think you'll like it." She moved her hand, sliding it down, and bent her head over his erection. She put her lips around its crown and took him inside her mouth. She inched down, but gripped him hard at the root so he couldn't push deeper without her permission. It took her a few seconds to get used to his size, then she dipped another inch lower, her lips gliding firmly down the hard rod that was encased in velvety-smooth skin.

With her free hand, she reached for his balls and took them into her palm, squeezing them gently.

Eric let out a few jerky breaths. "Oh, fuck!"

Enya pulled up and let his cock escape from her mouth as she looked up at him. "Is there a problem?" she teased, knowing full well what a man in lust looked like. And Eric was a picture of lust.

He pinned her with his eyes, looking at her as if he could see into her core. The intensity of his stare made her shudder. "Put your lips back around my cock and suck me, or I might just have to toss you on that couch and fuck you until you can't walk anymore."

The words send a jolt to her clit, igniting it. She loved seeing Eric lose control, loved that he went all primal on her. The one-night stands she'd had in the last few years had never shown their animalistic side, never dared to be so wild. She'd never before encouraged it, had always been the one in control, the one deciding what happened. But suddenly, the thought of allowing a man to take charge of her, was... tempting.

"Make me," she challenged him.

There was a flicker in his eyes, then he lifted his hands from the armrests and placed them on her head. He pressed her head down to his groin. "Suck me!"

His cock pressed against her lips.

"Open," he demanded. "Take me into your mouth." His words were like a growl, and to her surprise, she felt herself respond to it.

She parted her lips and allowed Eric's cock to push into her mouth, deeper and faster this time. She'd barely had time to adjust to him when he was withdrawing, moving her head up and down on him. He thrust again and again, their movements in sync with each other, and then she felt his hands on her shoulders and realized that she was the one dictating the rhythm now, the rhythm he'd set before. Her body was instinctively continuing it, even though he'd taken his hands off her head.

She sucked him harder now and inhaled his manly aroma. With one hand around his root, she pumped him, while she cradled his balls with the other.

All of a sudden, Eric pushed her shoulders back and freed himself from her mouth. "Stop!"

She stared up at him, stunned at the sudden command.

"I'm too close."

He jumped up and grabbed her. A few moments later, she found herself on her hands and knees, her dress hiked up to her waist, her G-string on the floor. Eric was on his knees behind her, gripping her hips tightly, while he plunged deep into her drenched pussy. Had he not held her so tightly, the impact of his thrusts would have catapulted her to the other end of the living room. No man had ever fucked her this hard, this unapologetically. She felt as if the entire building was shaking from the force of his thrusts.

Her body felt as if an earthquake was rippling through her, sending shock wave after shock wave through her each time Eric plunged deep and hard. She clawed her fingers into the carpet, holding on, jerking backward each time he thrust forward. With every movement, her heart beat more frantically, and the blood rushed through her veins with such speed that any vampire close by would have been able to hear it. But there was no vampire in the condo, just a human who fucked with more vigor and stamina than any supernatural creature she'd ever been with.

"You like it rough, don't you?" he asked.

A moan was her only answer, for words to describe what she felt had deserted her, together with her sense of restraint. Every rule she'd put in place when it came to men, and particularly one-night stands, flew out the window. All because this man showed her what could happen when she gave control over to somebody else, when she finally let herself go and surrendered to her darkest desire. To for once just be a woman. Not a warrior. Not a fighter. Not a guardian. Just a woman who wanted what all women wanted: to be desired, to be taken care of, to be loved.

And though she recognized the danger in that simple wish, for tonight, she couldn't deny it. Tomorrow, she would scold herself for these stupid thoughts, for making herself vulnerable, but right now, she wanted only one thing: Eric.

"Take me. Take me as hard as you can. I need to feel you."

As if Eric had expected her surrender, he increased his tempo and let out a moan that sounded like the growl of an animal. The sound shot through her like a spear and made her arousal spike. She couldn't hold back her orgasm, couldn't stop the waves that crashed over her, buried her beneath their force, while her body trembled uncontrollably. A moment later, she felt Eric's cock spasm inside her and his hot semen fill her, igniting another climax as if it contained a secret elixir that heightened her arousal.

"Oh God," she murmured, and collapsed, her knees shaking, her arms losing all strength. She was spent. Utterly and completely spent. It was a feeling she could get used to.

7

When Zoltan entered the living room, now fully clothed, Enya stood at the floor-to-ceiling windows, looking down onto the city of Baltimore. She didn't turn around when he approached, giving him a chance to admire her in the figure-hugging dress she wore. The ocean-blue fabric clung to her body like a second skin, and her long blond hair reached down to mid-back. The blue suited her perfectly, making her look regal, yet sexy. She'd worn the same color a few months earlier when he encountered her at a cosplay event, of all places. She'd fought his demons, killed several, but luckily, she hadn't seen his face: it had been hidden behind a Batman mask.

Zoltan walked up to Enya and put his arms around her, pressing his front to her back, her ass fitting perfectly against his groin. He slid a hand over her stomach down to her pussy, still remembering vividly how it felt when her interior muscles had gripped him during her orgasm. Enya didn't stop his possessive movement. Instead, she pressed against him, arching her back. He couldn't resist sliding his other hand to her breast, squeezing it, first lightly, then firmer.

He bent his head to hers. "You've exceeded all my expectations." He pressed a kiss to her neck. "No woman has ever allowed me to take her like that."

Enya put her hand over the one that still cupped her pussy. "I didn't know hu—uh, men like you existed."

Human, she'd wanted to say, he realized. Good; he hadn't aroused any suspicions in her. His cover was still firmly in place.

"You're a rare breed, Enya. So full of passion." He rubbed the heel of his hand against her mound. "Without inhibitions." He kissed the skin below her earlobe. "I'm glad you decided to call me."

"So am I." She turned her head to look at him. "I hope I didn't spoil your homemade dinner by attacking you like this. I hope it's still edible."

Apparently his kitchen looked sufficiently messy for her to believe that he'd actually prepared the dinner himself. He chuckled. "No worries."

"You went through so much trouble."

He sighed. "Enya..."

"What?"

"I have to confess something. I lied to you."

Twisting out of his hold, she spun around and stared at him. Her eyes shot suspicion and disappointment in equal measure.

He'd expected her reaction. It was all going according to plan. By confessing one small lie and playing a man with scruples, Enya would never suspect that he was keeping a much bigger secret.

"I didn't cook the meal." He ran a hand through his hair. "Fact is, I can't cook to save my life. I ordered it from a restaurant. I wanted to impress you. I'm sorry."

Enya's chin dropped. A breath of air rushed from her mouth, and then she started laughing. "Oh my God. That's your lie? That you can't cook? Join the club! I even manage to burn water."

Zoltan grinned. "So you're not mad?" Bingo! She now believed he was an honest man, one who didn't even want to lie about an inconsequential thing.

She took a step toward him and put her hands on his chest. "No. I'm not mad. But why didn't you just take me out to a restaurant? That would have been enough."

He chuckled. "Sure, but I wanted to make sure that you'd come to my condo, where we could be alone."

Her eyelashes swung up, and her blue eyes were full of mischief. "So you planned all this, greeting me at the door with just a towel, still dripping from your shower."

"Well, if I may point out, you did arrive a half-hour early, so it's technically not my fault." Zoltan pulled her hands to his lips and kissed her knuckles. "Though I have to admit, it couldn't have worked out more perfectly if I'd planned it."

Which he had. He'd timed it so that she'd seen him masturbate in the shower. It had had the desired effect and catapulted Enya directly into his arms. Now all he had to do was to pull her deeper into his net, first tying her to him with his sexual prowess—which she clearly responded to—then plying her with promises of love and devotion, until she trusted him and shared her true identity and the location of her compound with him. And once he was inside, he could finally execute his plan. Everything was running smoothly, like a well-oiled machine.

A dull ache suddenly crept up from the top of his spine into the back of his skull. The momentary pain made him squeeze his eyes shut and suck in a breath. Fuck! Not now! He didn't need one of his crippling migraine attacks right now.

"Eric?"

He opened his eyes and focused. But he couldn't think straight. Who was Eric?

"Eric," Enya said again, and cupped his cheeks with her warm palms. The soothing touch made him temporarily forget about the pain. "Are you all right?"

He forced himself to smile. "Yes, I'm fine. Just a bit of a headache. Nothing to worry about. I probably just need to eat something." He motioned toward the kitchen. "Shall we have dinner?"

"Are you sure you're okay? How about an aspirin?"

He shook his head. He'd tried every conceivable drug— legal and illegal—and nothing had ever helped. "No, no. It'll go away."

Enya pulled his head to her and tenderly pressed her lips to his. Oddly, her kiss seemed to push the migraine back down to where it had come from. He responded to her kiss, swiping his tongue along the seam of her lips until she parted them and granted him access. Suddenly, the pain was forgotten and their tongues danced, mated. Reluctantly, he severed the kiss.

"Mmm. That helped. Thank you." He pulled her hand to his mouth and pressed a kiss into her palm.

A few minutes later, they sat down at the dining table and began to eat. The sun had set while Enya had given him the most incredible blow job he'd ever had. Candles on the dining table and soft music from the sound system contributed to the romantic ambiance he'd created to make her welcome.

That Enya wouldn't need any romancing to get her into bed, he'd gathered from their first encounter. But it wasn't simply about getting her into bed; it was about making her feel special. So special that she would fall for him and trust him. Fucking wasn't the problem. They had plenty of chemistry when it came to that—more than he'd expected. Now it was time to romance her and to play the man a woman like her needed: strong and demanding, yet totally devoted to her and fulfilling her every wish. In other words: pussy-whipped. The strong and demanding part came naturally. The rest he could fake. The prize was worth it: the annihilation of the Stealth Guardians, and making Enya his personal sex slave, something he'd dreamed of from the day he'd first laid eyes on her.

"I needed this after the week I had," Enya said after taking a sip from her wine.

Seeing an opening to get her to talk about herself and hopefully the Stealth Guardians, Zoltan asked, "Trouble at work?"

She gave a one-shouldered shrug. "I wouldn't call it trouble." She seemed reluctant to elaborate.

"Well, stress might not look like trouble, but it's all the same. I should know. Some weeks I barely have time to eat. Hey, but I knew what I was in for when I went into business for myself."

He'd not only taken Eric Vaughn's condo, but also his life, then researched the real Eric's backstory to make sure he kept as close as possible to the truth, while wiping out as much of the man's electronic footprint as possible, erasing records that could lead somebody to believe Zoltan wasn't who he pretended to be. He knew that Enya would do a background check on him eventually, if she hadn't done so already. "Sometimes the workload can get overwhelming."

"It's not that. In fact, it's been quiet the last week. Just like the week before."

"Well, that's good, isn't it?"

"Not really. I get nervous when nothing is happening."

"Hmm." Had Enya noticed that he'd pulled demons off Baltimore so that they didn't get in the way of his plan? "You didn't mention what sector you're working in"—he raised his hands—"and I'm not gonna ask now, but could it just be seasonal and that's why it's quiet right now? I mean, in my field, it gets frantic just before the year-end, and then there's a bit of a lull."

She cast him a hesitant look, as if she was assessing how much to tell him. Zoltan shoved a forkful of food into his mouth so he didn't appear too eager for her answer.

"I work in security," she said. "There's never a quiet time in my business. That's why I'm worried. It feels like the calm before the storm."

This wasn't good. Maybe he should send a few demons to Baltimore, sacrifice a few pawns to alleviate Enya's suspicions that something bigger was brewing.

"Have you talked to your boss?" he asked.

"That's just it. I brought it up with my superiors, and they don't seem to be too concerned."

He shrugged. "Then maybe it's nothing." He lifted his glass. "It would mean you can spend more time with me."

She clinked her glass to his. "When you say spend time, did you mean…" She motioned to the living room, where only minutes earlier they'd fucked like rabbits.

"That's a start. But sex isn't all I'm after. I enjoy your company."

Enya smiled and drank from her glass, then ate a bite from her plate. "By the way, this is delicious."

"Thank you." He winked at her. "I picked it up myself."

Enya's eyes sparkled with humor. She looked even younger when she smiled, something she didn't do much when she was in the company of the other Stealth Guardians and fighting his demons. Tonight she was different, more relaxed. Was it the sex that had softened her? Or the fact that there was no audience? Nobody who could judge her?

"Do you do that a lot, getting food from a restaurant and pretending you cooked it?"

He finished chewing. "Why don't you ask what you really want to ask?"

"Which would be?"

"Whether there are a lot of women in my life."

To his surprise, Enya blushed at that and focused her eyes on her plate. "That's really none of my business. I was just curious whether that's something men do these days to impress women."

Enya was cute when she was lying. "I don't know if that's what men do. It was my first try." Zoltan waited until she lifted her head again and met his gaze. "And clearly I'm not very good at hiding the truth from you."

She chuckled softly. "Maybe that's a good thing. No woman likes to be lied to."

"And I don't like to lie to you. You deserve better."

"Do I?"

Before he could answer, a bolt of pain shot through his head. He dropped his utensils on the plate and gripped the edge of the table for support. But another wave of pain hit him out of nowhere, jolting through his body. "Sorry, Enya, I have to..."

He shot up from his chair, intent on fleeing, on leaving the room so she wouldn't witness his debilitating condition, his weakness.

"Eric! What's wrong?"

He pressed his hands to his temples and tried to move, tried to walk, but his legs didn't cooperate. He stumbled over his own feet. If only he could make it to the sofa. But another wave of searing pain nearly paralyzed him. His knees buckled.

All of a sudden, he felt Enya's arms around him, supporting him, guiding him. "I've got you. Let's get you to the couch." She steered him to the sofa and lowered him with an ease that no human woman could have managed with a man his size. "Just lie back. Is it the headache again?"

He couldn't open his eyes. "Migraine."

Enya helped him stretch out and sat down on the edge next to his hip. "Do you have meds for it? Shall I get them? In the bathroom?"

"No."

"In the bedroom, then?" She squeezed his hand, and he held on to it for dear life.

"No. No meds. They don't work."

"But—"

Another wave of pain made his body spasm as if he was having an epileptic seizure.

"What can I do?" Enya asked, her voice full of concern, full of… pity.

He couldn't let her see him like this. No woman wanted a weak man, least of all Enya. She was a warrior. How could she ever look up to a man who was weak? This could destroy his plan. "Leave. Please, leave."

"Are you crazy? You need help." She grabbed him by the shoulders and bent over him. "There has to be something that can be done."

He knew there was no remedy for his condition. He had to get through this without any help. Alone. "I don't want you to see me like—"

She pressed her finger over his lips. "Hush." Then she put her palms to his temples and cupped his head, holding him still. "Just relax. Think of something that makes you happy. And just breathe, in and out."

She brushed her lips to his in a featherlight kiss, her torso now fully touching his. Her breasts rubbed against his shirt, and he felt her warmth and softness calm him.

"That's good," he murmured, and put one arm around her waist, holding her close. "Your weight on me, it helps."

Enya came to lie on top of him, one leg wedged between his thighs, rubbing against his balls.

He let out a deep sigh. With it, some of the pain left his body.

"Again," Enya murmured. "Just breathe."

He followed her instruction and took a deep breath, then let it out. Enya rubbed his temples softly. More pain seeped from his body. He inhaled again, his stomach lifting with the intake of air, then felt Enya shift on top of him. Arousal instead of pain suddenly charged through his body.

Zoltan opened his eyes and put his arm around her back, while he slid his other hand to her ass. "You're a miracle worker. Normally these attacks last a half-hour."

"I didn't do anything," she said. "I only reminded you to breathe and relax."

"Wow."

"Hasn't your doctor taught you any relaxation techniques?"

He shook his head. He had no doctor. As a demon, that option wasn't open to him. One blood draw and he would be exposed for his green blood.

"Maybe I should thank you," he said, and pulled Enya's face to him.

When their lips met, the last vestiges of pain fled and made way for the lust now coursing through his blood. His hands weren't idle. He was already shoving her dress up to her waist and yanking on her G-string.

Enya lifted her head. "You can't possibly—"

He pressed his cock against her soft flesh to make her aware of how hard she'd gotten him. "I can. That is, if you want me to."

Now more than ever, after seeing him at his worst, at his most vulnerable, his most defenseless, he had to prove to her that he was the man she needed.

Enya sat up. "Eric—"

"Don't say it," he interrupted. "No woman wants a man who's weak." He silently cursed the migraine attack. Had it screwed up his carefully laid plan?

"Weak?" Her forehead furrowed. "You think you're weak because you have migraines?" She blew out a breath and shook her head. "Idiot!"

Instead of jumping up and leaving, to his surprise, Enya pulled her dress over her head and tossed it to the floor. She wore no bra.

"Are you—"

She gave him a look that said more than words.

"You still want me," he murmured.

"Obviously, you've been with the wrong women until now. You're not gonna frighten me away with a migraine."

"Obviously." He put his hand on her nape and pulled her to him for a kiss. "I have the feeling not much is gonna frighten you." Though he knew that one thing would drive her away for certain: finding out that he was a demon. That he was Zoltan, the Great One. But for tonight, he had to put that fact out of his mind. Enya had just shown him that his vulnerability could bring them closer.

"You'll never frighten me," she promised.

With a few movements, she freed herself from her panties, while Zoltan opened his pants and shoved them and his boxer briefs down to mid-thigh. He didn't have time for more, because Enya was already straddling him and lowering herself onto his cock, impaling herself impatiently. He didn't mind, because he was just as impatient.

Being with Enya was exciting, exhilarating, electrifying. She gave herself so freely, without restraints, without boundaries. And for now, he didn't want to change the way she saw him, because once she found out who he really was, everything would change.

He would become her master, she his slave.

8

Enya looked over Pearce's shoulder at the computer screen. They were alone in the command center. The others had already left for their various assignments.

"Who else is on the detail?" Enya asked.

Pearce scrolled farther down. "Just you and Jay."

"Will Jay be carving the portal?"

Pearce chuckled. "Are you kidding? Cinead is gonna do it himself. He was around back when we had the dagger the first time. He knows how it's done." He winked at her. "He's probably champing at the bit already. He's wanted to move out of his old house for decades, and all that's been keeping him there was the fact that he couldn't move to a place without a portal."

"Well, all that's changed now. Finally we can open new compounds and new residences for our people."

"Yep, the source dagger makes it all possible."

It was the only tool that could create portals, the teleportation devices the Stealth Guardians relied upon to securely travel from one compound to another. The dagger had been lost for centuries, but only months earlier they'd recovered it—and not a moment too soon, or it would have fallen into the hands of the demons.

"You'll meet Jay at the council compound," Pearce said. "There, they'll sign out the source dagger to you. You'll travel to the compound in Seattle via portal. From there—"

"I know the drill. Jay and I will travel invisibly from there until we reach Cinead's new home. I assume he's already there?"

Pearce nodded. "He traveled there last night, taking the same precautions as you will be to make sure the demons won't get a whiff of you. After you're done, you and Jay will bring the dagger back to the council compound. I'm told there's a long list of applicants who've applied for a personal portal."

"I assume the approvals go by seniority?" After all, Cinead was one of the oldest living Stealth Guardians and a valued member of the Council of Nine, their ruling body.

"Not necessarily. The locations for the new portals are thoroughly vetted for any security concerns. If you must know, Cinead's first choice of location was denied, because the council deemed it not secure enough."

"Even though Cinead's on the council?"

Pearce shrugged. "Didn't matter."

"So what was his first choice?"

"Vancouver Island."

"What was wrong with that?"

"The council will never approve an island, because there's no escape route via land, should the portal have to be destroyed in case of detection by the demons."

"Makes sense."

Pearce pointed to the clock. "You should get going."

"See you later."

"Good luck."

Enya turned and left the command center. The sound of her heels hitting the stone floor echoed in the long corridor of the compound. She descended two flights of stairs to reach the level where the compound's portal was located. She'd placed her hand on the symbol of a dagger that was etched into the stone and already felt a warmth underneath her palm, indicating that the portal responded to her command to open, when she heard footsteps behind her. She looked over her shoulder and saw Winter hurrying down the stairs.

She wore her long red hair down, and it looked like she'd just awoken. "Enya!"

Enya took her hand from the portal and turned. "Is something the matter?"

"I heard you're going to see Cinead."

She nodded. "Yes, he's moving to his new place, and we're installing a new portal."

"Logan told me." Winter hesitated. "Cinead called me last night."

"About?"

Winter met her gaze full-on. "The same as always."

"Hmm." Enya knew what this meant. Winter, a true psychic, who'd once been kidnapped by the demons who wanted to exploit her gift, had visions of events from the past as well as the future. One of these visions had saved her own life, another had led to the discovery of the source dagger and indirectly saved Pearce's life. But there were other visions that had led nowhere, as in the case of Cinead's kidnapped son.

"He said that while he was packing up the house, he found an old toy that belonged to his son, and he wanted me to have it. Would you mind bringing it back for me?"

"No problem." Enya sighed. "He's not giving up hope, is he?"

"Would you? As long as there's even a one percent chance that his son is still alive, he'll keep looking." Winter let out a long breath. "And hoping that I'll have another vision. I don't have the heart to tell him that I doubt I'll ever have another vision about his son's abduction. He keeps sending me things baby Angus might have touched in the hopes that it will help me conjure a vision and tell us if he's still alive."

"Maybe the move will be good for him. There are too many memories in his old place. It's time he moved on, physically and emotionally." Despite her words, Enya understood the elder statesman. His baby son had been believed killed by demons over two hundred years earlier, and only a few years ago, one of Winter's visions had established that the baby had been abducted, not killed. Ever since then, Cinead had tried to find his son. His wife, heartbroken after the loss of her child, had killed herself on her son's first birthday, unable to continue living with her grief. Cinead had never bonded with another.

"Thanks, Enya." Winter turned on her heel and walked back up the stairs.

Moments later, Enya stepped into the portal, willed it to close, and allowed the darkness to surround her. She concentrated on her destination, the secret council compound, and felt the air around her stir. Seconds later, everything was quiet again, and the portal opened, allowing light to stream inside. The sudden light made her sway, and for a fraction of a second, she felt dizzy. Damn it, she should be used to this. Besides, only creatures other than Stealth Guardians felt the disorienting movements of the portal.

Enya stepped out into the corridor and was instantly greeted by Jay, her fellow Stealth Guardian, who'd been assigned to the Baltimore compound a few years earlier and was now on assignment at the council compound.

"Hey, Enya. Long time."

"Yep." She wasn't particularly keen on Jay. While assigned to Baltimore, he'd made a couple of passes at her, and she'd rejected him. She hadn't exactly been very diplomatic about it either, which meant Jay had been rather frosty to her ever since.

"So it's just you and me. Let's get it over with, then."

He motioned her to follow him into the direction of the archive. Considering that she had seniority—Jay was a good three decades younger than she—it irked her that he made it look like he was giving the orders. Not wanting him to get any ideas, she sped up and walked past him, then moved into the center of the narrowing corridor so he had to walk behind her. When she heard him huff, she grinned to herself. One-nil Enya.

In front of the archive, two heavily armed guards were posted. This hadn't always been the case. The coded entry system had been sufficient to protect the contents of the council compound's archives before the source dagger had been recovered and placed there. Protecting it was now the council's highest priority.

"State your name and business, guardians," the female guard demanded.

"Enya and Jay to retrieve the source dagger and bring it to council member Cinead," Enya said before Jay could open his mouth.

The female guard nodded at her colleague, who pressed a small receiver in his ear and spoke into the microphone extending from it. "We have an Enya and Jay here to retrieve the source dagger for council member Cinead."

For a moment, there was silence, then the guard looked at them. "Council member Norton is on his way. Please wait over there." He pointed to a bench several feet from the door.

Enya made her way there, but didn't sit down. Neither did Jay.

"Tight security," Jay murmured.

"As it should be," Enya replied tightly.

"But to waste a council member's time to sign out the dagger? That's a bit over the top, don't you think?"

"And who else, in your opinion, should have the authority to sign it out?" she snapped. "Pearce nearly died for this dagger. Our compound fought to get it back. And you think it's a waste of time for a council member to have to come down here to verify our credentials and sign it out to us? Think again." She crossed her arms over her chest.

"Hey, you got a bee in your bonnet or what?"

"What the fuck's that supposed to mean?" She glared at him. She didn't know why he irritated her, but he did.

To his credit, Jay quickly said, "Nothing."

It didn't take long until Norton walked toward them. "Enya, Jay, good to see you both." As always, he was casual. "I reviewed your assignment." He pointed to the door of the archive. "Shall we?" To the two guards he said, "Please open the archive for us."

The female guardian entered a code into the keypad next to it, then pressed her thumb onto the scanner. Apparently, the automatic entry system had also been upgraded. When Norton caught Enya's look, he explained, "Another layer of security. Only the guards assigned to the archive are able to operate the keypad. And only during their hours of duty. It's all programmed in. The guards change every two hours, and rotate in an unpredictable pattern, making it impossible for an outsider to figure out."

"You're leaving nothing to chance," Enya said. "I like it."

Norton opened the door and walked in ahead, then held the door open for her and Jay. Inside, it smelled musty. The large, cavernous room was made of thick stone walls on two sides and butted up against the mountain that the new council compound was located on. As they walked deeper into the space that contained row after row of steel shelving with boxes and crates, overhead lights, activated by motion sensors, flicked on. They were neon lights, and as long as they worked, the Stealth Guardians could be sure that no demon had entered, because neon lights burned out instantly in the presence of demons.

Norton led them to a corner of the room that penetrated the mountain the farthest. There, the symbol of a key was carved into the stone, but there was no keyhole. Norton placed his hand over the symbol, and a few seconds later, part of the stone was gone. Behind it was a small space laid out with dark green velvet, and in its midst lay the source dagger.

Even Enya had to admit that the vessel the dagger was kept in was genius. "So even if the demons got in here, they could never open the dagger's hiding place."

"That's right," Norton said. "Only a Stealth Guardian can open it."

"But isn't this like a tiny portal?" Jay asked. "One that's connected to all other portals?"

Norton shook his head. "No. All portals carry the symbol of the dagger to connect them. This doesn't. It might look like a portal, but believe me, it can't be accessed from anywhere else. It's safe, even if this compound were to be compromised."

Norton reached into the opening and retrieved the dagger, then turned to face Enya. "Guard it with your life."

Enya took the dagger and nodded.

"I'll contact Cinead and let him know that you're on your way."

Less than an hour later, Enya and Jay entered Cinead's new residence several miles outside Seattle's city limits and made themselves visible the moment they were inside the foyer and away from prying eyes.

Cinead was already expecting them and put away his pocket watch. Despite being several centuries old, he looked like a virile man in his late fifties. "Right on time."

"Cinead, it's good to see you," Enya said.

Jay stretched his hand out and shook Cinead's. "It's an honor to be chosen to witness the creation of a new portal."

Enya stopped herself from rolling her eyes. She'd never thought that Jay was one to suck up to the elders, but it was all too clear now why he'd gotten one of the assignments at the council compound, where rarely anybody ever saw combat. She preferred to work in the field, to slay demons, to defend her people. Unfortunately, there hadn't been much demon slaying lately. Perhaps today was her chance to speak to Cinead directly and tell him about her concerns. But first things first.

Enya reached into the inside pocket of her leather jacket and pulled out the dagger. "Here it is."

Cinead took it from her hands, his mouth dropping open. "Every time I see it, it takes my breath away. The power, the magic this weapon possesses... I can feel it seep into me just by holding it in my hands." Then he caught himself and smiled. "I'm sorry. You must think me an old fool, talking like this. But you're both still young; you weren't around when we lost the source dagger. It was a tragedy. And the circumstances under which it disappeared are still hazy today." He sighed. "Hmm. Let's get to work. The less time the dagger spends out of its hiding place, the better."

Cinead walked through a door that led down a staircase. At the bottom of the stairs, he turned into a corridor that split in two directions. He took the one to the left, and Enya and Jay continued following him until they reached a large room with several doors. Cinead opened one door and marched through it. He flipped a light switch. They stood in a small room that at one time had been a coal cellar. Coal dust still stuck to the crevices between the bricks.

"This is where the portal will go," Cinead said, and pointed to a wall that was fashioned from large flagstones. He approached the wall. Enya and Jay flanked him.

Cinead took a bow before the wall, then he set the blade to the stone and began the etching. Enya watched him and was surprised to witness that Cinead didn't seem to need much force to scratch the symbol of a Stealth Guardian dagger into the stone. As if the dagger did it on its own and only needed a guiding hand.

"Unbelievable," Jay whispered, and for once, she had to agree with him.

"It's like magic," she murmured.

"Ancient magic," Cinead said, and continued etching the symbol of the dagger into the stone. It didn't take long for it to take shape. Only minutes passed instead of hours, like Enya had expected.

"And now to the final stroke." Cinead opened his left hand, and before Enya knew what he was about to do, he was cutting into it with the source dagger.

"Cinead!"

But Cinead didn't even seem to hear her. Instead, he pressed his bleeding palm over the symbol he'd just carved. Instantly the stone beneath his hand began to glow. A few seconds later, the flagstone was gone. Behind it was a space the size of an elevator shaft.

"A new portal," Enya said with awe. "You did it."

Cinead turned around and smiled at her. "The dagger has lost none of its power. Now our people can fulfill their destiny and save mankind from the demons."

"Amen to that," Jay said.

After wiping the blood from the dagger, Cinead handed it back to Enya and wrapped a cloth around the wound.

"You should let me bandage you properly," Enya said. It would give her the opportunity to talk to him.

Cinead looked at her, already shaking his head, when their gazes connected. "Oh well, why not? You're probably better at this than I am."

They made their way upstairs and entered the great room, a large room that served as kitchen, dining, and living room.

"There should be some bandages in the top drawer of that cabinet over there," Cinead said, and pointed to one of the kitchen cabinets. "Jay, why don't you get them?"

While Jay walked into the kitchen, Cinead sat on the sofa, and Enya took a seat next to him.

"You're here to pick up the toy for Winter?" he asked in a low voice.

Enya nodded and replied just as quietly, "Yes, but that's not all. I need to bring something to your attention. It's important."

Cinead raised an eyebrow.

"It's not in here," Jay called from the kitchen.

Cinead turned his head. "Oh, I must have put it somewhere else. You know, I think after the move I decided to put bandages into the bathroom. Upstairs, second door. Would you be so kind, Jay?"

"No problem."

The moment Jay left the room, Cinead said, "That should give us a few minutes. He'll never find them, 'cause they're in the downstairs powder room."

Enya chuckled. "You're terrible."

"Resourceful. Now, what is it you wanted to talk to me about?"

"The demons. Over the past few weeks, they've been too quiet. There have been no run-ins with them in Baltimore, not even any sightings. As if they've disappeared. That's not normal. Baltimore is a hotbed for them. So why would they suddenly all disappear? Something is up."

"You had Aiden speak to Barclay about it, didn't you? Primus brought it up with the council."

"And?"

Cinead shrugged. "The lack of demons isn't evidence enough that they're planning something big. We've had no worrisome reports from other compounds. It's an anomaly for sure, but at this point there's nothing we can do, even if they are planning something. Just remain vigilant."

"But—"

He put his hand on her forearm. "You're a good warrior, Enya. I commend you for your diligence. But sometimes a lull in the action is just that: a lull. Use it to recharge your batteries. And live a little." He rose. "Now let me get the toy I found." He walked to a mahogany armoire and opened its doors.

Enya approached. Inside the armoire were stacks of papers, small trinkets, and other items that most likely only had sentimental value.

"I haven't put everything back on the shelves yet," Cinead said, turning, his eyes displaying a telltale sheen. Dealing with old memories was hard for him.

He held an old rag doll in one hand, a small framed painting in the other. Enya glanced at the painting. It was that of a naked baby lying on its stomach. She'd seen it several times. Cinead and his wife had it painted a few weeks before Angus's abduction. She reached for the doll. The colors had faded, but she could still make out that it had been a knight.

"My wife made it for him, while she was pregnant. She knew we'd have a boy."

"She was very talented." Enya put the toy into the same pocket as the dagger. "I'll give it to Winter the minute I return to Baltimore."

"Thank you." He didn't look at her. He looked at the picture of his son.

"One day, I hope you'll find him," Enya said, though she knew there was little hope of ever finding out what happened to the baby, let alone finding him alive.

9

Zoltan had chosen two of his weakest and most gullible demons for this mission. They were also the most expendable. Now he could only hope that they followed his instructions to the letter and showed up exactly when and where they were needed. They would serve two goals. The first was to squash Enya's suspicion that something was going on due to the lack of demon activity in Baltimore. She had said as much during their dinner a week earlier by telling him that work had been too *quiet*. She'd called it the calm before the storm, and she wasn't wrong. Things were brewing in the demon world.

The second goal was even more important: the two demons he'd chosen would make sure that his relationship with Enya graduated from a purely sexual one to one where she would see him as a partner whom she could trust with her life. Not that he minded the sex. Hell, he enjoyed it more than anything else. The way she got him hot with just one look, one touch, was addictive, and just thinking of their last encounter got him randier than he'd ever been. And then there was another thing about Enya: the way she'd soothed away his migraine by rubbing his temples, by pressing her body to his, and by whispering calming words to him had been unexpected.

Oddly enough, he'd felt a connection to her at that moment, and his nefarious plan had vanished for the rest of the night. When she'd straddled him after his migraine dissipated, something changed. He hadn't simply fucked her; he'd made love to her. It was a first for him. Even now, he didn't know what to think of it. Had he gone completely mad? There was only one reason why he was with Enya: so she would get him inside the world of the Stealth Guardians, so he could destroy them.

Actually, there was a second reason: he liked fucking her. He wanted to make her his sex slave. Nobody else would ever touch her but Zoltan. He would chain her to his bed and take her whenever he wanted to. Which was all the time. Yes, he would fuck her for eternity.

But right now, he had to move things along in the trust department, because for his liking, Enya was still too reluctant to open up to him, even though she was surrendering to him sexually in every way. So he'd devised a plan to give her a gentle shove in the right direction.

He'd chosen a restaurant that was bordering on a bad neighborhood, yet had excellent food. Since he'd confessed to Enya that he couldn't cook worth shit, she'd been all too happy to agree to go out for dinner. For a proper date, as he'd suggested. The restaurant stood at the end of a cul-de-sac, which meant he knew from which direction Enya had to approach. She'd declined his offer to pick her up from her home, which, of course, he'd counted on.

At the entrance to the cul-de-sac, Zoltan had already smashed one of the streetlights, of which there were few to begin with. His action ensured that no light filtered into his hiding place, the entrance to an auto shop. He'd arrived thirty minutes prior to the time he'd made the reservation for, though he didn't expect Enya to show up early. She had no reason to believe that he wanted anything more than to spend the night in bed with her. Nor did he think that she would arrive invisibly. At the very least, she'd make herself visible as soon as she entered the cul-de-sac to ascertain that no restaurant patrons became witness to her supernatural skill.

The stage was set. The curtain was about to rise.

Zoltan felt his heart pound. A lot of things could go wrong; however, he not only counted on his own demons' inadequacy, but also on Enya's fighting skills. He'd seen her fighting demons often enough to know that she could handle two of them, if with a little difficulty.

His ears perked up. He heard the clickety-clack of high heels on the uneven pavement grow louder as the person walked closer. A few seconds more, and he could make out Enya's lithe form in the darkness. She wore a short dress again, showing off her slender legs. Her leather jacket was open in the front, and he had to assume that the only reason she wore it on this rather warm night was so she had a place to hide her weapons.

Enya walked to the entrance of the cul-de-sac. Nobody else seemed to be in the vicinity. Zoltan glanced around. Where were his demons? He held his breath and listened. But there were no sounds other than the distant humming of cars that drove by on a nearby street. A movement from the corner of his eye made him snap his head in that direction. It was them. They were approaching silently, staying in the shadows of the buildings, and in a few seconds they'd be at the entrance to the cul-de-sac with Enya facing the opposite direction. She wouldn't see them coming. Nor would she hear them: the demons weren't wearing their usual boots. They'd donned... *tennis shoes*? What the fuck?

Shit! He couldn't interfere yet. Couldn't simply call out to her. The demons would see him and most certainly blow his cover. But he had to do something. He bent down and grabbed a couple of small stones, a little larger than gravel, and tossed them in the direction of the demons. The sound of the stones hitting the pavement made Enya spin around.

The two demons, though appearing startled, immediately charged at her. They'd lost their element of surprise, but they still had an advantage: they were already holding their daggers in their hands, while Enya had to dig into her inside pocket to remove hers. But she was fast, ready to defend herself in an instant.

From his hiding place, Zoltan watched the fight, his heartbeat accelerating. Despite wearing a dress and high heels, Enya kept her two attackers at bay, delivering kicks and blows. She catapulted one of the demons against a wall, while trying to stab the other. But demons were strong, even the two losers Zoltan had chosen for this suicide mission. He counted on Enya, on her hate for the demons and her skill as a fighter, to hold her own. She'd done so before, killed more than her fair share of his underlings. At least tonight, she had Zoltan's permission, even though she didn't know it.

One of the demons landed a blow, then followed it up with a swipe of his dagger. Enya blocked it with her forearm, while kicking back to fend off the guy who was attacking from behind, but she couldn't prevent the blade from cutting into her leather jacket. Had she not worn it, a deep gash would now grace her arm. Enya managed to grab the guy's wrist and twist the dagger from his grip. It clattered to the ground, while Enya tried to drive her own dagger into the demon's chest. The other demon attacking her from behind prevented her dagger from reaching its target.

Enya whirled around, simultaneously kicking back at the demon who'd lost his dagger, while she swung her blade at the other one.

Time to intervene.

Zoltan left his hiding place and ran toward the melee. The unarmed demon searched the ground for his dagger, but Zoltan had seen where the weapon had landed and was already heading for it. They got there at the same time. Zoltan kicked his underling in the stomach, catapulting him back, and reached for the weapon. His subject stared at Zoltan, his eyes wide with disbelief, his mouth opening. Zoltan flicked his wrist and let the dagger fly, planting it in the demon's throat, cutting off the words that were going to make it over his lips.

"Eric?"

Enya's panicked cry told him that she'd seen him join the fight. Good. But her surprise had also given the second demon a moment to gather his wits and thrust his knee into her stomach. She had to make a step back to keep her balance, then tried to kick back, but her leg was stuck. Zoltan focused on the spot—her high heel was caught in between the cobblestones. Her attacker grinned and lunged forward, his dagger in his hand, ready to stab Enya.

"Shit!" Zoltan yelled, and barreled toward his subject. There was no time to snatch the dagger from the dead demon. No matter. Zoltan charged the demon and wrestled him to the ground. But the bastard was stronger than Zoltan had previously thought. The demon blocked Zoltan's next blow, and then their gazes connected. Surprise and disbelief flashed in his subject's eyes in equal measure.

"Oh G—"

A dagger came flying and landed squarely in the demon's throat, cutting off his words before he could betray Zoltan's identity. From the corner of his eye, Zoltan saw Enya approach. He took a deep breath and pulled the dagger from the demon's throat, ready for his next performance: to appear surprised at seeing green blood. He stared at it, then turned his head to Enya to give her a confused stare, and saw a movement behind her. Green eyes lit up in the darkness just a few yards behind Enya. A third demon.

"Eric, oh my God. Are you okay?" Enya asked.

Zoltan jumped up, dagger still in hand, and pushed Enya out of the way, making her crash to the ground. Just in time, because the third demon's dagger flew through the air, aimed at Enya's back. Seeing Zoltan, the demon turned tail, but Zoltan couldn't let him escape. This third demon wasn't part of the mission. Somebody else had sent him. And if this demon reported back that Zoltan, the Great One, had saved a Stealth Guardian's life, his days would be numbered. In single digits.

"Eric, no! Stop!" Enya called after him. "He'll kill you!"

He heard her footfalls behind him, but he couldn't stop. His life now depended on killing this witness. He turned the corner and saw the demon already casting a vortex, but Zoltan couldn't allow it. He aimed the dagger and flicked his wrist. The dagger hit the demon in the back before he could step into the vortex. As life seeped from him, the vortex collapsed as well. Zoltan breathed hard. This had been close. Too close.

"Eric, oh my God." Enya stopped beside him. "You killed him?"

Zoltan turned his head to her, doing his best to turn his face into a mask of surprise and fear. Mimicking fear wasn't too hard, since he'd truly been afraid that his plan would backfire. Besides, he didn't want Enya dead. She was worth more alive.

"He tried to kill you. They all did." He let out a ragged breath and looked at his hands and the green blood on them. "What is this? What are these people? What did they want from you?"

She looked at him, a strange expression on her face. "You're very good with a knife."

He shrugged. He had an explanation for that too. "I wasn't always an investment manager. I grew up on the wrong side of the tracks, so to speak." He sighed. "But you haven't answered my questions. Who are these people? Because for sure they don't look normal."

"They're not. But… Listen, I can't talk about this now. I need to get a cleanup crew here first. Contain the scene."

"Well, let's call the cops," Zoltan suggested. That was what a human would say, wasn't it?

Enya shook her head. "No cops. My… uh company will deal with it."

"I just stabbed two men, and you killed a third. We have to tell the police now, or they'll never believe that we acted in self-defense."

Enya put her hands on his biceps. "We can't. The police can never find out what happened here. Nobody can. Please, I'll explain everything. Later. Tonight, I need to get this cleaned up. And you have to get cleaned up too. If any of your clothes got stained, toss them. The green will never come out."

"What is it?"

"Blood."

"Come on, Enya, don't play a prank on me now. I'm kind of on the edge here."

"It's the truth. It's green blood. And the three men we killed are evil. Truly evil. I can't tell you anything else right now. I have to take care of all this before somebody comes across the bodies." She pulled out her phone and pressed a button. "I need a cleanup… Yeah, guess they're back… Three. All dead." She gave the address. "Thanks. I'll wait." Then she disconnected.

"Who are we waiting for?"

"You're not," she said. "You need to leave now. It's better if my colleagues don't find you here."

"But I can't just let you wait here on your own. It's dark and dangerous."

She pointed to one of the dead demons. "I think I'll be all right for tonight." She put her hand on his nape and pulled his face to hers. "Please. Go home. I'll see you tomorrow. Then I'll answer all your questions. Okay?"

He nodded and kissed her. "Dinner tomorrow?"

"You bet."

He turned around and walked away. Tomorrow Enya would open up to him. She trusted him now. Trusted him because he'd killed for her. He'd saved her life. His plan was playing out nicely. There was only one problem: who had sent the third demon and why?

10

While she waited for her brethren to arrive, Enya dragged the three dead demons, one by one, behind a dumpster around the corner. Luckily, nobody saw her. The blood the demons had spilled in the alley was substantial, but she couldn't do anything about that before her colleagues were here.

Her heart was still thundering from the adrenaline pumping through her veins. She hadn't been prepared for this fight. She'd let down her guard. How stupid of her to wear high heels and a dress! It had impeded her movements, made her slower, and nearly cost Enya her life when one of her heels had gotten stuck in the cobblestones. If Eric hadn't shown up just in time and killed two of her attackers... She didn't even want to think of the possible outcome. But he'd jumped right in as if a street fight with daggers was his hobby. She'd never seen such a brave human. Would he have been just as brave had he known that the creatures were demons? She shrugged. It didn't matter. What mattered was that he'd helped her out of a bad situation.

A dark, unmarked van approached, and Enya recognized it immediately. She stepped out of the shadows and waved at the driver, directing him toward the dumpster, where he reversed to line the back of the van up with it. Moments later, Hamish stepped out of the driver's side, while Aiden walked around from the passenger side and already opened the back doors.

Hamish looked at the bodies. "Nice job." He pointed to her dress. "Guess the dress is a goner."

She looked down at herself. Several green bloodstains were visible on her dress. "Sucks! I just bought it. Fucking demons!"

"Weren't you the one complaining that there hasn't been any demon activity lately?" Aiden asked.

"Whatever."

"And what's with the dress anyway?" Aiden asked. "Not exactly the right outfit for patrolling."

She narrowed her eyes and pointed to the dead bodies. "You gonna lift them into the van or not? I've got to clean up the blood in the alley." She reached into the van and pulled out a heavy can with a hose and a nozzle attached to it, without waiting for Aiden's reply.

"Well, let's get to it, then," Hamish said.

While Hamish and Aiden loaded the dead guys into the back of the van, Enya walked back to the scene of the fight and washed down the green blood, directing it into the drains along the sidewalks, until all evidence was gone. She placed the half-empty can back into the van and shut the doors.

"You coming to the incinerator with us?" Hamish said.

"No, but you can give me a ride halfway home."

Enya squeezed onto the front bench of the van, next to Aiden, and pulled the door shut. Hamish got in on the other side, started the engine, and drove off.

"So three, huh?" Aiden asked. "That's impressive, even for you."

"Particularly in those heels," Hamish added with a grin.

Enya looked out of the side window. They would soon realize that she couldn't have killed those three without help.

"Yeah, well, I got lucky."

"Cut the crap," Aiden said. He motioned to her dress. "Who were you with? Because for sure you weren't patrolling in this."

"Maybe I was playing bait."

"Enya, stop," Hamish said calmly. He'd always been more like a brother to her than all the others at the compound. But their relationship had changed when Hamish bonded with Tessa, the mayor of Baltimore. "As much as I admire your fighting skills and know how good you are, defeating three demons in a dress and high heels is nearly impossible. What really happened?"

She glanced past Aiden, met Hamish's sideways look, and let out a sigh. Here it went. "I had help."

"Who?" Aiden asked.

There was silence for a few heartbeats before she answered, "A guy. He managed to grab one of the demons' daggers and stab him with it. And when the third ran off, he chased him down and killed him."

Hamish stopped the van. "Human? Vampire? What is he? And more importantly, where is he now?"

"Human. I told him to go home."

"After what he witnessed? Damn it, Enya. You know the protocol," Aiden grunted with displeasure. "Grayson or Ryder could have tried to wipe his memory. How could you just let him go? What if he talks to the press? Or the police?"

"Don't get your knickers in a twist," Enya snapped. "I know what I'm doing. He won't say anything."

While Aiden glared at her, Hamish shook his head. "You know him." Then his gaze dropped to her dress. "You're dating him."

"What the fuck, Enya?" Aiden cursed. "When were you gonna spring that on us?"

"How about never?" She crossed her arms over her chest. "I don't have to tell anybody if I'm dating someone."

"You do, if that someone becomes a witness to what we're doing," Hamish said, though he seemed much calmer than Aiden. "What did you tell him? Did you reveal who you are?"

Somewhat pacified by Hamish's calm tone, Enya shook her head. "Of course not. I told him they were evil guys and that we can't go to the police. I sent him home and told him I'd talk to him tomorrow and explain everything."

"We have to check him out, see if we can trust him," Aiden said. "Pearce should run a background check on him."

"I did that already," Enya said. Well, not a full one, but a cursory one, and together with a search of his condo that had turned up nothing odd, she was confident that she could trust Eric.

"When?" Aiden asked.

"A few weeks ago, after I met him."

"You might have overlooked something," Aiden said. "Pearce can run another one." When she opened her mouth to protest, he cut her off. "He's the best. If there's something to find, he'll find it."

"There's nothing to find. He's just a guy, okay?" And after what Eric had done for her tonight, she trusted him. How close to death she'd come because of her stupid high heels, she didn't even want to tell her colleagues.

"We're just looking out for you," Hamish said. "Let Pearce run the background check the moment you get back to the compound, and tomorrow morning we'll discuss how much to tell this guy and how to proceed. Agreed?"

Reluctantly, she nodded. It didn't mean she had to do what he said. After all, none of her brethren had asked her opinion when it concerned their love life and how much to reveal to the women they'd fallen in love with. So why should she be restricted to how much to tell the man she…

She stopped herself. She wasn't in love, of course not. She was in lust. Yes, and she enjoyed Eric's company. Plus, she trusted him. And now, she also owed him her life. That was why he deserved to hear the truth from her.

"All right if I let you out here?" Hamish asked, pointing at the next stoplight. "We've gotta get these bodies burned ASAP."

"The stench is unbelievable," Aiden groused.

"Yeah, let me out here. It's just a few blocks. I'll be all right," Enya said.

Moments later, she hopped out of the van and walked to the compound. She covered the green bloodstains on her dress with her leather jacket. Ten minutes later, she was back in the compound.

Pearce was still in the command center. He swiveled in his chair when she entered. "Hey, you're back. Where are the others?"

"Incinerator. Got three bodies to burn."

"Good job." He turned back to his computer screens.

"Yep." She hesitated.

Pearce looked over his shoulder. "Something else?"

"Yeah, I need you to do a background check on a man named Eric Vaughn. I'll write down his address for you."

"What are you looking for?"

She sighed. "He was there when I killed the demons tonight. In fact, he helped me."

"You—"

"Yes, I'm dating him, okay? Damn it, why is everybody so curious about my love life?"

"I wasn't asking about that. But thanks for filling me in."

She felt her face flush.

"You wouldn't know where he works, would you?"

"He's an independent investment manager. Works for himself."

"All right, then, let's see what we can find. Let's start with the Maryland Motor Vehicle Administration."

"Already did that."

"So why are you asking me to do a check on him?"

"Because Hamish and Aiden insist that you do it. I told them I'd already checked him out. I even searched his condo. He's clean. Nothing to worry about. But unless you can back me up, you know those two will never get off my back."

"Fine. So, the MVA record was clean?"

She shook her head. "He doesn't have a driver's license in Maryland. I saw a driver's license in his wallet, but honestly, I can't remember which state it was from. So, don't bother with that."

"Okay, then." He typed away on his keyboard and looked through the results he got. "Social security records look okay." A few minutes later, he'd hacked into the FBI's systems. "No criminal record."

While that surprised her a bit, because Eric had said that he'd grown up on the wrong side of the tracks, it didn't have to mean anything. If he had a juvenile record, it would have been sealed. Or he'd never been caught if he got into knife fights when he was younger.

"Okay, here are his tax returns. He makes quite a bit of money. Pays his taxes. Pretty straightforward."

She'd already seen the records previously and nodded. "As I said. And he doesn't have Facebook or Instagram. I asked him about it. He said social media is for teenagers." She was getting impatient. "Are we done? I wanna take a shower and get the stench of those demons off me."

"Let me just verify that he doesn't have any social media accounts." Moments later, Pearce pointed to the screen. "Well, well, well. No Facebook and Instagram, you're right. But he's got a LinkedIn page." Pearce clicked on the link. "So that's your type, huh?"

Enya stared at the photo posted on Eric's profile. The name matched, and the profession did as well. But the man in the photo wasn't Eric. He was dark-haired, yes, but everything else was different. He was skinny and looked nothing like the Eric she'd been seeing.

Pearce scrolled down the page. "I always thought you'd go for someone, I don't know, hunkier? Oh well, to each his own."

She couldn't tell Pearce that the man on the picture wasn't Eric. Not yet. Not until she knew what was really going on.

"Yes," she mumbled. "Okay, then. I'll take a shower now and go to bed. Can you tell Hamish and Aiden that everything's good?"

She barely waited for Pearce's confirmation before she rushed out of the command center. She raced to her quarters and entered, her breaths now unsteady, her heart beating a panicked rhythm against her ribcage. Who had she slept with? Because she hadn't slept with Eric Vaughn, the man in the picture. The Eric she knew was an imposter. Was he a criminal who'd committed identity fraud? A con artist who used his good looks to trick women into a financial scheme? Or had she stumbled into an even more serious situation?

One thing was clear: she wouldn't be able to sleep until she knew the truth. And whatever it was, she would deal with it one way or another. Nobody lied to Enya and got away with it, particularly not a man whom she'd just started to trust.

11

After getting changed and getting rid of any trace of his subjects' blood, Zoltan cast a vortex in an alley behind his condo building and descended into the Underworld. He was still seething from the events of less than an hour earlier. Somebody had sent the third demon and undermined his brilliant plan.

And the demon hadn't been surprised to see him. As if he'd expected Zoltan. Had he been sent by the same person who'd sent an assassin after Zoltan only a few months earlier? Ever since then, Zoltan had been extra cautious about not announcing his movements to anybody, not even to his closest associates—not even to Vintoq, his right hand. Which meant somebody was tracking his movements. How, he wasn't sure yet. None of his demons knew of the cell phone he used in the human world, and he never carried any other electronic devices with him when he left the Underworld.

Zoltan felt solid ground under his feet, stepped out of the vortex, and closed it behind him. He stood in the middle of one of the three vortex circles, the only places in the Underworld where a demon could cast a vortex. In the human world, there was no such restriction. As long as the demon had a visual of the place he was traveling to—either by having been there before, or by having seen it in a photo, such as on Google Street View—he could teleport anywhere he wanted. However, the place of arrival had to be directly connected to the ground—making it impossible for Zoltan to teleport directly from his twenty-fifth-floor condo to the Underworld or vice versa.

Richard, one of the vortex guards reporting to Yannick, greeted Zoltan. "Welcome home, oh Great One."

"Yeah, yeah," Zoltan said impatiently. "Where's Yannick?"

"In his office, oh Great One."

Without a thank you, Zoltan hurried down one of the seven corridors that originated from the vortex circle and into the direction of the cave Yannick had turned into his office. Recent improvements had made it possible to tap into the geothermal energy of the earth, and now many of the living quarters of the demons had electricity and were slowly joining the twenty-first century.

Zoltan didn't knock and entered Yannick's office without announcing himself. After all, this was his empire. Everything in the Underworld belonged to him. He didn't see the need to ask permission for entry. Besides, he liked to keep his subjects on their toes. It was harder to plot against him when he could show up anywhere at any time he chose.

Yannick looked up from his computer. He'd recently computerized the comings and goings of the demon population, a suggestion Zoltan had made in order to have easy access when he needed to find out which demons had used the vortex circles and on what business.

"Oh, Great One," Yannick said, and jumped up, bowing.

"Yannick." Zoltan marched toward him. "I need information."

"Of course. How may I help?"

"Get me a list of anybody who's left the Underworld in the last two hours and hasn't gotten back yet. I want to know what business they stated when they left."

"No problem, oh Great One. I'll bring the list to your study the moment I've compiled it."

"I want it now." Zoltan grunted and pointed to the computer. "The reason I had you computerize the records and sync them with the data terminals at each vortex circle was so I'd have instant access to the information." He hovered over Yannick's desk. "Is that a problem?"

"Not at all, oh Great One. I'll do it right away."

"Good. I'll wait here." Zoltan crossed his arms over his chest and widened his stance while he watched Yannick stare at the monitor, his fingers flying over the keyboard.

Due to the fact that there was no Wi-Fi or internet in the Underworld, Zoltan didn't have his own computer to receive such information electronically. The data terminals that the guards used at the vortex circles were hardwired along the tunnels to connect to the computer in Yannick's office. It was archaic, but the only way to transmit data from the vortex circles to the computer for Yannick to compile the information.

"What's taking so long?" Zoltan asked.

"Just another minute, oh Great One. I have to set the correct parameters so the data you'll receive is exactly what you're asking for."

"Hmm."

It seemed to take forever until the printer next to Yannick's computer began to sputter. Moments later, it spat out one printed sheet. Zoltan snatched it from the tray and turned on his heel.

"Is there anything else I can assist you with, oh Great One?" Yannick called out after him.

"No."

Zoltan opened the door and exited. He didn't look at the sheet until he reached his study and shut the door behind him. At his desk, he switched on a lamp and perused the piece of paper. Martin and James, the two demons he'd sent up top to attack Enya, were on the list. Next to their names, their business was stated: *supply run for the Great One.* The description was innocuous and would raise no suspicion. Zoltan often sent demons up top to run errands. He crossed the two names out.

There were about a dozen more. Several of them he knew and could cross out too, since he hadn't recognized the third demon who'd attacked Enya tonight. Only one name remained on the list, one demon whose face Zoltan wasn't familiar with: Phillip. He had to be the third demon, the one who'd attacked Enya. The one who'd been sent by somebody other than Zoltan. He looked in the column reserved for the reason to use the vortex. Authorized by Vintoq, it said.

Vintoq. Zoltan's right hand had sent the demon?

Zoltan slouched back in his chair. Vintoq had been with him ever since he'd become the Great One. He'd been his most trusted adviser, a man loyal to him above else. But also a man with ambitions, a man with a superior intellect. Could Vintoq be the man plotting against him, the traitor who wanted the throne to himself, the one who'd sent an assassin after Zoltan a few months earlier?

He needed certainty. Zoltan returned to Yannick's office, once more entering without knocking. Yannick was busy taking a stack of papers out of a box and placing it on the desk.

"Oh, Great One," he said in surprise.

"I need something else. I need you to go back a few months and get me a list of everybody who was up top on a specific day. Can you do that?"

"Sure. What's the date?"

Zoltan bent over the desk and grabbed a pen, then scribbled the date on a piece of paper. Yannick looked at it. "Is there anything special about that date?"

"Just get me the information."

"Of course. However, there's a slight problem."

"A problem?" Zoltan growled.

"Data that far back hasn't been entered into the system yet." Yannick motioned to the boxes behind him. "They're on the paper records. I'll have to go through those first and enter them before I can run a complete list."

"How long?"

"A week?"

"You have three days!"

Zoltan pivoted and stormed out, slamming the door behind him. He had to wait three days to find out if Vintoq had also sent the previous assassin after him? Fuck! He was in his right mind to kill Vintoq right now, but he knew it was imprudent. Sending one demon up top, who then showed up at the same place as Enya and Zoltan, could be a coincidence. Sending one to attack Zoltan a few months earlier would show a pattern, and be sufficient proof to act.

He was already walking to his private quarters when he stopped himself. He had to go back into the human world. Tomorrow Enya would tell him the truth about herself, and he didn't want to miss her call. Besides, he preferred sleeping in his luxurious condo to spending the night in his rather basic accommodations in the Underworld. He'd grown accustomed to the amenities in the human world, the pleasant smells, the soft sheets, even the views over the city.

The moment he teleported back to Baltimore, his tense neck muscles started to relax. This was where the Great One should rule from, a city full of crime and fear, and not from the caves and tunnels deep within the earth that smelled of sulfur and never saw daylight.

Once he'd overthrown mankind, he'd live here permanently, never to return to the dark and squalid hellhole the previous leaders of the demons had created. Why nobody before him had ever thought of setting up mission central in the human world and enjoy its amenities, he couldn't fathom. But then again, he was a new breed of leader, a leader who looked to the future, a leader with true ambitions. And soon, they would all be fulfilled.

12

Enya was prepared for everything. She'd dressed accordingly. Gone was the dress, which was ruined by green demon blood anyway, and gone were the high heels that had nearly killed her. She wore boots that hid a dagger—a second one was stashed away in her leather jacket—and her hair was braided again. She'd thought long and hard about how to confront Eric about his shady background—because it had to be shady if he was using somebody else's identity— and decided that she couldn't wait until morning. She had to talk to him now, catch him by surprise so he didn't have time to make up a story to explain away her findings.

On her way to Eric's condo building, she remained invisible. Only once she'd entered his apartment did she make herself visible. It was dark and quiet, past midnight, and seeing that there were no lights in the living area, she walked to his bedroom. The door was closed. She looked down to her feet. No light coming from the bedroom either. Eric had to be asleep. Not wanting to make any noise to announce her arrival, she stepped through the door.

Her eyes had already adjusted to the darkness, helping her recognize Eric sleeping in the king-sized bed. The sheets were covering his lower half. His chest was naked, and judging by the contours of his body beneath the thin sheet, he slept in the nude. For a moment she simply stood there and looked at him, watching his chest rise and fall with every slow and steady breath. He looked so peaceful, so innocent. But looks could be deceiving. Eric was a liar, most likely a crook and a conman. But he was also fearless, had saved her life only hours earlier.

Don't get soft now, she chided herself. *He lied to you.*

There could, of course, also be an innocent explanation why he was using another person's name. Perhaps he was in witness protection. It was the only explanation she would accept.

You're stalling.

She hated it when her inner voice pointed out the obvious. It was time to confront him. Time to find out the truth.

She inhaled and took a step toward the bed. Her boot kicked against a shoe and pushed it against the bedframe, making a sound.

It took barely a second before Eric jumped out of the bed, brandishing a blade in his hand, and slammed her against the wall, the dagger already at her neck. He blinked. "Enya?"

Almost immediately, he pulled back and lowered his weapon. But she'd already seen enough. Her pulse raced, her heart beat into her throat, and adrenaline shot through her veins. This had to be a dream. No, a nightmare. This couldn't be true.

"Fuck! Sorry," he said, and ran his free hand through his ruffled hair. "How did you get in here? I didn't mean to scare you. But you gave me quite a shock."

She glanced at the dagger in his hand, then back at his eyes. His green demon eyes. There was no mistaking them. She'd seen plenty of demon eyes to know for certain. Eric was a demon. She'd slept with a demon. Let her guard down with a demon. Enjoyed his hands on her, his cock inside her.

Slowly, hoping he wouldn't notice, she moved her hand and slid it into her leather jacket, where she'd stashed her dagger, but she noticed him follow her movement and shake his head.

"I suppose the secret's out. Forgot to change my contact lenses before I went to bed. The old ones must have dissolved by now. How careless of me. But then, I wasn't expecting you to break into my place in the middle of the night. What happened to dinner tomorrow night?"

Finally, she found her voice again. "News flash: I don't date demons."

A sly smile played around his lips. "Correction: you fucked this demon. And you liked it."

It was true, but the thought disgusted her now. "Don't flatter yourself."

"You wouldn't be in my bedroom in the middle of the night if you didn't want more of the same. I'm game." He looked down to his groin.

Big mistake. She used the split second to pull her dagger from her leather jacket and press it to his neck. As if he'd expected her move, his dagger was at her throat an instant later. But he didn't press the blade into her throat, didn't break the skin with it, only held it there as a warning, while he took a step closer and brought his groin flush to hers. His cock was hard. It appeared demons got sexually aroused by danger. No surprise there.

"Step back," she ordered him.

"Make me."

She pressed her blade harder against his neck, but he neither flinched nor budged.

"You knew I was a Stealth Guardian from the moment you met me. So what were you planning? Huh? The demons we fought tonight... they were a setup, weren't they?"

"I saved your life, didn't I?"

"After endangering it."

"I admit trying to gain your confidence by saving you was part of my plan, but when that third demon showed up and nearly killed you, my priorities changed—"

"Bullshit! How stupid do you think I am?" She gritted her teeth. He was still playing with her, still playing the suave seducer. But it wasn't working anymore. "So you wanted to impress your leader by bagging a Stealth Guardian, is that it? You figured I'd be easy prey."

"I don't think you're easy at all, Enya. In fact, you're a very complicated woman. And as I said before, I love complicated women." He let his demon-green eyes roam over her chest. "As for your body... I've never had bet—"

"Don't! You're disgusting! You're a fucking demon!"

"Yes, and you *were* fucking a demon. It won't be the last time. You and I, we have something."

"We have nothing. You've failed in your attempt to serve the Great One by bringing him a Stealth Guardian. I wish I could see his face when he finds out that another one of his stupid subjects has bought the farm."

Eric chuckled. "Oh, you haven't guessed yet. I'm surprised. You really thought some run-of-the-mill demon would come up with a plan to seduce a Stealth Guardian and actually succeed?" He attempted to shake his head, but the dagger at his throat prevented him from doing so. "I guess introductions are in order."

Her throat went dry. Before he opened his mouth again to speak, she already knew what he was going to say.

"I'm Zoltan. I'm the Great One, the ruler of the Underworld."

Shit! This was Zoltan, the demon she and her fellow Stealth Guardians had been hunting for years? What the hell was she waiting for? She had to kill him, even if she lost her life in the process.

His demon eyes bored into her. "And the man you fucked with more abandon and more passion than you've ever shared with anybody before."

She hated the fact that he was right, hated that it made her hesitate. Any other demon she would have killed twice over already. But Eric? No, Zoltan! If anybody deserved to die, it was him.

"You're responsible for Finlay's betrayal, for Tessa's drug overdose, for the destruction of the council compound, for Winter's abduction, for Logan risking his life to rescue her. You killed Kim's mother to get at one of our books. You killed countless innocents! You stole the source dagger! You're—"

"I'm not behind all of those atrocities. Tessa, the mayor? I never hurt her."

"Liar!"

"It's the truth, and I'm still trying to figure out which of my demons went behind my back. However, I admit I invited the psychic to join me in the Underworld, yet she declined."

"Invited? I don't call kidnapping an invitation."

"As if the Stealth Guardians have never done anything against a person's wishes."

"We do it for the greater good!" Enya protested.

"And who decides what's good?"

She glared at him. "I'm not letting myself be drawn into a conversation about good and evil with you."

"Too late! Damn it, Enya, it's not all black and white."

"It is for me." But even as she said it, she knew she was lying. When it came to her feelings for Eric—no, Zoltan— things had turned a shade of gray. She hated *what* he was, a demon, but she desired him for *who* he was, her lover.

"Is it?"

He met her eyes, and despite the evil green color, she saw something else there, something she'd seen when he'd made love to her. Something that looked like affection. She shook her head. She was losing her mind. Zoltan was using his powers on her, the power to influence a person, to turn them to his side.

"Stop it! Your powers don't work on me. I'm not human."

"You thought I was trying to get you to do my bidding?" Unexpectedly, he laughed. "Enya, the only way I can get you to do anything I want is to fuck you until you surrender to me. That's the only time you'll ever be compliant. And even that won't last for long. Which means I'll have to fuck you daily."

Enya grunted. "That's never gonna happen again. Because you'll be dead. And dead demons don't fuck."

He cast an eye at the dagger at his throat, then lowered his own dagger and tossed it to the floor. "Go ahead, then. You want to kill me, then do it. Just one last thing."

She hesitated. "What? Spit it out!"

"Are you gonna tell your colleagues that you fucked Zoltan? Or are you gonna live with that secret for the rest of your life?"

"None of your fucking b—"

"And when you lie in bed alone, awake night after night, will you think back to this moment and wish you'd never found out that I was a demon?"

Her throat tightened. She didn't want to breathe. Because breathing meant giving her brain the oxygen it needed to think of the scenario where Zoltan was still Eric, a scenario where they were happy. But she couldn't allow that, because nobody could ever be happy with a demon.

"You were using me! Why would I waste a thought on you once you're dead?"

"I'm not blind. I've seen you fight, Enya. Not just tonight, but many times before. At the cosplay event, you massacred my subjects. You're fearless, you're skilled, you're strong." He opened his arms wide. "Yet here I am, still alive, where you could have killed me several times by now. I laid down my weapon. I'm defenseless. But you can't kill me." His lips curved into a smile. "Because you care about the man you made love to. You care about me. Just like I care about you."

She pressed the knife harder against his throat and broke the skin. A few drops of green blood stained the blade. "A demon cares about nobody. And you're a demon! A demon!"

"Funny, how you focus on a demon's inability to feel, when you could have just told me you didn't care about me." He slowly put his hands on her shoulders, cupping them gently. "You didn't deny it. You do care about me. Because there's something between us that defies everything, even the fact that we're archenemies."

She pushed him back with such force that he landed on the bed. She couldn't take any more of this. "You know nothing." Enya spun on her heel.

"I know one thing: the next time we fuck, you'll be screaming my real name when you come."

She charged through the door and hurried out of his place, making herself invisible in the process. Moments later, she was outside his building, the cool night air enveloping her heated body. She braced her hands on her knees. Damn it, she should have killed him, should have done what was her duty as a Stealth Guardian. But she hadn't. Instead, she stood here, doubts and disappointment colliding within her, while her stomach growled in protest.

Nausea rose and hit her out of nowhere. Since she hadn't eaten since lunch, she threw up only bile. It should have made her feel better, but it didn't. Tears welled up in her eyes. She didn't have the strength to stop them. But they couldn't wash away the pain of having lost something she'd never hoped to find in the first place.

~ ~ ~

Zoltan sat on the edge of his bed, in the dark, his head in his hands, replaying the confrontation with Enya in his mind. How could this have happened? He'd been so careful, so why hadn't he put new contact lenses in before he'd gone to bed, knowing the old ones would dissolve from the secretion of his eyes while he slept?

Why the fuck had Enya even shown up in the middle of the night? Something had sparked her suspicion, but she hadn't told him what. Had he been too efficient in killing his own demons? It didn't matter now. The damage was done. His original plan was destroyed, his location compromised, his assumed name worthless. He should leave now, hightail it out of Baltimore and find another hiding place in the human world, before the Stealth Guardians raided his condo and finished what Enya couldn't.

Tonight changed everything, and everything changed tonight.

Enya had called him disgusting. The word cut deeper than the dagger at his throat had. Still, he couldn't let her go. Couldn't accept what had happened. He had to salvage what could be salvaged. So what if his original plan was shot? It didn't change anything about the fact that he wanted Enya in his bed—and he'd take her any which way he could.

Still naked, he grabbed his phone from the bedside table and pressed the programmed number. It went straight to voicemail. He wasn't surprised. Why would she take his call?

"It's Enya. Leave a message."

"Enya, it's me." He didn't want to say his name in case one of the other Stealth Guardians heard the message. "Listen, we need to talk. I'm sorry for what happened... for how it happened." He infused his voice with a pleading tone, a tone men used when they groveled. Women seemed to respond to it and were more inclined to forgive a man who used that tone. Of course, he had no actual experience in this, had only observed it in others. After all, he was the Great One. And the Great One didn't grovel. "I can't change *what* I am. But for you, I can change. I can be who you need me to be. Please, give me a chance to explain."

He disconnected the call and sighed. What now? He couldn't just sit here and wait for the second shoe to drop. He had to do something. Perhaps he could find out where she'd gone. Back to her compound? Somehow he doubted that. How would she explain to her comrades that she'd discovered where the Great One was hiding, and at the same time admit that she hadn't been able to kill him because she had scruples? No, Enya wouldn't put herself in that kind of situation with her brethren. She was a warrior like the men in her group. She didn't want to come across as a weak female. Admitting that she couldn't kill Zoltan because she'd slept with him would cost her the respect she'd worked so hard to earn.

In a hurry, Zoltan got dressed, put colored lenses over his green irises, and left the condo. To save time, he cast a vortex behind his building and transported to an apartment building in a rather decent part of the city. There, he looked at the names on the doorbells and found the one he was looking for. He rang three times. When there was no reply after thirty seconds, he pressed the doorbell again repeatedly.

Finally, an annoyed voice came through the crackling intercom. "What the fuck?"

"It's Eric. I need you to do something for me."

"In the middle of the fucking night? Come back tomorrow." The intercom went silent.

But Zoltan couldn't give up. Not now. He pressed the doorbell and held it down, until after an eternity, the buzzer sounded. "Well, was that so hard?" he grumbled to himself.

He pushed the door open and entered. The apartment was on the fourth floor. By the time Zoltan reached it, the door was already open, and Mick was waiting for him, a shabby bathrobe thrown over his pajama bottoms.

"You'll be paying double," Mick said, and walked back into his apartment.

Zoltan followed and closed the door behind him. "I thought you computer guys are up all night."

"Yeah, right," Mick said. "What do you need?"

"I need you to find somebody for me." And Mick was the only person Zoltan could trust with this job, because Mick was human and had no idea who or what Zoltan was. All he knew was that Zoltan always paid, and he paid well for the services Mick provided. Even if there were a demon with Mick's computer skills or equipment, he couldn't trust a demon, not with this.

"Who's the lady?"

Zoltan snapped his head to Mick and narrowed his eyes. "How do you know it's a woman I'm looking for?"

Mick did an eye-roll. "Oh please, you're not the first guy showing up here after midnight wanting me to trace his girlfriend who just walked out on him."

Girlfriend? Zoltan wouldn't call Enya his girlfriend, but he didn't owe Mick an explanation. Besides, the situation was complicated.

"Well, then you should know how to find her."

Mick's computer was already booting up when Zoltan gave him Enya's phone number. After a few keystrokes, Mick looked over his shoulder. "It's a burner. And it's switched off. Do you have anything else? Place of work? Home address? Facebook account?"

Zoltan shook his head. "She wasn't exactly very forthcoming with information."

Mick chuckled. "Fuck, you're screwed. How about a name?"

"Enya."

"And?"

"I don't know her last name."

"Hate to break it to you, buddy, but she doesn't wanna be found. Hope she didn't steal anything valuable from you."

"Well…" No, she hadn't stolen anything, though she had destroyed his chance at infiltrating the Stealth Guardians.

"I could put a trace on the burner, see where it shows up when she switches it back on."

"Do that. Call me the minute you get anything at all."

Mick nodded. "All right, then. Close the door on your way out." He turned back to the computer and started hammering away on his keyboard.

Zoltan would have never tolerated one of his subjects speaking to him like this, but he couldn't afford to disgruntle Mick. He needed him to find Enya. However, Zoltan couldn't rely on Mick alone. He had to do some legwork himself and comb the city for her.

13

Enya felt as tired and worn out as if she'd fought a battle all night. And in a way, she had. Only the battle was mental, not physical. Over and over, she'd replayed her decision not to kill Zoltan when she had the chance. She couldn't decide whether letting him live was the most harebrained idea in her entire life, or a sign that behind her tough-woman façade was a vulnerable woman. Either explanation was bad. And what was worse was that she couldn't tell her brethren. The humiliation would be too hard to bear. Not only that, she'd be brought before the council.

What was she to say? *Hey, guys, guess what? I met Zoltan, had a few quickies with him, and then decided to let him live 'cause the sex was so hot.*

Fuck!

Well, at least she hadn't been entirely stupid after she left his condo: she'd switched off her cell phone immediately so he couldn't trace her—in case he was smart enough to do that—and only switched it back on inside the compound, where a powerful scrambler made sure no phones could be traced to this location. For anybody trying to find any kind of electronic activity at the location of the compound, it was a dead zone. Nevertheless, the Stealth Guardians were able to receive calls and messages inside the compound. Just like she'd received Zoltan's message.

Enya, it's me. Listen, we need to talk. I'm sorry for what happened... for how it happened. I can't change what I am. But for you, I can change. I can be who you need me to be. Please, give me a chance to explain.

What a crock of shit. As if a demon could change! Demons were evil through and through. Zoltan was her

enemy, and he'd always be her enemy. No amount of great
sex and sweet words could ever change that.

Annoyed at herself that she had allowed Zoltan to wrap
her around his little finger, Enya marched out of her private
quarters and headed toward the communal kitchen. When
she entered, several of her colleagues were finishing their
breakfast. Leila was packing lunches for her twins, who had
started kindergarten recently— a special one for only Stealth
Guardian children, which was located in a secure location in
Scotland and only a short portal ride away. Stealth Guardian
children from all over the world were educated there.

Looking at Julia and Xander caused a little twinge in the
pit of Enya's stomach. As a Stealth Guardian female, her
duty had been to bear children for her race, yet she'd decided
to become a warrior instead. She'd never regretted that
choice, but for some reason, this morning, she couldn't help
but wonder how her life would have turned out had she taken
that path instead. For certain, she wouldn't be in the situation
she'd gotten herself into with Zoltan.

"Morning, Enya," Hamish called out to her, and waved
her to the table.

She approached and poured herself a cup of coffee, then
added a little cream. "Morning." She sat down and took a
sip. "Ugh, who made coffee today? It tastes bitter."

"If you say that a little louder, you'll offend Daphne,"
Hamish warned her. "Besides, the coffee tastes fine. Same as
always."

Enya pushed the cup away. "Yeah, whatever."

"Pancakes, Enya?" Logan called from the stove.

"No, thanks. Not hungry." After the night she'd had, she
didn't think she could ever eat anything again. Finding out
her boyfriend was a demon could do that to a girl.

"So, what are you gonna tell him?" Hamish asked,
nudging a little closer.

"Whom?"

"That Eric guy. Pearce told me he ran the background
check and he came back clean."

Enya shrugged. "Just what he needs to know to explain what he's seen."

"Okay… You want one of us to come with you when you meet him?"

"I'm perfectly capable of handling it," she snapped.

"Whoa, whoa. What's that all about?"

Enya caught Leila and Daphne looking at her, having noticed her outburst. "It's nothing." When the two women turned their attention back to the twins and their own breakfast, she said to Hamish, "I'm gonna break up with him anyway. So there's no need to tell him what's really going on." This lie would hopefully get her colleagues off her back and off Zoltan's scent. Because if they dug deeper, they'd eventually figure out who he was. Several of them would even recognize his face: Aiden, Hamish, and Logan for certain, as well as Leila and Winter. And there was a chance that some of the others had also seen Zoltan's face before.

"You sure?"

"Yeah. He's not really my type anyway." True: demons weren't her type.

"If you say so." He cast a look at the women. "But you know that nobody here would fault you for wanting a relationship. I mean, you're the only—"

"The only one who doesn't have anybody?" Enya interrupted. "Yeah, I'm not blind. But maybe I don't want anybody. Have you ever thought of that? Maybe I'm not interested in domestic bliss." She rose from the table and carried her mug to the sink, where she poured the vile liquid down the drain.

Logan sidled up to her. "Hey, could you do me a favor today?"

She gave him a sideways glance. "Depends."

"Winter needs to see Cinead urgently, but I can't take her, because I'm on assignment. Would you take her to him and stay until she's ready to come back?"

Enya nodded. "Sure. So the doll worked? She had a vision?"

Logan looked over his shoulder, but all the others were chatting at the dining table. "She did. It upset her, but she didn't want to tell me what she saw. She said Cinead should be the first to find out."

"Sounds ominous."

"She was shaken by it. I've only ever seen her like this when she had visions about her own death."

"So you think...?" Enya stopped herself from putting into words what she suspected.

He shrugged. "Don't know, but I assume so. In any case, it's best if you take her rather than one of the guys. She might need a shoulder to cry on afterward. The pregnancy is hard enough on her. The hormones make her more emotional than before, and that's when she needs her girlfriends."

"You think I'm Winter's girlfriend?"

"Of course you are. All the women here are. But she admires you the most. So do that for me, please?"

"Sure. She'll be in safe hands."

Logan squeezed her shoulder and turned back to the stove.

At least accompanying Winter to Cinead's new house would take Enya's mind off her problems. It was better than sitting around, waiting for an assignment to fall into her lap. And she liked seeing Cinead. She loved the older man's deep voice and the soothing effect it had on her. But if Logan was right, today would be a difficult day for the respected statesman. Winter had so far always shared her visions with the compound inhabitants first, the good ones and the bad ones. For her not to share this vision and insist on speaking to Cinead first meant two things: it was a vision about his baby son, and it was bad news, very bad news. Just how bad, Enya would have to wait patiently to find out.

~ ~ ~

Winter looked a little worse for wear when Enya picked her up from her private quarters. The baby bump was barely visible, but her face looked ashen. As if she'd seen death. Maybe she had.

"Hey," Enya said softly. "Are you ready to leave?"

"Not really, but Logan already called Cinead, and he's expecting us." Winter sighed. "Sometimes I hate my gift. It seems I'm always the bearer of bad news."

Enya forced a smile. "Don't say that. You've helped lots of people with your visions. Logan, Pearce. And so many more. But not everything can have a good outcome."

Winter nodded. "I know that. But I'd so hoped for good news for Cinead. He's lost so much." Tears welled up in her eyes. She sniffed and took a breath.

"You can do this," Enya said.

Winter pasted a smile on her face. "I can do this."

"Okay, then." Enya led the way to the portal, which was located on one of the lower levels of the vast compound. In front of it, she stopped.

"I hate taking the portal these days."

"You're not afraid of it anymore, are you?" Enya asked, and laid her hand over the symbol of the dagger that was etched into the stone.

"No, it's not that. But ever since I got pregnant, I get so dizzy in there."

Underneath Enya's hand, the stone warmed, and suddenly, it was gone, revealing a small, cavernous space behind it. "It'll pass. And it's only a few seconds." Enya stepped through the opening and took Winter's hand. "Just hold on tightly if that makes you feel better."

Winter entered the portal and put one arm around Enya's waist. "Thank you."

A moment later, it went pitch-black around them. Enya concentrated on their destination and felt the portal respond to her command. Underneath her feet, she felt the ground wobble.

"Ugh!" Winter exclaimed. "I'll be sick."

"Almost there," Enya said, though she felt a queasiness too, as if Winter's feelings were contagious. "A couple more seconds."

Just in time, they arrived and stepped out of the portal. Winter took a deep breath, and Enya did the same.

"Better?" Enya asked.

"Better."

Enya looked at the camera that pointed at the entrance to the portal. It appeared the security system had already been hooked up, which meant Cinead would be alerted to their arrival. Having been in the house only a day earlier, Enya guided Winter through the cellar to the steps that led up to the first floor. In the foyer, Cinead was waiting for them. Two workmen were carrying a heavy painting covered in protective wrapping through the door into the home.

"Which way?" one of the men asked Cinead.

"Excuse me for a moment, Enya, Winter." Cinead turned to the two men. "To the first landing on the main steps. Right there." He pointed up the wide steps that made a turn halfway to the second floor.

"Okay," the man replied, and he and his colleague headed toward the stairs.

Cinead turned back to his visitors. "Enya, Winter, so good to see you."

"It's been a while, Cinead." Winter took his hand with both of hers and clasped it.

Cinead looked at her hands and then back at Winter's face. "It's bad, then?"

Winter motioned to the open door that led into the living area. "Shall we sit down?"

Cinead nodded. "Enya, would you?" He pointed to the two movers, and Enya understood. She was to watch them.

"Certainly. I'll be out here."

Cinead and Winter disappeared in the living room and closed the door behind them, leaving Enya to watch the workers grunt and puff as they heaved the heavy painting up the stairs and leaned it against the wall on the first landing.

The older of the two pulled out a box cutter and started slicing open the cardboard wrapping.

Both men were human, but belonged to the Stealth Guardians' network of trusted individuals. They'd been vetted extensively to make sure they didn't have anything in their background that made them particularly vulnerable to the influence of demons. In addition, they were only given sufficient information to perform their duties, not more, not less.

Movers were always used only once to make sure they could disclose at most two Stealth Guardian locations, should the demons get their claws into them. Only items too large to fit into the portals were moved by humans. There were other security procedures too. Ever since the Stealth Guardians had allied themselves with Scanguards, a vampire would wipe the men's minds of memories associated with the move. Computer geeks at the various compounds around the world—like Pearce—would do the rest to wipe out any electronic records.

When the two men finally freed the life-size painting from the wrapping that had protected it during its journey, Enya looked back up to the landing. The painting was of Cinead as a young man. His dark hair was unruly, his brown eyes piercing. They drew her to him, demanded she look at him, admire him. The magnetism that emanated from the man in the oil painting was palpable. Together with his deep voice, what woman would have been able to resist him back then? He reminded her of the man she hadn't been able to resist. But she didn't want to go down that path. Couldn't. So she continued watching as the two movers mounted the painting on the hooks provided.

Cinead had truly been a handsome man in his younger years. Even now, he was virile and looked no older than a human man in his late fifties, when in reality he was several centuries old. And now truly alone. Would Enya end up just as alone?

Behind her, a door opened. She cast a look over her shoulder and saw Winter emerge from the living room. Her eyes were puffy. She'd been crying. She pulled the door shut behind her and met Enya's eyes.

"We should leave. He needs to be alone," Winter said, her voice laden with pain.

Enya nodded. "And the movers?"

"The council sent a guard—"

The sound of footfalls came from the corridor.

"There he is," Winter said.

Enya recognized the young man who approached as a Stealth Guardian and nodded to him. "We'll see ourselves out."

A nod and a short greeting, and Enya led Winter back down into the basement. When they reached it, Enya squeezed Winter's hand.

Winter forced a smile, but it was one of sorrow.

"How did he take the death of his son?" Enya asked.

Winter's eyes widened. "Death?" She shook her head.

Enya stopped in her tracks. "But… uh, Logan said it was bad news, and you also—"

"He's not dead. It's much worse. Cinead's son is a demon."

Enya's heart stopped beating. She felt as if choking on the air she couldn't expel. Before her eyes, everything became blurry, as if she was being whirled around her own axis. But then everything came back, clearer than before.

The baby picture, a small oil painting, which showed Cinead's son lying naked on his belly. The painter had captured the birthmark in the shape of an axe on the baby's bottom.

The painting depicting Cinead as a young man, who shared features with another man in Enya's life. How had she not seen this before? How could she have been so blind when the signs had been there all along?

She stopped and turned to Winter. "I just remembered I forgot something upstairs. I'll be back in a second." Not waiting for Winter to respond, Enya walked toward the stairs and, once out of Winter's line of sight, made herself invisible.

14

Zoltan stared at the five demons coming at him. They didn't look friendly, nor did they seem to have any respect for their leader.

The sun had just set, and he was only a few steps away from his apartment building. He'd taken the back way, through the alley, because his contact lenses were on the verge of disintegrating, and he was hoping to avoid being seen. Apparently that was his first mistake. His second was that he hadn't slept and was exhausted. He'd combed the city for Enya. Without success. Mick hadn't delivered any better news. So Zoltan had decided to return to his condo, rest for a few hours, and then try again. He wasn't going to give up. He needed to talk to Enya. But the way things appeared now, it didn't look like he'd get the chance.

Five demons and five deadly daggers against one exhausted Great One. The odds weren't good. Whoever wanted him dead was stepping up his game and had clearly gotten some good intel. To encounter assassins only steps away from his hideout in the mortal world meant Zoltan's antagonist knew about the place. Not that this fact was the most important one right now. After all, a dead leader didn't need a condo anymore. To his own surprise, one regret surfaced: Zoltan would never know what it would be like to have Enya in his bed every night.

Zoltan gripped his dagger tightly. He wasn't going down without a fight. He'd take a few of these bastards with him. Turning to his left, he charged the demon on the outer flank first, a move the idiot hadn't anticipated. Zoltan slammed into him, dagger first, lifted him off his feet, and tossed him toward the other four. Three of them managed to get out of the way; only one got knocked off his feet by the injured demon. Both crashed onto the asphalt, while the other three advanced.

Zoltan glanced around, but there wasn't much he could do. Turning tail and running back to where he'd come from wouldn't get him far. Besides, he wasn't going to die a coward.

With a grunt, his jaw clamped shut, he lunged forward and let his dagger fly. It hit its target: the chest of one of the approaching demons. The bastard tumbled backward. But the two others were unimpressed, and the demon who'd crashed to the ground earlier was on his feet again. Zoltan ducked to pull his second dagger from his boot. The action cost him a valuable second, allowing one of his attackers to lunge for him, his dagger pointed at Zoltan's heart. Temporarily off balance, Zoltan swayed. With his free arm, he instinctively blocked the assassin's dagger hand, but he felt its tip rip his sleeve.

Already, a second attacker came charging from the other side.

"Fuck!" Zoltan cursed.

He pushed the demon whose knife had almost sliced into his arm away from him, and to his surprise, the bastard stopped in mid-motion. His mouth opened wide, and his eyes glazed over with utter surprise. An instant later, he fell to the ground, green blood bubbling from his mouth.

"What the—"

But Zoltan had no time to figure out what had happened. The second attacker was upon him, wrestling him to the ground, while a third joined the melee. Zoltan thrust his knee up and managed to toss one of his attackers off, but the other made a downward motion with his dagger. Zoltan couldn't get his arm up fast enough to block the attack.

"Shit!" This was it.

But the dagger stopped an inch away from Zoltan's chest, and the attacker's head was jerked back as if by invisible hand. In the next second, somebody slit the assassin's throat, and green blood spurted over Zoltan. Now he knew he wasn't alone. Somebody was helping him. Somebody who was invisible.

Confused, the third demon who'd lunged for him froze for a split second. It was long enough for the invisible rescuer to plunge a dagger into his heart. Zoltan jumped up, grabbed a dagger from one of the dead demons, and charged for the only demon still standing, but somebody tripped him, making him fall forward. Zoltan ripped his head toward the asshole: the injured demon on the ground. A punch landed in his face, whipping it to the side. Zoltan rolled, then jumped up and whirled back to the injured demon. Just in time, because the assassin had gotten back on his feet and was coming for him. But this time, Zoltan was prepared. He barreled past the bastard, pivoted, and plunged his dagger into the demon's back, twisting it for good measure, then pulled it out and kicked the dead creature to the ground to join his dead brethren.

Behind him, he heard grunts, some definitely belonging to a woman. And she was in trouble. Green demon blood had splattered on her, and even though she was still invisible, the specks of demon blood weren't and gave away her position.

"Enya, duck!" Zoltan called out, and lifted his dagger hand over his shoulder. When he saw the specks of green demon blood move, he took the shot and threw the blade. It found its target. The last of the five demons stumbled for a few seconds, before he fell forward, dead.

Zoltan breathed hard and braced his hands on his knees. Adrenaline was pumping through his veins the way a bullet train cut through the landscape. He'd survived, but not thanks to his own doing. He looked up, and in front of his eyes, Enya became visible.

"You saved me." He shook his head. Had his groveling actually worked on her? Had he known of the power of groveling before, he would have used it earlier.

"We've gotta hide the bodies. Help me." She motioned to the large trash containers lining one side of the alley.

Together they heaved the first demon into the container.

"I was looking for you," Zoltan said. "Looks like you got my message and decided to agree that we talk."

She huffed. "Don't flatter yourself." She pointed to the next body and gripped the dead guy's legs.

Zoltan hooked his hands under the demon's arms, and they carried him to the container, swinging him back and forth to get enough momentum to heave him over the ledge.

"Listen, Enya, we clearly have something here. You and me. We want the same." At least when it came to sex.

She tossed him an annoyed look. "If you're talking about getting your dead friends off the street, then yeah, we want the same."

He lifted up the third guy. "They're clearly not my friends."

"And there I thought all demons stick together." She took the dead guy's legs. "Guess there's trouble in the Underworld."

"You could say that. Somebody wants me dead."

"That's pretty evident."

The third body landed in the garbage container.

"Somebody wants to usurp me. Whoever it is, he's getting pretty desperate."

She raised an eyebrow. "A revolution? So they want a more lenient leader?"

"On the contrary. They want a tougher one. One who can deliver results when it comes to annihilating the Stealth Guardians."

She shook her head. "I see. So you figured you'd bag me and cement your reign on my back. What girl wouldn't like to hear that from the guy she's been sleeping with? Nice one, Romeo."

Zoltan let out a sigh and ran a hand through his hair. "Enya, it's not like that. Not anymore."

"Oh really? You're telling me you changed? Bullshit! Demons don't change." She gave the fourth demon an extra-hard kick before they tossed him into the container.

"You keep saying that, but it doesn't look like you believe it yourself. Or you wouldn't have come to my aid tonight. Damn it, Enya, you saved my life. You can't tell me you had no reason for it. You feel something for me, and you know that I care about you." It wasn't a complete lie. Because he desired Enya, he was concerned for her wellbeing, therefore he cared about her.

"It was quid pro—"

"No it wasn't, and you know it. You know I sent the two demons last night to attack you so I could save you, hence it doesn't count."

"There were three demons, not two."

He nodded. "I didn't send the third." He motioned to the container. "Whoever sent these assassins also sent the third demon last night."

"This is fucked up!"

When Enya turned away from him and headed for the last dead demon, he snatched her bicep and made her pivot. "I agree. It's fucked up. But it doesn't change the fact that you saved the Great One tonight, the one person you claim to hate the most." He pulled her closer. "And don't tell me it's because you think you owe me something. Tell me the truth."

Enya glared at him. "You want the truth? I'll give you the fucking truth." Her nostrils flared. "There's a chance that you were born a Stealth Guardian and kidnapped by the demons."

Zoltan let go of her arm as if he'd been burned. His heart thundered into his throat, cutting off his ability to speak.

"Yes, I think you're Angus, the son of one of our council members. That's why I had to save your life. Because if you are who I think you are, I have to try to save you."

"That's impossible. I would know if I was a Stealth Guardian once, or if I was kidnapped. Trust me, I was neither."

"There's an explanation for it, but this isn't exactly the right place for a long chat. So if you don't mind..." She pointed to the fifth body.

"Fine, let's finish this," he growled. But the whole notion of him having been born a Stealth Guardian was still ludicrous, no matter the explanation. He was a demon through and through.

~ ~ ~

Enya noticed the skeptical look on Zoltan's face. She couldn't blame him. To find out that the leader of the demons had once been a Stealth Guardian would throw anybody for a loop. No wonder he didn't look convinced. But soon, once she showed him the proof she had, he would have to accept the truth.

When they'd disposed of the fifth dead demon, Enya pointed to Zoltan's jacket. "Take it off and toss it in the trash."

He cast her a puzzled look. "You suddenly don't like my taste in clothing?"

"See the specks of green demon blood? If you want me to get you to a safe hiding place without being seen, you need to get rid of it." She rid herself of her own jacket, which also had blood splatter, then started to collect the demons' daggers. She carefully wiped the green blood off, then tucked them into her boots and pockets.

Zoltan threw his jacket into the dumpster. "That's why the fifth demon saw you. You can't make demon blood invisible."

For a second, Enya hesitated. Had she told him too much already? After all, he was still a demon.

"Don't worry. We figured it out eventually. You haven't told me any state secrets."

"Well, then let's move. Don't talk once you see other people around, or they will discover us."

"This will be interesting. I've never been invisible before."

"News flash: you already are. Now shut up and follow me."

Zoltan looked at his hands, turned them, then met her gaze. "I don't think it's working. I can still see myself. And you, for that matter."

Enya rolled her eyes. "Trust me, to everybody else, we're both invisible. So let's go, before I regret this." She started walking, and he sidled up to her. "Your eyes turned back to demon-green during the fight. Did you lose your colored lenses?"

"They dissolved. It's the chemical that causes the green color. It eventually burns through them."

She and her colleagues had assumed something like that. "How long do they last?"

"The ones I wore, about eight hours. But my subjects don't have access to them. They use commercial colored lenses. And they disintegrate…" He hesitated. "…faster."

She shook her head. "You don't like your subjects very much, do you?"

"They're expendable. And stupid."

"Have you always seen them like that?"

He shrugged. "Why not? I'm smarter than them, stronger than them. Why else do you think my opponent sent five assassins?"

She let out a chuckle. "Arrogant much?"

"You think I'm big-headed? Is that how you like your men?"

"We're not talking about my taste in men." Luckily, several people came walking toward them, so she had a good reason to shut him up. "People ahead—quiet."

For the next ten minutes, while Enya navigated them through several busier streets until they reached a more deserted area, they didn't talk. Ahead of them, close to a freeway onramp, stood a motel. Enya pointed to it. At a traffic light, they waited for it to change, then crossed the street and entered the property. Just outside the office hung a neon sign.

She pointed to it. "We'll stay far away from it."

"So you know?" he asked.

"That neon lights burn out when a demon comes close? Yes, the warning has saved many a Stealth Guardian's life." She pointed to a room at one end of the T-shaped building. It was their best choice. The office window from which the manager could have had a direct view of the unit was boarded up. It appeared somebody had smashed in the glass.

At the end unit, Enya stopped. "I'll see if it's empty. Wait here."

She walked through the closed door. As she'd hoped, the room was unused. There was no luggage anywhere, the towels were clean, the wastebasket empty, and the bed unused. The blackout curtains were already drawn. Perfect.

She walked back to the door and opened it. "Quickly."

Zoltan entered and locked the door behind him. "Light?" he asked.

"Only use the bedside lamp."

He flipped the switch, while Enya took the daggers she'd taken off the dead demons out of her boots and pockets and placed them on a small desk.

Zoltan looked around in the dimly lit space. She noticed his gaze fall on the bed and a grin form on his lips. Figured.

"Don't even think about it."

To her surprise, he dropped the grin and turned serious. "Tell me why you think I was once a Stealth Guardian and why I have no recollection of it."

"You were a six-month-old baby when it happened."

"When what happened?"

"You were kidnapped, though back then your parents believed you were killed by the demons. There was blood in your crib, sufficient to suggest that they'd slaughtered you."

He raised an eyebrow. "So how would you know that that baby isn't dead after all?"

"Because Winter saw it."

"The psychic."

Enya nodded. "Yes, I believe you met her." She stopped herself. "No, let me rephrase that. You kidnapped her."

"I did. But only to make her an offer. Unfortunately, somebody snatched her right out of the Underworld. One of these days, you'll have to tell me how you guys did that."

"In your dreams," Enya said curtly.

"Fair enough. So, Winter had a vision. What did she see?"

"The boy as an older child, maybe a twelve-year-old, but with green demon eyes."

"That could have been any child. What makes her think the boy she saw was the baby the demons took? From what I know about babies, they all look the same, and you can't really tell me you can predict what a child would look like twelve years later. No offense. There's nothing to connect her vision to me."

"There is. In fact, there are several things." She lifted one finger. "Winter had her first vision about the baby being taken when she was in the Underworld, I believe at the moment you struck her when she defied you. That physical contact may have triggered the vision."

He shrugged. "Is that it?"

Enya shook her head and pulled out her phone. She opened her pictures app and scrolled to the photo she'd taken when visiting Cinead's house earlier. She turned the screen to him.

"This is your father as a young man, most likely about the same age as you're now. When I saw it earlier today, there was something so familiar about it. I just couldn't put two and two together until Winter told me about her latest vision about the boy having turned demon. That's when I knew."

She looked directly at him, but Zoltan didn't meet her gaze. Instead, his eyes were glued to the picture on her phone. He reached out and took it from her hand, stunned silence accompanying his action. Then he shook his head as if he didn't want to believe it.

"Many people have similar looks. I bet if we searched the world, we'd find several other men who look similar to me. That's not proof."

"Fine." Enya took the phone back. She wished she didn't have to issue her next command, but it appeared that Zoltan was more stubborn and harder to convince than she thought. "Turn around and drop your pants."

"Excuse me? Does that mean we're done talking and are going straight to sex?"

"This isn't about sex."

"Okay, making love, then. Whatever you wanna call it."

"I said turn around and drop your pants."

Slowly he turned and started opening his pants. "Be careful, or you're gonna turn me on, and we both know where that leads." He pulled his pants down to mid-thigh.

"The boxers too."

He complied with her command. "Like what you see?" He couldn't have said the words in a cockier tone if he'd tried.

Enya decided not to answer, pointed her phone camera at him, and snapped a photo.

Zoltan whirled around. "Did you just take a picture of my ass? Is that your idea of kinky foreplay? 'Cause I can give you better ideas, if you'd just ask."

She scoffed. "I took a picture of your birthmark."

"What for?"

She turned the screen to him. "This is your birthmark."

He shrugged. "You think I've never seen it? I do look in the mirror occasionally."

"I can believe that." What man didn't check himself out to see if he measured up? And Zoltan did measure up when it came to most women's expectations. He certainly did for her.

She swiped to a photo she'd taken earlier in the day and pointed to it. "This is a photo of a painting of Angus, Cinead's baby son. Look at the left butt cheek."

Zoltan dipped his head to look closer, then he took the phone from her hands and pinched the screen to zoom in. His eyes widened. He swiped to the picture Enya had just taken, then back again, then he suddenly lifted his head and stared at her.

"That's impossible."

"It's not," she said. "That's you at six months old. You're Angus. You're Cinead's son, and you were a Stealth Guardian when you were born."

Angrily, Zoltan pressed the phone back into her hand. "Fine! So what if it's true? Do you really think that my father would welcome me with open arms? Hate to remind you"—he pointed to his eyes—"but I'm still a demon." He pulled up his pants.

"There has to be a way to change that." She put away her phone. "We can find a way."

"If you know anything about demons, and I think you do, then you know this one thing about us: once a demon, always a demon. There's no redemption."

She knew that. But against all odds, she hoped that there was a way to save him.

Suddenly, Zoltan's fingers were under her chin, and he tilted her face up so she had to look at him.

"You know there's no redemption for a demon, and still you came to save me tonight. Not for my father, not for the Stealth Guardian race, but for yourself, Enya. You still want me, but you can't face the fact that I'm a demon, and I'll always be a demon. It's time you acknowledged that."

"I can't." She tried to free herself from his grip, but he backed her against the wall.

"Yes, you can. If I, the leader of the demons, can admit that I'm falling for a Stealth Guardian, for my mortal enemy, then you can do it too."

15

Shit!

The words were out, before Zoltan's brain could register them. He hadn't meant to say them. Love had no place in his mind, and even less in his heart. So why on earth was he suddenly talking about falling in love? Was it just a means to manipulate her further so she would come back to him? It had to be. The evidence was clear: he wanted Enya back in his bed. Hence, any means was fair game. Even declaring he was falling in love with her? Certainly. However, he hadn't made the conscious decision to use this particular tactic to get her to come back to him. So why had the words rolled off his tongue so easily, so smoothly? And why had they sounded so sincere?

"That's bullshit! You're not in love with me!" she said with a raised voice.

Something about her attitude riled him up, made him want to contradict her. Just for the hell of it. "We wouldn't be the first star-crossed lovers. *Romeo and Juliet*? *West Side Story*? Why can't it be Zoltan and Enya?" And all of a sudden, he was wondering himself: why couldn't it be *Zoltan and Enya*? What was so wrong about that?

"Because suddenly we'd only have enemies. My people would cast me out and hunt you down. And yours would do the same."

He smirked, inexplicably pleased with the direction the conversation was taking. "And again you don't deny that you care about me. Don't you think that's telling?" He dipped his head, bringing his lips to within an inch of hers. "You want me, babe, just as much as I want you. If you don't, then all you have to do is push me away."

She could end it all here. Give up, take his offer, walk away. But he didn't want her to. And why should he? He'd lusted after Enya for far too long, and he was so close to getting what he wanted. So what if he started developing feelings for her? Considering how hot the sex between them was, it wasn't exactly a surprise that their desire for each other was turning into something else, something more intimate. It didn't change anything for him. He was still the Great One. Where was it written that the Great One couldn't fall in love and still rule the Underworld?

He scrutinized Enya's face. Even though he wasn't quite sure what she would ultimately decide, of one thing he was certain: she wasn't anywhere near regretting what she'd done. She'd enjoyed the fight, enjoyed killing the demons—and frankly, so had he—and not just because she thought Zoltan was born a Stealth Guardian and she needed to save him.

That part, he believed now. The evidence was too convincing to deny, even for him. When he looked at the photo of his father as a young man, he'd thought he was looking in a mirror. But even knowing that what Enya said was true didn't change anything for him. He could never turn back into a Stealth Guardian. He'd always be a demon. And it was that fact—a fact Enya knew better than anybody—that made him believe that Enya had saved him for her own selfish reasons.

She cared about him, and if he could get her back in his bed, he'd make her face just how much. He'd make her realize that although their relationship had started out with deception and a good dose of sex, there could be more to it. After all, he'd fantasized about Enya for years, and while he'd always thought of making her his slave once he'd overthrown the Stealth Guardians, that thought rang hollow now. He didn't want Enya against her will. He wanted her to want him with the full knowledge of who and what he was. No ifs and buts about it. He realized now that taking her as his slave would have never been enough. He wanted her as his queen.

"Enya," he murmured. "You have to make a decision. Show me that you're not indifferent toward me, or push me away."

"I need time," Enya said, her breath brushing over his lips.

He recognized her words as a cry for help. "I'll give you all the time you need, until you're ready to tell me what you feel. But I need you in my bed now. I can't wait another second. So I beg you, even if all you feel right now is lust, share it with me."

She lifted her hands to his face and cupped it. "Will that be enough?"

"No. But I can be a patient man." He slid one hand down to her ass and drew her to him, so she had to feel his cock. "My body, on the other hand, isn't quite as patient. When I'm with you, I can't keep my carnal side in check. When I'm with you, I'm not in control of that part of myself." In fact, he already had a full-blown erection, and they hadn't even kissed yet.

"Are you just saying that to get me into bed?" she asked.

He drew his head back a little, and she dropped her hands to his chest. "Oh, Enya. Getting you into bed would be so easy. All I would need to do is tie you to it and ride you for as long as I want to. But that's not enough. It was my fantasy for a long time... from the moment I first saw you. But everything's changed. Now I want so much more. I want you to want me, *me*, Zoltan. I want you to come to me of your own free will. I want you to crave my cock inside you. My mouth on your tits. My hands on your skin. Because that's what I crave: to be imprisoned inside your tight pussy, and to feel your hands and lips on me. To look into your eyes when you come, when only the two of us count. That's what I want."

An unsteady breath rolled over Enya's lips. "You need to stop talking, or I'll come without you even touching me."

"I take that as a yes to sharing my bed."

Enya didn't answer. Instead, she slanted her lips over his and kissed him, while she slung her arms around him and pressed herself to him as if she was afraid he would try to escape.

Zoltan welcomed her by delving his tongue into her mouth and dancing with hers. He loved kissing her, teasing soft moans from her, until she was breathless, until her body was soft and yielding. He felt her breasts crushed against his chest, felt her hard nipples poking him through his shirt. He squeezed her ass, loving how her firm flesh felt in his hand. There was nothing tentative about Enya. When she surrendered to her carnal need, she surrendered fully, held nothing back. He loved that about her. She wasn't playing games with him, wasn't coy or calculating, but sinful and passionate.

He loved how she shoved his pants down and rubbed herself against his cock, practically rode the hard ridge where pre-cum leaked from its tip and seeped through his boxer briefs. He wasn't idle either, pulling her top out of her pants and sliding one hand underneath it. Like the times before, she wore nothing beneath it, no bra to hinder his access. Her clothing was as uncomplicated as her attitude to lovemaking.

He captured one breast and kneaded it in his palm, enjoying the way the firm flesh responded to his touch, and the way Enya yelped into his mouth when he tweaked her nipple hard. And although he knew she liked it rough, tonight wouldn't be about that. Tonight he would show her that he cared about her, that he could be a tender lover, a tender man.

Getting hot, Zoltan let go of Enya for a moment and freed himself of his shirt, then reached for Enya's top and pulled it over her head.

"My God, you've got gorgeous tits," he said, and pulled her back into his arms. "Everything about you is perfect."

He captured her lips again while he busied himself with opening Enya's pants and pulling them down sufficiently to slide one hand into her panties and touch her pussy.

Enya gasped and tilted her head back, her eyes closing. "Oh, God."

He rubbed along her wet slit, then slid his dew-covered finger upward to her clit. "Look into my eyes and I'll make you come." He wanted her to see his demon eyes while he pleasured her, wanted her to recognize that even though he was a demon, he wouldn't hurt her. "Please."

Enya opened her eyes and looked straight at him.

"That's it, babe. Just like that." He held her gaze while he painted circles over her clit, rubbing the little organ harder and faster. Enya panted, her lips parted. Perspiration collected on her brow. He increased his tempo, caressing her center of pleasure with mounting eagerness. He'd never thought he'd love pleasuring a woman without wanting anything for himself. But in this moment, all he could think of was Enya's pleasure.

"Oh, oh…" Her eyelids fluttered, and her body stiffened.

He knew she was close. "I wanna hear my name when you come. Can you do that for me? Can you cry out my name?" Nothing would give him more pleasure.

Her eyes went wide as if for a moment she'd forgotten who he was. But then he pinched her clit, and Enya spasmed. Zoltan slid his middle finger into her channel while pressing his thumb to her clit.

"Oh… oh… Zoltan, yes, yes!"

Her muscles contracted around his finger, granting him an exquisite moment of her surrender, making him part of her pleasure.

"Beautiful," he murmured, and dipped his head to kiss her.

She collapsed against him, and he caught her against his body, holding her until her orgasm subsided. He managed to shuck his boots and pants, then lifted Enya and carried her to the bed, where he laid her down gently.

Slowly he freed her of the remainder of her clothing and stripped himself of his boxer briefs. Now naked, he lowered himself over her, and as if they'd done this a thousand times, Enya spread her legs wide and welcomed him. He plunged into her with one thrust, seating himself to the hilt.

Enya looked up at him, her hands on his hips. "I love your cock inside me, Zoltan. Make love to me."

The way she said his name nearly made him climax. She truly saw him now, and there was no disgust, no fear in her eyes when she looked at him. Maybe they had a chance.

"Anything you want," he said.

He braced himself on his knees and elbows and began to move inside her, withdrawing an inch, then sliding back into her welcoming warmth. He took his time. There was no rush now. "I love how tight you are. I love how you cradle me." He shifted so he could dip his head to her breasts and kiss them. "And I love feeling your breasts rub against me and your hard nipples tickle me."

He drew his hips back and thrust forward, faster than before. Enya let out a moan and arched her back. He smiled at her. "Didn't want you to think that I'd forgotten about your sweet pussy." He delivered a few rapid thrusts, then followed them with a much slower rocking motion meant to ignite her clit again.

"I like that," Enya murmured.

"Good." He shifted again, lifting one leg over her thigh so their legs were intertwined like scissors. "Then you might like this too." He rocked against her, squeezing his leg against her outer thigh, creating the feeling that her pussy was even tighter. At the same time, his groin pressed harder against her clitoris, the friction heightening Enya's arousal.

"Zoltan," she cried out breathlessly.

He repeated the motion while dipping his head to one breast and sucking the nipple into his mouth. He licked it and simultaneously plunged in and out of her wet channel. He was well aware that Enya couldn't move much, but she wasn't complaining. He'd guessed right: she wanted to be dominated in bed, wanted to be taken care of so she could let go. And he loved seeing her like this, free to enjoy her body.

Again and again, he drove his cock deep into her, and every time, sounds of pleasure rolled over Enya's lips.

"Talk to me," she said, breathing hard. "Your voice. I need to hear you."

A smile formed on his lips. "You want me to talk dirty to you?"

She panted. "Yes. Your voice turns me on. From the moment we met in the bar, before I even saw your face, I felt it."

He plunged deep and hard. "You would have let me fuck you in the street, wouldn't you?"

Her eyes widened, but then she admitted what her eyes were already telling him: "Yes."

"I wanted to." He increased his thrusts. "I wanted to strip you right there and fuck you, no matter who was watching."

Enya shuddered, and her nipples hardened even more.

"And you would have sucked my cock right there if I'd demanded it, wouldn't you?"

Enya pressed her head into the pillow and arched her back. "Yes!"

"Yes, 'cause you're wicked, Enya. You like to be bad." He delivered several more thrusts, but soon, his control would snap. Knowing what Enya would have allowed him the moment they met made him hornier than he'd ever been. "I should have fed you my cock right there on the street."

"Why didn't you?" she asked, moaning.

"Because I had no idea how wicked you are." He dipped his head to her face. "And how hungry for sex. Just as hungry as I. Now be a good girl and squeeze my cock really tightly."

He felt her muscles respond to his command and close around his cock like a tightening fist. It was just what he needed.

"Fuck!" he said, his semen already shooting through his cock and exploding from the tip.

Beneath him, he felt Enya climax a second after him, her muscles twitching, her chest heaving. He looked at her face and saw an expression of pure joy and happiness. Relieved and satisfied, he collapsed and rolled off her, then pulled her to him so her back was aligned with his chest and her ass was tucked into the curve of his body, resting against his groin.

Even though he'd just climaxed, his cock was still hard. He lined up his shaft with her pussy and slid back into her from behind. Her channel, now drenched in their combined juices, instantly tightened around him.

"Hmmm," Enya said, and pulled his arm around her front.

"Is that a *hmmm, that's good*, or a *hmmm, what's he trying to do now*?" Zoltan asked.

Enya turned her head to look at him. "It's a *hmmm, I'm surprised*."

"Surprised how?"

"I hadn't thought of you as a man who likes to cuddle after sex."

"Maybe I'm just getting ready for the next round," he teased.

"No, you're not."

"May I tell you a secret?"

"Sure."

"I've never done this before. You know, cuddle with a woman after sex." He'd never seen the point. Or the need for it. Nor did he understand why he was telling her this. Had his orgasm robbed him of his mind?

"Are you saying that demons don't cuddle?"

He chuckled. "No, I'm not saying that at all. But I never felt the need to hold a woman after sex. I never wanted that. But with you, I don't know, it's different. I want to spend the night with you. Fall asleep with you, wake up together."

"Are you just saying that to prove to me that you're not a bad demon?"

"I'm telling you the truth." He understood why she was skeptical. After all, he'd deceived her before.

She nodded. "Okay, so since we're telling the truth, may I ask you something?"

"Of course."

"Demons don't get sick, right?"

"Right. We're immortals, like you."

"Then what about your migraine attack? Did you fake it to draw me in?"

He put his hand on her shoulder to turn her halfway to him. "No. It's not something I would ever fake. What man wants to look weak in front of the woman he's trying to seduce? Believe me, if I could make those migraines disappear, I'd do it in a heartbeat."

"But I don't understand how you can have migraines as a demon. That's an illness. Demons don't get sick. You just said so yourself."

He shrugged. "I don't know. And it's not exactly as if I could ask anybody, is it? My subjects don't know about them. So far, I've been able to hide them from everybody, but if they ever get wind of my affliction, I'm as good as dead. Nobody wants a leader who's weak."

"You're not weak."

It was sweet of her to say that, but it didn't change how these attacks made him feel: vulnerable. "Tell that to the other demons. A ruler is only on the throne for as long as he can defend his position."

"Do you think somebody may have found out about your migraines, and that's why they sent the assassins tonight?"

"No. If anybody found out, they'd tell all demons. There wouldn't be a need for sending assassins. Everybody would be after me then. It wouldn't take much to topple me. They wouldn't do it here in the human world. They'd do it in the Underworld for everybody to witness."

"Why?"

"Because whoever kills me will take the throne. He'll be seen as the strongest demon, the rightful heir. I think the person who's behind the assassination attempts is much more devious. He doesn't want to be seen as the one who killed me for no good reason. It would mean a revolt among those who're loyal to me. My guess is that his own following is small. He'll have me killed and will then expose his own assassins and bring them to justice, thus earning the position as the Great One, because he avenged my death."

"Do you have any suspects?"

"Several, but my main suspect is Vintoq, my right hand. He's smart and ambitious. But I can't prove anything yet. I'm working on it."

"About that…"

"Yeah?"

Enya sighed. "I don't think you should return to the Underworld. Stay here and—"

"I'm the ruler," he interrupted. "If I don't return, somebody will make himself the Great One." And he wouldn't let his throne go without a fight.

Enya turned fully to him, making his cock slip from her sheath. She sat up. "But that's not important anymore. Haven't I proven to you where you came from? Who your father is? Cinead is a council member. He's respected. I'm sure that together we can somehow figure out how to turn you back into a Stealth Guardian."

Zoltan gripped her shoulders, wanting to shake the impossible dream out of her. "No demon has ever turned back to what he was before. Least of all a demon like me. I've done too many evil things. I'm beyond redemption. Why can't you accept that?"

"Because I don't want to, okay? I don't want to accept that you can never turn back." Tears welled up in Enya's eyes. "Why won't you even try to find a way?"

Zoltan pulled her into his arms and cradled her. "I'm sorry. I don't mean to hurt you. I'm just realistic." He pressed a kiss into her hair. "Please don't cry, babe. It makes my heart hurt."

She lifted her head and looked at him. "That's because you're not evil through and through. There's still good inside you."

He gave her a sad smile. "My feelings for you are the only good thing inside me." And even those were hardly strong enough to turn him into a good person. "Everything good that's happening to me is because of you. You even made my migraine disappear that night. When you touched me, you pushed it away." He kissed her softly. "It was probably your virta that helped me."

Her eyes widened. "You know about a Stealth Guardian's virta?"

"Yes, we're aware of it. Don't worry; we can only take a human's life force, not the virta of a Stealth Guardian."

She nodded absent-mindedly. "But I didn't use my virta on you to soothe your migraine. I didn't dare, or you would have felt and seen the effects, and would have asked questions."

That surprised him. "Then what did you do?"

"Nothing. I only touched you and spoke to you. Maybe you just relaxed and that's why it went away. What triggered it in the first place? Perhaps that's what you should look at."

He thought back to that moment, his memory crystal-clear. But he hesitated to voice what he'd been thinking about then.

"You know what triggered it…" She looked at him. "What was it?"

He avoided her gaze. "I'm sorry, Enya…"

She put her hand under his chin and forced him to look at her. "Tell me."

He took a deep breath. "I was thinking how close I was to achieving my goal, to getting you to trust me so that you would soon take me to your compound. So that I could destroy the Stealth Guardians from within."

For a long while, Enya said nothing. Had he destroyed the little trust they'd built?

"And during the migraine, when I tried to soothe you, what did you think then?" she asked.

He shrugged. "What does it matter now?"

"It matters."

"I forgot all about my plan. I forgot that I was trying to con you. All I could think about was that I wanted to spend the night with you, not because it was part of my plan, but because I wanted you. I still do."

"That must have been it," she said, as if to herself.

He glanced at her. "What must have been it?"

"You dispelled the migraine yourself. You brought it on by thinking about your plan of harming me and my brethren, and you made it vanish by forgetting about your plan."

"But that's impossible."

"Maybe not," she said excitedly. "Don't you see? I think there's still a part in you that's Stealth Guardian. And that part is rebelling when you try to harm us."

Could that be the reason? Were the migraines trying to tell him that there was another path he could take? One that would lead to redemption? Even if that were true, would he even want that? He'd been a demon for as long as he could remember. Who would he be if he wasn't the Great One anymore?

Could he give up that kind of power? And for what? An uncertain future?

16

Enya stretched her tired limbs and started opening her eyes. Her long hair fell like a thick curtain of big locks over her face. She'd undone her braids before falling asleep, wanting to be more comfortable. The blackout curtains were still drawn, but on one side, a little bit of light filtered into the room. It was morning. She'd slept well and felt safe in Zoltan's arms, but she'd also dreamed. In her sleep, her brain had been trying to come up with ideas of how to save Zoltan. She tried to remember a face she'd seen in her dream, the face of somebody who might be able to help her.

She turned to the other side and reached for Zoltan. But her hands touched only an empty pillow. She shot up to sit and flicked on the bedside lamp. Her eyes flew to the spot on the floor where Zoltan had dropped his clothes the night before. They were gone, as were his boots.

Fuck! He'd left. Without a word. Like a thief in the night. Had the previous night meant nothing to him? By telling her that it was impossible for him to change what he was, had he been trying to tell her that there was no future for them? No future together?

Naked, she jumped out of bed and hurried to the table. The daggers she'd placed there the night before were still there. She reached for one and saw the piece of paper held down by it. She picked it up, and her pulse settled instantly.

Gone to get breakfast. Wait for me. Back soon. Z.

"Stop being paranoid," she murmured to herself. After what they'd shared last night, Zoltan wouldn't just disappear. He'd told her that he had feelings for her, even though he hadn't actually said what kind of feelings. And he'd told her about his nefarious plan, shared secrets with her he'd never share with an enemy.

She took a few breaths and headed for the shower.

Zoltan cared about her. And she cared about him.

Enya turned on the water and stepped under the spray. She always had her best ideas in the shower. The steady flow of the water washing over her body felt like a meditation. It was almost hypnotic and transported her back to her dreams.

Before her mental eye, she saw old books and manuscripts. Maybe something in the old history books would give her a clue. There had to be some ritual, some potion, that could turn a demon back to his original form. She froze. Or a spell. Yes, a spell. All of a sudden, the face of the person in her dream appeared before her. That was it. She knew what she had to do.

Quickly, she finished her shower and dried off. A towel wrapped around her, her hair falling down her back, she left the bathroom and found her panties. She slipped them on and tossed the towel on the bed. Her top was wrinkled, but she didn't care. She pulled it over her head and tried to detangle her hair. Not having a comb or anything else to aid, she quickly pulled all hair to one side and braided it into one long tress. She would have to give it a good combing later. But right now, there were more important things to do.

Enya stepped into her cargo pants and pulled them up. She felt something heavy in one of her pockets and patted it. It was nothing more innocuous than her cell phone— switched off, of course, so her colleagues couldn't track her, in case they found it odd that she hadn't returned yet. However, she doubted they were looking for her yet. After all, Hamish knew that she had planned to speak to her boyfriend "Eric" the night before to explain what he'd seen. Neither Hamish nor the others would find it strange that she hadn't slept at the compound. It was buying her time until they came to ask questions. Time she needed, because as soon as Zoltan was back with breakfast, she'd have to make a short trip.

A sound as if somebody was kicking against the door with a boot made her snap her eyes to the door. Before she could wonder who would do such a thing, she realized that it could only be Zoltan. He had no key and probably had his hands full with cups of coffee and whatever else he considered breakfast. Barefoot, she hurried to the door, not wanting him to stand outside for too long, in case the maid was already cleaning rooms.

She turned the knob fully, but didn't get a chance to open the door, because somebody was already kicking it in. The door hit her. One man wearing sunglasses muscled his way in, followed by two others who also hid their eyes behind dark shades. She didn't have to be a genius to guess that the three weren't human. Their weapons identified them as demons.

"Fuck!" She scrambled to jump up and spin around to lunge for her dagger she'd left on the bedside table. The daggers she'd taken off the dead demons the night before were out of reach—getting them would mean charging directly toward the demons.

She vaulted over the bed and reached for her dagger on the nightstand, and had touched its hilt when one of her attackers gripped her ankles and yanked her back. She fought against his grip.

"Stop fighting, bitch!"

A second demon snatched one of her arms and nearly jerked it out of its socket when he twisted it back.

Enya cried out in pain. "I'm gonna kill you fucking bastards!"

The third demon jumped onto the bed and snatched her braid. He pulled it back so rapidly that she would have gotten whiplash were she not an immortal.

"Not if we kill you first," one of her attackers grunted.

She tried to punch him with her free arm, but the other two did a good job holding her down, one of them now shoving his knee into her lower back so she couldn't take a swing. Before she could yell another curse at them, one demon shoved a piece of cloth into her mouth.

"Shut up, Stealth Guardian!"

Enya struggled and fought so hard that it took all three demons to lift her off the bed. Finally, her feet on the floor again, she tried to dig her heels in, but the demons just dragged her with them, out the door and around the corner of the end unit.

Right there, next to a big tree, one of them made a movement with his arm and cast a vortex.

Fuck! They were taking her down to the Underworld! She tried to scream, but the rag in her mouth prevented her from doing so.

Zoltan, you're gonna pay for this betrayal! I'll kill you even if that's the last thing I do.

She was certain it was Zoltan who'd told the demons where to find her. Nobody else knew, and he was the one who'd so conveniently left the motel like a thief in the night. Christ, just by leaving her a note that he'd bring breakfast, he'd made sure that she'd wait for him. What a fucking idiot she'd been. How could she have trusted him?

~ ~ ~

Zoltan turned the corner of the building, a cardboard tray with two cups of coffee in one hand, a bag of various pastries in the other, when he looked at the motel across the street. His heart stopped at what he saw just a few yards away from the door to the motel room he'd shared with Enya the night before. A vortex was open, and three demons yanked a struggling, gagged Enya into it.

He dropped the breakfast and raced across the street, neither caring that cars were swerving to avoid him, nor paying any attention to their angry honking. All he was concerned about was reaching the vortex in time to pull Enya back. Despite his speed, he knew he would be too late. The last demon was already disappearing in the vortex, and the swirling mass of dark fog and air shrank.

"No!"

Nobody heard his scream. By the time he reached the spot where the vortex had been, the dust on the ground had already settled, and not even footprints from the demons' boots were visible.

His heart pounded like a jackhammer, and fury charged through his veins. How dare those bastards touch what was his? How dare they put their dirty paws on his woman? Nobody had the right to touch Enya! Nobody but Zoltan! She was his, and his alone! Whoever had ordered Enya's abduction—and he was sure the three demons were only henchmen—would pay for it.

He ran a shaky hand through his hair. Fuck! Everything seemed to spin around him as if his life had just been upended. A ragged breath tore from his chest, and with it, a realization manifested out of nowhere. He didn't want to acknowledge it at first, but even he couldn't deny what stared him in the face now: he did indeed have feelings for Enya. The reason he knew it was because the thought of somebody harming her sliced through his heart with more ferocity than an assassin's blade ever could. However, this news wasn't entirely welcome. If he accepted it as true, and acted upon it, his entire life would change. Everything he'd worked for, all his plans, his goals, his aspirations, would turn to cinder like the bodies of the many demons he'd tossed in the lava pits. And there was no guarantee that following his heart would yield success. Nevertheless, he knew he had to try.

Although he wanted to descend into the Underworld right away, he stopped himself and headed for the motel room instead. The door was left open, and Zoltan quickly entered and shut it behind him. He had to devise a plan to free Enya, and he couldn't do that if he charged after her without thinking things through.

How the fuck had his subjects found Enya? He and Enya had been invisible from the moment they'd left the alley where they'd killed five demons. Zoltan's phone was switched off, eliminating the possibility that he'd been traced electronically. Besides, nobody in the demon world knew of this phone. He only used it when transacting with humans. Knowing Enya, she was equally cautious when it came to having electronics on her that could be traced. Had Enya gone outside and been spotted by accident, even though he'd ordered no demon activity in Baltimore?

He looked around the room. There wasn't much evidence of a struggle, though a chair lay on its side. However, Enya's shoes were near the bed with a damp towel. She'd showered, gotten dressed, but hadn't put her shoes on yet. She hadn't gone outside, not voluntarily anyway. He glanced back at the door. The lock was intact, as was the doorframe. She'd let the demons in, which confirmed that the demons had known she was here. They'd targeted her, which suggested that his adversary knew that he'd been with Enya. But just how much did the traitor know about his relationship with her?

The kidnappers had left in such a hurry that they hadn't even bothered collecting the daggers that Enya had taken off the dead demons the night before. They still lay on the table near the window. Zoltan walked toward it and accidentally kicked one of Enya's shoes, turning it sole up. There, on the back of its heel, was a large green blotch. He reached for the shoe and touched the spot. It was dry. Blood from the night before. Blood that Enya couldn't make invisible. Had another demon lain in wait, watching the five attack, then followed Zoltan and Enya after they'd disposed of the dead demons? The green bloodstain on Enya's shoe would have made it possible for somebody to follow them at a safe distance without them noticing. If this was true, it meant the demon following them had reported back to his master with every detail he'd observed.

Enya and the demons who'd snatched her hadn't seen Zoltan approach, which was a good thing. It meant he could prepare, work out a story that his demons could believe, and in the process free Enya. Most of them were gullible enough to believe anything if the Great One said it with authority. But the traitor who wanted his throne wouldn't be as easily fooled. Zoltan needed a plan to deal with him. But he couldn't lose time, because sooner or later, his underlings would start torturing their prisoner. And the thought of somebody hurting—or worse, abusing—his woman boiled his blood. He had to get to her before that happened.

17

Less than an hour after witnessing Enya's abduction, Zoltan arrived at the vortex circle closest to his quarters in the Underworld. He'd gotten himself a new jacket to wear over his shirt, so he could hide the daggers he'd brought back. He wore no contact lenses, but for emergencies, he'd stuffed a pair of sunglasses into a pocket, together with a few other items, which might come in handy should things blow up in his face.

Zoltan closed the vortex and looked at the man who was on duty. He was surprised to see Yannick and not one of his subordinates monitoring the vortex circle himself. Just as well. Yannick was one of the men Zoltan wanted to talk to anyway.

"Oh Great One, you've returned." Yannick gave him a quick bow.

"Yannick," Zoltan said. He didn't want to sound too eager with his next question, so he lent his voice a casual tone. "Any unusual comings and goings while I was gone?"

"Not until an hour ago."

Zoltan raised an eyebrow. "Which means what? Talk straight; I've got lots of work to do."

"A patrol brought back a prisoner. A Stealth Guardian."

Zoltan managed to fake surprise. "A Stealth Guardian? Where is he?"

"In the lead cell, but he's not a—"

"Who captured him?" he interrupted, emphasizing that he assumed it was a Stealth Guardian male, when he knew all too well that it was Enya. "I want to reward the man."

"Uh, well, it's not a man—it's a female Stealth Guardian they captured."

"A female?"

Yannick nodded. "But I'm not sure who exactly brought her back. I was told just a short while ago that it was a routine patrol of three men arriving back with a prisoner. I can find out the details, oh Great One."

"Very well. Later. I'd like to see the prisoner for myself." Zoltan rubbed his hands together. "Finally, some progress! Take me to her."

"Right away, oh Great One." Yannick called down one of the corridors, where Zoltan could make out the faint outline of a guard, "One vortex guard for relief immediately."

A moment later, Zoltan heard the heavy footfalls of a man running toward them. When he reached them, he stopped and bowed. Zoltan recognized him. It was Richard.

"Oh Great One." Then he nodded to Yannick. "Richard reporting for duty."

Yannick nodded, then motioned to the corridor that led to the cells. Torches at various intervals illuminated the path. The Underworld had a whole host of cells for all kinds of prisoners, but only one was adequate to hold a Stealth Guardian. Its inside was lined with lead so Stealth Guardians couldn't use their powers. They could neither walk through walls nor turn themselves invisible. Rumor had it that a lengthy incarceration in a lead cell could erase a Stealth Guardian's powers permanently. Unfortunately, Zoltan had no idea how long such an exposure had to be, or even to what extent the rumor was true. In any case, he had to get Enya out of there as quickly as possible.

When Zoltan turned the last corner before reaching the doors that led to the various cells, he recognized Silvana standing guard in front of it—together with a huge Doberman. Zoltan wasn't surprised to see a dog guarding a Stealth Guardian prisoner. After all, no demon had ever been able to reliably verify that the guardians could indeed not make themselves invisible when blocked by lead. The dog was a fail-safe. Plan B, so to speak. Should Enya escape invisibly, the dog would immediately follow her scent. However, he hadn't expected that Silvana, the master of dogs herself, would be present. That would have to change for his plan to work.

"Oh Great One!" Silvana said.

Zoltan didn't get a chance to reply, because at that moment, somebody came toward them from the other end of the tunnel. He immediately recognized Vintoq.

"Oh Great One, you're back." Vintoq motioned to the lead cell. "I trust you've been informed that our men have captured a Stealth Guardian?"

Zoltan nodded. Of course Vintoq would show up just as Zoltan was about to look at the prisoner. Most likely Vintoq wanted to see his leader's reaction to seeing Enya. Zoltan denying that he knew her would be fruitless. If Vintoq was the traitor, he would have already been informed by the demons who kidnapped Enya that Zoltan had been with her, though clearly the three had been too chicken to confront him as well, and had waited until he left the motel before grabbing Enya. Yeah, that was brave of them: three large men against one petite woman.

"Vintoq, good timing. I was just about to take a look at our prisoner." Zoltan motioned to Silvana. "Unlock the door."

He watched carefully as she pulled a large key from her breast pocket and slid it into the old-fashioned lock. The creaking sound that followed when she turned the key echoed eerily against the tunnel walls. Silvana pulled on the heavy ring that served as a door handle and opened the door. Inside there was no light source, but a little light from the corridor streamed into the cell. Zoltan motioned to Silvana to stand aside and took a few steps until he stood under the doorframe, which he almost completely filled. He had no intention of stepping inside the cell. He wasn't that stupid. If Vintoq was the traitor, it was entirely possible that Silvana was on his team. Together they could easily lock the door behind Zoltan and kill Yannick should he protest.

Zoltan's eyes finally adjusted to the darkness, and he recognized Enya. Not that he needed confirmation that she was indeed the prisoner, but he had to get a message to her that he would get her out.

"You!" She suddenly pounced, eyes full of fury and jaw clenched. "You fucking asshole!"

He looked into her eyes and lifted his hand, waving a finger to make the sign for no, while he formed soundless words with his lips. *Trust me. I'll get you out.*

But either Enya couldn't read his lips or she didn't believe him, because she continued glaring at him. "I'm gonna kill you!"

Before she could say anything more that might put him in a situation where he'd have to explain more than he wanted to, he pivoted and took a few steps into the corridor, then slammed the door shut.

"Lock it!" he ordered Silvana, who immediately executed his order.

Once the key turned in the lock, he motioned to Yannick and Vintoq to join him a few yards farther down the corridor. Out of earshot of the cell, Zoltan turned and faced his lieutenants. "Who the fuck did this?"

"Oh Great One?" Vintoq asked, a clueless expression on his face. Oh yeah, he was quite an actor.

"Is there a problem? She's a Stealth Guardian for certain," Yannick added, apparently just as surprised.

"Yes, there's a problem!" For emphasis, Zoltan pointed back to the cell. "That Stealth Guardian female is the one I've been working on! She has no idea that I'm the Great One; she thinks I'm a run-of-the-mill demon who wants to change for the better. She believed me, because I played my role well. And now, some idiots kidnap her and destroy my plan. I was this close"—he held up his thumb and forefinger—"from getting her to trust me enough to invite me to her compound! And some fucking overeager grunts grab her. What the fuck were they doing in Baltimore? Didn't I issue an order that there was to be no demon activity in Baltimore?" He narrowed his eyes at both of them, not wanting to give away that he was suspecting Vintoq of going behind his back.

"Yes, oh Great One, you did," Vintoq said. "I pulled all patrols off Baltimore weeks ago, just as you demanded."

"Then who the fuck sent them up?" Zoltan looked at Yannick. "Get me the fucking vortex records."

"Of course, oh Great One." Yannick bowed.

Zoltan grunted. "I swear, when I find out who did this, heads will roll."

Yannick cleared his throat.

"What else?" Zoltan snapped.

"You might want to speak to Ulric. My understanding is that the three men who brought back the prisoner were on an intelligence mission. That's Ulric's domain."

Zoltan nodded. "Send him to my study. Now!"

He spun on his heel and marched off. Within minutes he was in his study, where he took a few breaths to relax. He'd played the angry leader well, because it hadn't been too hard to fake anger. After all, his demons had snatched Enya, and now he had to come up with a plan to free her. His heart thundered at the thought that he might fail. But he couldn't allow himself to go down that path.

He had to remain calm, not let his emotions get the better of him. At the same time, it was important that he found out who was behind the assassination attempt on him, and Enya's subsequent kidnapping. It was evident that these two events were related. The same traitor was responsible for them. It was time to find out who he was.

A knock at the door announced his visitor.

"Enter!"

The door opened, and Yannick came in. "Ulric is here, oh Great One."

"Then what are you waiting for? Send him in!"

"Uh, there's just one thing, oh Great One." Yannick nervously cleared his throat.

"What?"

"The news that we've captured a Stealth Guardian is spreading fast among your subjects. They are already asking what you're planning to do with her."

"I've not decided yet."

"It's just… they want a public spectacle. They want her tortured to pay for the many demon lives she and her people have taken."

"We all want her punished, but for now, she's staying in the cell. Nobody touches her. Do you understand that?" Zoltan jabbed his finger into Yannick's chest. "I make you personally responsible if anything happens to her. I need her alive, and I need her compliant. And that's not gonna happen if she's being made a spectacle of. Is that clear?"

Yannick nodded. "Yes, oh Great One."

"And bring me the records from a few months ago that I had you compile."

Yannick gestured past Zoltan. "They are on your desk."

Zoltan grunted. "Send Ulric in."

Yannick pivoted and walked out in the corridor. A moment later, Ulric entered and bowed.

"You wanted to see me, oh Great One."

"Shut the door!"

Ulric flinched, then closed the door quickly.

"I was informed that the three demons who captured the Stealth Guardian female were on an intelligence mission in Baltimore. Is that right?"

Ulric blinked. "I'm afraid I don't know."

"What's that supposed to mean? It's an easy question. Did you send them on an intelligence mission to Baltimore or not?"

He cleared his throat. "Yes and no. I mean, they were on an intelligence mission, but not in Baltimore. At least, that's not where they were supposed to be."

"So, how did they end up in Baltimore?"

"I don't know."

"Well, then fucking ask them."

"I can't."

Zoltan glared at him. "You will obey my command!"

"They've disappeared."

"What?" Zoltan snapped.

"After the Stealth Guardian was locked in the cell, they left, presumably to go to their quarters, but they weren't seen again."

"They went back up into the human world?"

Ulric shook his head. "I checked all three vortex circles and was told that they didn't go up top. They must be hiding somewhere."

Zoltan let the news sink in. "Well, isn't that convenient?" The men who could have told him how they'd ended up following him and Enya to kidnap her were missing in action.

"Oh Great One?" Ulric asked, clearly not tuning into Zoltan's sarcasm.

"Leave!" Zoltan thundered.

Ulric hurried out of the study, leaving Zoltan wondering whether the demon responsible for intelligence had spoken the truth. Had he disposed of the three demons after they'd returned to the Underworld in order to erase any evidence that may lead to Ulric himself? Or was Ulric truly clueless, and another demon had used the three to do his dirty work, knowing that Ulric would be blamed for it if the three kidnappers disappeared without a trace?

"Fuck!" Zoltan said under his breath. With every new piece of information he discovered, he got further and further away from finding the traitor. His pool of suspects was expanding. In addition to Vintoq, Ulric, too, had had opportunity to orchestrate the kidnapping. But had Ulric been behind the assassination attempt a few months earlier?

Zoltan marched to his desk and scanned it. He found the sheet of paper that Yannick had left for him: a list of demons who'd gone up top that day, together with the purpose of their trip. He studied the list, trying to recall the face of the assassin in the abandoned building. Vintoq was indeed on the list. He'd been in the human world that day. Had he been there, killing the assassin before the poor bastard could reveal his master's name? There had to be a way to find out.

Zoltan walked to the door and opened it to leave his study and nearly collided with Wilson, the stocky demon in charge of weaponry.

"Wilson, is there something you wanted?"

"Uh, oh Great One. I wanted to mention to you that your subjects are getting impatient. They want to know what you intend to do with the Stealth Guardian prisoner."

Zoltan tilted his head a little to the side. This wasn't Wilson's domain. Why was he concerned with what happened to the prisoner? "Yannick already informed me about that. I told him just as I'm telling you now that I'm still deciding on my course of action."

"Very well, oh Great One."

"But since you're here, you might as well do something for me. I need to speak to the prisoner, alone. Go fetch her and bring her to my quarters."

Wilson raised an eyebrow. "To your quarters, oh Great One? How many guards do you want me to bring to watch her?"

"Just one." If Zoltan had said none, and Wilson had relayed this message to Silvana, who was currently guarding Enya, Silvana would have questioned Wilson and accompanied Enya anyway. She wouldn't be so easy to shake. However, he'd make Silvana wait outside his private rooms so he could talk to Enya alone.

"Uhm."

"What?" Zoltan snapped.

"Is one guard enough? What if she uses her powers and disappears?"

"Even with her powers intact outside the lead cell, she can't leave the Underworld without casting a vortex. And I doubt that one of my subjects is stupid enough to cast one for her. Or don't you agree?"

"I agree, of course, oh Great One."

"And have some food brought to my quarters."

"Right away, oh Great One." Wilson scurried away.

18

Enya's eyes had adjusted to the dark quite easily. There was no light in the cell, but there was a tiny sliver of space between the door and the uneven ground that allowed her to see if somebody moved in front of her door. Every so often, she saw a shadow blocking the light, and once she'd heard a dog growl. She wasn't surprised that the guard who stood outside the door was accompanied by a dog. It was common knowledge that the demons used dogs to sniff out Stealth Guardians who'd made themselves invisible. Not that she had a chance to do that here. In the lead-lined cell, she was powerless. There was no chance of escaping through the walls or door either, because just as she couldn't make herself invisible here, she couldn't dematerialize either. Which left her with only one option: to wait until somebody opened the door and hope they'd transfer her somewhere else. Then she'd take her chances.

She hadn't been locked up for very long yet when she saw several demons' shadows move in front of her cell, though she couldn't hear any part of their conversation. Enya jumped up and continued watching the door. Finally, she heard a sound of metal scraping against metal. Somebody inserted the key into the lock and turned it.

The door opened. Green eyes was the first thing she saw. A second later, her eyes adjusted and she was able to make out the person, a male demon just a few inches taller than herself, but at least thirty to forty pounds heavier. He stepped into the cell, and behind him, Enya now saw the other demon, a woman, hover with her Doberman.

A rattling sound made her snap her gaze back to the male demon. Only now she noticed the shackles in his hands.

"You give me any trouble putting the cuffs on you, and Silvana will tell the dog to go for your throat," the demon warned her.

She motioned to the shackles. "Let me guess, they're made of lead."

The demon chuckled. "We got ourselves a real smart cookie, haven't we?"

"Not smart enough," the female demon he'd called Silvana replied with a snort. "Now cuff her already, so we can get on with this." She spoke with a strong accent.

Knowing there was no use trying to fight the two demons without her powers, Enya stretched out her arms to be chained. The chains would have the same effect as the lead cell: they bound her powers just as they bound her hands. The demons were smarter than she'd given them credit for. Much smarter, or she would have never fallen for Zoltan's lies. Now all she could do was hope for an opportunity to free herself and hitch a ride into the human world with an unsuspecting demon—just like Logan and Winter had done, and Wesley and Virginia before them.

The demon tested the shackles. They held. "Now let's go." He shoved her out of the cell and turned her to the left, where Enya could see a long corridor with several branches leading in other directions.

"Stop, Wilson. I will take her," Silvana said.

Wilson turned around, and Enya noticed the silent battle between the two, until Wilson shrugged. "Whatever."

Wilson walked away, while Silvana sidled up to Enya, the dog on the outer flank. "This is how this is gonna work: you walk where I tell you to walk. Try to run, and I send Rex after you. He's not been fed today."

"And apparently neither have you."

Silvana rammed her elbow into Enya's side, making her lose her balance for a second. Then the demon leaned in as if they were suddenly best buddies. "Between you and me, I hope you'll run. I love watching."

Enya glared at her, but she didn't unleash the barrage of four-letter words she had at the ready for this bitch. It wouldn't help her cause. But later, when she was free—if she got free—she would make sure Silvana died a slow and painful death.

She didn't bother asking where Silvana was taking her. The she-devil wouldn't answer her anyway, so Enya used her energy to memorize the path they were taking. By her estimate, they walked less than five minutes before Silvana stopped at an unassuming door and knocked.

It took only seconds before the door was opened and a very familiar man appeared in the frame. Her jaw instantly tightened, and her hands balled into fists. Just the person whose face she wanted to pummel.

"Bring the prisoner in," Zoltan said.

Silvana gave her a nod to proceed, but Enya didn't budge.

"Fuck you!" Enya cursed and spat on the floor for good measure.

Silvana raised her arm and swung, but her fist never made contact with Enya's face. Instead, her arm was held back by Zoltan himself. Obviously stunned, Silvana turned back to Zoltan.

"But she insulted you, oh G—"

"Enough!" he said. "I'll deal with her. You may go."

He reached for Enya's shackles to pull her into the room. Enya had no choice but to move her legs, or she would have fallen right into his arms.

"Leave!"

"I shall guard your door with Rex." Silvana nodded sternly.

"As you wish." Zoltan slammed the door shut.

"You f—"

Zoltan put two fingers over Enya's lips to stop her from speaking. But she wouldn't be silenced so easily. Furious about his betrayal, she jerked up her bound hands and hit his chin with an upward hook, whipping his head back, before he even knew what was happening.

Zoltan pressed one hand to his chin. But instead of screaming at her or striking back, he slapped one hand back on her mouth and lifted her off her feet. Before she could do anything to free herself, he was already carrying her around the corner of the large suite and kicking open another door. He stepped inside the smaller room, a bathroom, and closed the door behind him. There, he set her back on her feet and removed his hand from her mouth.

"Damn it, Enya, keep your voice down. We can't afford for anybody to listen in on our conversation."

"Conversation?" she growled. "You think we were having a conversation, you piece of shit!?" She thrust her knee up, but Zoltan blocked her.

"Hey, not the family jewels. We still need those."

"We? In your fucking dreams, you two-timing bastard!" How dare he suggest that she would ever sleep with him again?

"Let me set the record straight: I didn't kidnap you."

"Oh no, of course not. You had your subjects do it for you! How stupid do you think I am? You were the only one who knew that I was in that motel, waiting for you to bring breakfast." She huffed. "Tell me, was it fun tricking me into trusting you? Did you enjoy yourself? Did you have a good laugh behind my back? Huh?"

Zoltan grabbed her shoulders and pressed her against the stone wall. "No, I wasn't laughing. I was too busy figuring out how I can free you and send you back to the human world."

"Liar!"

"I didn't order your abduction. It was the traitor who's vying for my throne."

"Oh, how convenient. That traitor probably doesn't even exist." Zoltan had probably planned every single incident from the start—like a well-directed stage play. And she'd played the main role, the heroine who was too stupid to live.

"Nobody else knew where I was. I didn't show my face outside. They came to the door. They knocked. They knew!"

Zoltan nodded. "Because there was demon blood on the heel of your boot. It remained visible while we left after we disposed of the bodies."

She slowly shook her head. "That can't be."

"But it's true. The blood was dry when I came back to the room, so it couldn't have been from when the three kidnappers grabbed you. There must have been a sixth demon that night who followed us."

Could this be true? Or was he lying to her again? But why lie now when she was already in his domain, when she had no chance of escape? What would it serve him?

"That's how they found us," Zoltan continued. "He must have brought in reinforcements while we… uh, slept… and then waited for a good opportunity to grab you." He sighed. "I wish I'd never gone to get coffee and pastries."

She looked into his eyes and only now noticed that he wasn't wearing his colored lenses. He was all demon.

"Please, Enya, I need you to believe me."

She hesitated, but his gaze intensified. His eyes became larger. It took her a few seconds to realize that the reason for it was simple: his face was coming closer. She could lift her bound hands to stop him from his intent—and she knew what he intended to do—but remained paralyzed.

"When I saw them take you, I was across the street. I couldn't get to the vortex fast enough. I tried, Enya. I tried to get to you. Because knowing what my subjects are capable of, knowing what they could do to you, it almost tore my heart out. I can't let them hurt you. It would kill me."

There was a wet sheen on his eyes now, and they looked like deep pools of water. Against her better judgment, despite her fear that Zoltan could still be lying even now, she continued looking at him. Something was drawing her to him. She felt a connection, something that told her that she was safe with him, even though she didn't understand it.

"Then help me," she murmured.

"I promise I'll get you out of here." A second later, his lips were on hers, and he was kissing her with the passion of a man who'd been given a second lease on life. She welcomed him and parted her lips, responding to him like she'd responded the night before. But just as quickly as the kiss had started, it ended.

"I wish I could make love to you right now, but we don't have much time," Zoltan said, and pressed his forehead to hers. "I need to get you back to your cell."

With her bound hands, Enya pushed him away. "What?"

"Let me explain."

"Yeah, you'd better."

"I still don't know who's behind all this. But I know that he's been working against me for years. And I'm nowhere near close to figuring out who sent the assassins or your kidnappers."

"Well, wouldn't it be easiest to just ask the three who grabbed me who sent them?"

Zoltan grimaced. "That *would* be the easiest, but the three demons who kidnapped you disappeared. And if I'm not mistaken, they're probably dead. The traitor doesn't leave loose ends."

"That's convenient."

"Yeah, it is." He ran a hand through his dark hair. "By now he probably knows that I have feelings for you, and he knows he can hurt me by hurting you. He'll use you to get to me. He'll never give up. I have to eliminate him."

"So he won't take your throne?" Enya shook her head. So all Zoltan was still interested in was his kingdom.

"My throne? You think that's what this is about? Me being worried about being deposed?" He blew out a breath. "This is about you. Your safety. As long as I haven't eliminated the traitor, you'll never be safe from him. He'll torture you. All because of me. Because I care about you."

Enya stared at Zoltan. Too many thoughts and questions bounced around in her head. "And once you eliminate him, will you continue sitting on the throne of the Underworld?"

To her surprise, Zoltan let out a mirthless laugh. "Enya, that's not important right now. Let's just figure out the best way to get you out of here."

Something in his expression made the wheels in her brain turn and click. She suddenly understood what he was doing.

"Once you've helped me escape, and eliminated the traitor, your days in the Underworld are numbered. Helping a Stealth Guardian escape... It's committing treason, isn't it?"

He shrugged. "It doesn't matter anymore."

"Zoltan, tell me the truth. What will happen?"

He hesitated for seconds that seemed to stretch to minutes. "I'll be fair game for any demon to kill me without repercussions. And whoever succeeds will take the throne."

Finally it sank in. Zoltan was risking his life for her. "Why?"

"That's the rule."

"No, not that. Why are you doing this for me?"

A genuine smile appeared on his lips, and he lifted his hand to brush his fingers over her cheek. "Because you're worth it. When I look at you, I feel a connection. I feel as if I've left a part of myself inside you. And all I can think of is to protect you." He laughed. "Crazy coming from a demon, isn't it?"

"No, not crazy. Because that's how I feel when I look at you. There's something that binds us together. I don't know what it is, but I can feel it."

He pressed a soft kiss to her lips. "Now let's figure out how to get you out of here and eliminate the traitor so he can't hurt you like he hurt so many others before you."

"What did you just say?"

"That he hurt others before you?"

She nodded. "What did you mean by that?"

"Just that he killed humans to interfere with my plans. Like he killed your emissarius Nancy Britton and—"

"And he gave Tessa an overdose of heroin!" Enya interrupted. "You said before that it wasn't you who did that."

"That's right. I wasn't going to turn Tessa into a martyr so she could win the election. Nor did I authorize to have Nancy killed." He raised his hands. "That was definitely not my plan."

"Then I have an idea of how to identify the traitor."

19

Zoltan stopped at the door and looked over his shoulder. "Ready?"

"As ready as I'll ever be," Enya whispered.

"Then let's get this show on the road," he replied, and gripped the shackles around Enya's wrists before he ripped the door open and dragged her outside.

As expected, Silvana stood guard, the Doberman standing next to her, its nostrils flaring at Enya's scent.

"Take her back to the cell. And then call a meeting for all lieutenants. We'll meet in twenty minutes. I want everybody there on time. Is that clear?"

Silvana motioned to Enya. "And who's guarding her?"

Zoltan narrowed his eyes. "You've got plenty of men at your disposal. Choose someone, for fuck's sake! And then get your ass down to the conference cave."

"Right away, oh Great One," Silvana replied, and grabbed Enya's shackles to pull her along the corridor leading to the cells.

Zoltan followed them with his eyes. With a little luck, his plan might just work out. All depended on a carefully choreographed sequence of events. Zoltan turned into another corridor and let his memory guide him through the labyrinth of tunnels. Many a newly minted demon got lost, but he'd grown up here. As a boy, he'd played hide and seek in the many corridors, tunnels, and caves. He knew every dead end, every shortcut, and every crevice that could be used to hide.

He used this knowledge to reach the tunnel that led to right behind the cave that housed the cells. He heard the distinct, heavy footfalls of Silvana and the decidedly lighter ones of Enya, though not the virtually silent ones of the dog. Moments later, there was a hushed conversation, then the cell door was opened. More rattling of chains: Silvana was taking Enya's shackles off, which meant she was now in the cell. A few more seconds, a few more sounds, and a key was turned in the lock.

Moments later, Silvana's boots clacking on the ground echoed against the rock walls and grew fainter and fainter. Then silence. Zoltan waited another minute to be certain that she'd turned into another tunnel from where she couldn't look back to see what was about to happen in the cell cave. One hand in his coat pocket, Zoltan emerged from the tunnel and marched into the cave. The demon who stood guard outside of Enya's cell was an experienced one. It didn't matter. Next to him, the Doberman sat at attention, its head turning toward the sound of Zoltan's boots.

"Oh Great One," the guard said.

"Todd, is Silvana not here?" Zoltan asked, and approached as quickly as he could without causing suspicion. "She was supposed to wait for me here to walk to the meeting with me."

"Oh Great One," Todd replied, and turned his head to the tunnel in which Silvana had disappeared. "You just missed h—"

The dagger Zoltan stabbed into the guard's heart cut his sentence short. "Yeah, I know." He twisted the blade, making sure the man was dead, then pulled it out and wiped it carefully on the guard's clothing, then let the body fall to the ground. He reassured himself that no blood had splattered on his own clothes and put his dagger back into his pocket.

The Doberman whined, and Zoltan turned to him. The good thing was that all dogs in the Underworld were trained to protect the Great One. They wouldn't turn on him. He pulled a piece of sausage out of his other pocket and gave it to the dog.

"Good boy, Rex."

The Doberman swallowed the sausage and what it contained: a fast-acting powder Zoltan had stuffed in its center to put the dog to sleep. In a few hours, Rex would be as lively as ever. While the dog grew calmer and lay down, Zoltan searched the dead guard's pockets for the key to the cell and retrieved it quickly, then turned to the door. He cast a last look at the dog and noticed its eyes closing, before he unlocked the door and pulled it open.

"Enya, quickly," he said.

She emerged from the dark cell. "You kept your word."

"You still doubt me? Enya, Enya. I have the feeling I'll have to pound it into you how much you mean to me."

"And by 'pound,' you mean…?" She dropped her gaze to his crotch.

"Don't look at me like that, or we'll never get out of here." He pulled his shirt from his pants, then pulled out a second shirt he'd stuffed underneath and handed it to Enya. "Put this on. It's unwashed and has my scent on it. It should help with the dogs." While Enya pulled the shirt over her top and buttoned it, he adjusted his own clothing. Then he looked back at the dead demon. "Take his dagger."

Enya retrieved the weapon from the dead guard and bent down, then stopped herself and pointed to her bare feet. "You wouldn't have a pair of shoes my size lying around, would you?"

"Afraid not. But maybe that's a good thing. Nobody will hear you walking."

"Okay." She slid the dagger into one of the pockets of her cargo pants, then pulled her phone from another and switched it on. "No signal."

Zoltan nodded. "Just like I told you. Good thing is you won't need a signal. Make sure it's on silent."

"Already set. I'm ready."

"Stay as close to me as you can at all times. My shirt will distort your scent, but not entirely."

"Don't worry, I'm gonna stick to you like glue. You're my ticket out of here."

He bent his head to her and smiled. "I hope that's not all I am to you."

She kissed him quickly, then stepped back. "I guess you'll have to figure that out later, won't you?"

"Tease."

"That's how you like it," she murmured, and in the middle of her sentence, she became invisible.

~ ~ ~

With a last look at the sleeping dog, Enya followed Zoltan as he took her through a maze of tunnels. That Zoltan hadn't killed the poor creature showed her that he had a heart. There was still some good in him, and she wouldn't give up until she found a way to change him back to what he was born as. But right now, her focus was on two things: identifying the traitorous demon who threatened not only her life, but also Zoltan's, and escaping from the Underworld.

To make sure that Zoltan knew she was with him, even if he couldn't see or hear her, Enya put her hand on his forearm and walked beside him whenever there was nobody coming toward him. Only when she had to make space for a demon to pass them did she walk behind Zoltan.

Despite the fact that Zoltan's reign was being threatened, she couldn't help but notice the respect with which his underlings greeted him. Nor the slavishness he seemed to inspire in them. For the first time since she'd found out who Zoltan really was, she saw the Great One in him. He moved with purpose, with determination, with the knowledge that his word was law down here. And they all knew it. His subjects were dispensable, exchangeable, and at the Great One's mercy. As if putting on a mask, Zoltan had slipped into this character only moments after the tender moment they'd shared outside the cell. Nothing of the man she knew was visible now. That was how it had to be. If his subjects knew what lay beneath his ruthless façade, she and he would both be dead.

Zoltan walked fast, and Enya knew why. He needed to get to the meeting in time, preferably before everybody was assembled, so nobody would suspect that he'd had time to free the prisoner. He needed an alibi.

After making a few more turns, he stopped in front of a door and opened it. He marched inside the cave the size of an upper-class dining room, not shutting the door behind him, allowing her to follow. Around a large stone table sat two men, as well as one woman she recognized: Silvana. A fourth man stood at the head of it, slightly leaning over it. The moment Zoltan entered, their quiet conversation stopped, and all faces turned to their leader.

"Oh Great One," they said nearly in unison, and rose from their chairs.

Enya used the temporary noise the chairs made as they scraped along the floor to hide her own movements and pulled her phone from her pocket. She unlocked it.

Zoltan cast a scolding look at the man who stood at the head of the table and now moved to the side. Clearly, this was Zoltan's place. "Vintoq, where are the others? Yannick, Ulric, and Tamara?"

Vintoq bowed. "On their way, oh Great One. In fact, I believe I hear them coming."

Enya took his picture.

Moments later, two men and one woman entered and greeted Zoltan.

"Sit," Zoltan ordered them, and sat down at the head of the table.

Enya took several pictures, then walked around toward the other end of the table to get a better angle on the demons who were with their back to her, then she came to a rocking halt.

Shit!

There, on the other side of the table, hidden by its stone base, a vicious-looking pit bull sat at Silvana's feet. Its ears perked up, and its nostrils suddenly flared. Had the animal picked up her scent? A low growl came from the dog, and it looked in Enya's direction.

Silvana snapped her gaze to the dog. "Easy, boy."

Zoltan jumped up and pounded his fist on the table. "You brought a dog in here? Explain yourself!"

Silvana cleared her throat while she petted the animal's head. "It's just a precaution, oh Great One. With a Stealth Guardian locked up in the Underworld, we can't be too vigilant. The dog is here for your protection. Surely, you can appreciate that, in case of an escape, the prisoner might seek you out to take her revenge."

"Yes, and whose fault is that?" Zoltan glared at the assembled. "If some idiot hadn't sent three men to Baltimore and messed up my carefully planned scheme, we'd be inside one of the Stealth Guardians' compounds by now. But no, somebody had to disobey my orders!"

Enya didn't dare move for fear the dog would pounce if its sensitive ears perceived a sound, forcing her to snap pictures of the remaining demons from where she stood.

"And when I find out who did this, there will be consequences." He sat back down. "Now all I can do is try to save what's to be saved. Getting the Stealth Guardian bitch to trust me now is impossible. She now knows that I'm the Great One. All we can use her for now is bait."

Hearing Zoltan talk in such a degrading way about her felt jarring, but she understood why he had to call her names: if he didn't, his lieutenants would wonder whether he'd developed scruples, or worse, feelings.

"I feel we've let you down, oh Great One," Vintoq said. "I will make it my first priority to find the three demons responsible for the Stealth Guardian's capture and question them myself to get to the truth."

Enya studied Vintoq's face. Was he just pacifying his leader, or did he mean what he said? She couldn't tell. If he was the traitor, he was very good at hiding his true feelings and playing the loyal subordinate.

Zoltan nodded, even though she knew he suspected that the three men who'd taken her were long dead. "Now... Any suggestions as to how we're going to use the Stealth Guardian female to our advantage now that my cover is blown?"

The five men and two women avoided looking in Zoltan's direction, casting their eyes either downward to the table or to a spot in the distance. Enya wanted to snort. It was clear that Zoltan was the brains of this operation. Without him, the Underworld wouldn't have nearly as much negative influence on the world. Except that there was one person— and she didn't want to assume that it was a man—among the assembled who was hiding their true intelligence, their true cunning: the traitor.

"Anybody?"

"We could torture her to reveal the location of her compound to us," a male demon said.

Zoltan gave him a bored look. "Torture, really? That's your brilliant idea? We're not talking about a human here. She's an immortal. Whatever we do to her, short of killing her, will be nothing but a temporary inconvenience. We can't inflict sufficient pain on a Stealth Guardian like her to make her reveal her secrets. Or would you reveal anything about the Underworld if you were tortured by one of them?"

"I'd rather die!" the demon responded without missing a beat.

Whether it was bravado that forced him to reply so forcefully or the fact that he feared Zoltan didn't matter. His response squashed his offered suggestion of torture. Just as well, because while Zoltan was right that torture wouldn't work on her, she still wasn't particularly keen on being at the receiving end of it.

"Anybody else?" Zoltan asked. "Just as I thought. First you destroy my plan, and now you can't come up with an alternative. Guess I'll have to do everything myself, just as always."

"Oh Great One, I'm sure we can devise a new plan," Tamara said quickly as if wanting to appease her leader.

Before Zoltan could say anything else, the door was ripped open and a demon stormed in. Enya noticed the dog instantly jumping up and looking toward the intruder. It gave her a chance to move as well—closer to the other corner of the room, farther away from the dog.

"What the—"

"Oh Great One, the man guarding the Stealth Guardian was found dead in front of the lead cell."

Zoltan jumped up amidst the stunned gasps of his subordinates, playing his surprise well. "And the prisoner?"

"Gone!"

Zoltan slammed his fist on the table. "Find her! Damn it, you imbeciles! Find the Stealth Guardian and bring her to me! Now!"

The demons around the table all jumped up, and Enya had to jump out of the way, pressing herself against the wall so nobody would bump into her.

Fuck! They'd found the dead guard too quickly. Now an escape would be doubly difficult and fraught with danger. She could only hope that Zoltan had a few aces up his sleeve.

20

Zoltan had hoped they'd have more time, but the discovery of the dead demon meant he had to improvise. Unfortunately, he had no idea where in the meeting room Enya was hiding out. He could only trust her instincts and hope she'd make herself known to him by touch as soon as she could.

"Everybody to your stations!" he said, wanting to clear the meeting cave as quickly as possible. "Alert your men and assemble search parties. Comb through every inch of the Underworld! I want her found!"

While the lieutenants rushed out, Yannick came toward Zoltan. "What about the vortex circles? What if she tries to hitch a ride with another demon?"

Zoltan growled. "Well, since you still haven't found a way of shutting down the vortexes temporarily, you'll have to double the defenses. And warn everybody as to what she may be trying to do! Now go!"

While doubling the guards at the vortex circles would make an escape somewhat harder, he had no choice but to order such a measure. Anything less and Yannick would smell a rat.

Finally, everybody was leaving the room, everybody but Silvana and her pit bull.

"I shall remain at your side," she announced. "Together with Baby." She petted the dog's head.

Figured that she'd name one of the most vicious dogs in her kennel Baby. But no way was Silvana staying by his side. "I'll take the dog myself. You're needed with the other dogs. If anybody can find the prisoner, it's you. I'm counting on you."

"But, oh Great One, you need protection."

"Baby here will protect me. Now go. That's an order!" he said.

Finally, she bowed her head, handed the dog's leash over to him, and left the room. He watched her hurry down the corridor then disappear into a side tunnel, before he turned around and walked away from the open door to a spot where he and the dog couldn't be seen from the corridor.

"Enya?" he murmured.

Almost immediately, he felt a hand on his back, then a breath at his ear. "What are you gonna do about the dog?"

Already, the animal was growling, smelling Enya, despite the shirt with Zoltan's scent.

"Don't worry about the dog," he said. "All dogs down here are trained to listen to my command." He looked at the dog. "Sit, Baby, sit." The dog followed the command. "Down." The pit bull lay down completely. "See?"

"Good. But we're not taking the dog with us."

"We have to, at least until we get to a vortex circle. If we run into Silvana and she sees me without the dog, she'll become suspicious."

"Doesn't matter," Enya said. "She won't see you. I'm taking no chances. We're getting out of here invisibly. Leave the dog here."

The dog growled again.

"See, he doesn't like me," Enya said.

"That's not it. He believes I'm in danger, because he can smell and hear you. He won't leave my side now. Protecting me overrides any commands I can give."

"Then drug him."

"Sorry, I'm out of the sausage."

"Fuck!" Enya cursed.

"Just walk on my other side, and if somebody comes toward us, walk behind me and put your hand on my hip so I know you're there."

"Fine."

Judging by her tone, Enya was less than pleased about the turn of events, but Zoltan knew it was the best way. Marching through the tunnels and encountering other dogs would mean drawing attention if he and Enya were invisible. If he remained visible, the dogs would simply acknowledge him and pass, and with some luck, his scent and footfalls would drown out Enya's.

"Let's go." He held out his free hand and felt Enya clasp it. It was still an odd feeling to touch somebody who was invisible, but he could get used to this.

"Come," he ordered the dog, and started walking.

The corridor was empty until they reached the first intersection, but as soon as they turned into the first side tunnel, there was lots of activity. He squeezed Enya's hand to reassure her that she would be fine, and marched along, while Enya fell in line behind him, her hand on his back. He kept the dog on a tight leash, making sure the animal didn't stop to sniff who was behind him.

Several demons rushed past, greeting Zoltan in passing with a quick nod and an even quicker "oh Great One." For some reason, he was starting to despise the salutation. He didn't feel like the Great One right now, because he wasn't behaving like the leader of the demons. He was betraying his own race, and he didn't even feel guilty about it.

And another thing suddenly hit him: he hadn't had a single migraine attack since he'd started to develop feelings for Enya. Feelings that he'd had to confront the moment she'd been abducted by his subjects. He hadn't put them into words yet, but he knew what they were. He'd never thought he'd be capable of feeling unconditional love for a woman, but here it was, black on white. He should confess his feelings to Enya, but what would be the use? In a few days he'd be dead anyway, either killed at the hands of a Stealth Guardian trying to save Enya from the mistake of being entangled with a demon, or—more likely—by one of his subjects once they tracked him down. He had no illusions about his future. He wasn't that naïve. But one thing he would do before he died: get Enya to safety.

Zoltan took another tunnel, using his knowledge of the vast maze to avoid areas that would be swarming with demons. In the short connecting tunnel that they entered, they were alone. Finally, an opportunity to exchange a few words with Enya.

"You okay?" he asked.

"Yeah, I'm good. How much farther?"

"A couple of miles. We have to take a detour to get to the vortex circle I have in mind. The less foot traffic we encounter, the better. I don't want to have to explain to one of my lieutenants where I'm going."

"You can always kill whoever questions you," Enya suggested.

Zoltan chuckled. "Did I mention that it gets me all hot when you talk bloodthirsty?"

A soft laugh came from Enya. "Anything I do gets you hot." An invisible hand landed on his butt and grabbed one cheek firmly.

The touch sent a bolt of heat through his body. "You're quite a woman, Enya. You could have anybody. Why still hang around me?"

"You're my ticket out of here."

"Yeah, you said that before. What about afterward?"

"Shh!" she suddenly warned.

A split second later, he heard footsteps and barking coming from a side tunnel a dozen yards ahead of them. Moments later, he saw a Rottweiler on a leash come around the corner. Behind the animal three demons emerged, all armed to the teeth and out for blood.

When their eyes fell on Zoltan, they immediately said, "Oh Great One."

But Zoltan didn't get a chance to reply. The Rottweiler charged toward him, teeth bared, snarling and growling. Its handler tried to hold him back, but the animal was so strong that it dragged him along.

"Get a hold of your fucking dog!" Zoltan ordered.

But the beast kept pulling on its leash and barking loudly. The pit bull joined in and moved in front of Zoltan, trying to defend him.

"I don't know what's wrong with him," the dog handler said.

Zoltan knew very well what was wrong with the dog: it had picked up Enya's scent.

"Hold him back, for fuck's sake!" Zoltan growled. "Or I'll unleash the pit bull on him." He narrowed his eyes at the man. "If you can't control a dog, you shouldn't be handling one." Attack was the best defense. "Now get out of my fucking way!"

Zoltan turned sideways, so Enya was now between him and the tunnel wall, the pit bull in front of him, the three demons with their Rottweiler only three yards away from them.

A second demon grabbed the leash, and together they pulled the dog closer to them, so it couldn't lunge toward Zoltan and the invisible Stealth Guardian behind him.

"Now, pass! And if your fucking dog so much as brushes me, you'll all pay for it!"

Sufficiently intimidated, the three demons rushed past, dragging the protesting Rottweiler with them, even though the animal continued looking over its shoulder and barking at the invisible foe.

"That was close," Enya murmured behind him.

"Come," he whispered, and hurried along the tunnel.

It took another few minutes until he could finally see the vortex circle he'd been heading for. "You know what to do," he whispered to Enya.

"You bet."

He nodded, then marched the last fifty yards toward the circle as if he owned the place—and, actually, he did. And as long as he behaved like the Great One and not like a man who'd betrayed his subjects for a woman, they wouldn't know what hit them.

The vortex circle was guarded by more men than usual—three in fact. Yannick was clearly not taking any chances, and were the situation any different, Zoltan would commend the man. But today, a little less initiative by Yannick would have been nice.

The guards had already spotted Zoltan and greeted him with a bow of their heads. Time to distract them.

"Guards," he said in a firm voice, approaching them. "I was told I'd find Yannick here. Where is he?"

"Yannick, oh Great One?" one of the demons replied. "But he only ever guards the main vortex circle himself."

Zoltan knew that Yannick had a preference for the vortex circle closest to Zoltan's study. It was the reason Zoltan had decided to use this one instead.

"He told me to meet him here." Zoltan glared at the three guards and walked even closer, until only a couple of feet separated them. "Are you fucking telling me he's not here?"

The demon who'd first spoken averted his eyes. "He didn't tell us to expect you, oh Great One. My apologies."

"Then what are you still doing here? Go get him!"

The demon quickly took a step to the left, away from Zoltan, while Zoltan continued with the next part of his deceptive maneuver. To the demon on his right, he said, "Here, do something useful and hold the dog for me." He pressed the leash into the man's hand.

It was his sign for Enya to act.

Zoltan turned to the third demon, pulled his dagger from where he'd strapped it inside his sleeve, and plunged the blade into the demon's heart. He didn't have to look back to know that Enya was stabbing the demon who was about to fetch Yannick; he could hear the grunt Enya expelled upon thrusting her dagger into him and the gurgling sound the dying demon made.

Zoltan spun around, ready to attack the demon who was hindered by the leash in his hand, but he needn't have worried: green blood was already soaking his shirt, and his fist opened to release the leash.

"Got 'im," Enya said, still invisible.

"Thanks!" Zoltan grabbed the leash and quickly tied it around a small boulder. Then he moved his hand and cast a vortex in the middle of the circle. "Give me your hand."

Enya clasped his hand, and together they stepped into the swirling mass of fog and air, the pit bull howling in protest.

Zoltan wrapped both arms around Enya and held her tightly while he concentrated on their destination.

21

Enya held on to Zoltan as the vortex seemed to swallow them. This was different from traveling in a Stealth Guardian portal. And very disorienting, not to mention nauseating.

She's safe. Thank God she's safe.

She knew instinctively that those were Zoltan's words, though he hadn't spoken. Which could mean only one thing: she could hear his thoughts.

Zoltan, I can feel what you're thinking.

But there was no reply. Instead, more of his thoughts penetrated her mind.

I'll kill whoever wants to harm her. I can't lose her.

His words made her realize that Zoltan couldn't hear her thoughts, even though she could hear his. And one other thing became clear despite her having a hard time believing it: his feelings for her ran deeper than she'd expected. Could it be possible? Was it possible that a demon could... love another being?

"We're here," Zoltan announced.

At the same time, the disorienting feeling subsided. Zoltan dropped one arm, but still held on to her with the other, then pulled her with him to step out of the vortex.

The vortex now behind her, Enya made herself visible and stared at a wall. She quickly oriented herself. They'd transported to the back of a building, where industrial-sized garbage containers stood next to a large metal garage door. They were at a loading dock. She glanced down to the opposite end of the alley and could see the gold-tipped rotunda of City Hall.

"This way." She pointed in its direction and looked over her shoulder.

The vortex was collapsing into itself, and Zoltan reached into his inside pocket. For a fraction of a second, she wondered if he was reaching for his weapon, and her heart stopped. A moment later, he slipped dark sunglasses over his demon-green eyes, and Enya's heart began to beat again.

He caught her gaze and tilted his head a little. "Enya, by now you should know that you're safe with me."

Feeling stupid, she put her arms around him and kissed him. "I'm sorry, but I just escaped the Underworld. Guess I'm still a little jumpy."

"Yeah, you and me both. Let's get off the street before they figure out that I helped you escape." He took her hand in his.

She looked at their intertwined hands.

"Something wrong?" he asked.

She shook her head. She'd never held hands with a man, not even in private. And now here she was, holding hands with a demon in daylight for everybody to see. "No, nothing is wrong. Nothing at all."

They made their way out of the alley. Enya continued to scan the area, observing the pedestrians they encountered on the main street, prepared for an ambush. When nothing happened, she started to relax.

"I heard your thoughts in the vortex."

Zoltan whipped his head to her, but she couldn't see his eyes behind the dark glasses. "You what? How?"

"I don't know. But it gels with what some of my colleagues reported. When they were in one of your vortexes, they heard the demons' thoughts. They always wondered whether you could hear them too."

"I had no idea," Zoltan said, genuinely surprised. "I never hear any thoughts of the other demons riding with me. And I didn't hear yours. Of course, now that I know, I have to try to remember what I was thinking when we were traveling in the vortex." When she didn't answer right away, he added, "Was it something along the lines of *once we get out of this mess, we need to have sex?*"

She chuckled softly at his attempt at levity. "I think you know very well what you were thinking of, and it wasn't sex."

He squeezed her hand. "We'll talk about all that later."

"Yes, after we find out who's trying to kill us both," Enya said, glad that they weren't discussing their feelings in the middle of downtown Baltimore.

Once they were only a block away from their destination, Enya remembered something. "Oh, crap, we're armed. We won't get into City Hall. They've got metal detectors now."

"Then make us invisible, and we'll just sidestep them," Zoltan suggested.

Enya looked around. "Too many people. I can't just make us invisible in broad daylight."

Zoltan motioned to a sign for a parking lot. "See those two vans parked in the corner? They can shield us."

Enya nodded, and together they walked to the lot. Nobody took any notice of them when they walked into the narrow space between the vans. Enya assured herself that nobody saw them standing there before she made herself and Zoltan invisible.

Minutes later, they arrived at City Hall, followed another visitor inside, then stepped over a cordon, bypassing the metal detector, and found themselves in the large entry hall of the building. Without saying a word, Enya pointed to the sign for the restrooms, and it appeared that Zoltan understood, because he nodded.

Down a short corridor, a small foyer opened up, showing a door for the men's room and a second one for the ladies' room. Nobody was around.

"Okay, we're visible again," she said.

"What now?" Zoltan asked.

"Tessa's office is one floor up. You can come up to the second floor with me, but it's best if you don't come in with me." They started walking up the staircase. "Hamish might be there, and there's a chance he'll recognize you. I believe the two of you had run-ins before."

"The mayor's husband?" Zoltan asked. "Yep, we've met. He thwarted my plan to make somebody else mayor of Baltimore." He shrugged. "No worries, I'll stay out of his way." Arriving on the second floor, he pointed to a sign for the restrooms. "When you're done, look for me back there."

"Okay." She was already turning toward Tessa's office when Zoltan pulled her to him and kissed her. She couldn't help but respond to him.

When he released her a few breathtaking moments later, he said, "Just so you won't leave without me."

"Not a chance," she murmured, feeling her cheeks flush.

"Good."

Her heart still beating excitedly, Enya walked toward the mayor's office and entered the ante office without knocking. Collette, Tessa's assistant, sat at her desk, sorting a mountain of envelopes. She looked up.

"Oh, hey, Enya," she said with a friendly smile.

"Hi, Collette. Is Tessa in?"

"She's pretty busy right now." Collette had been working for Tessa since before she'd become mayor, and was very protective of her and her time.

Nevertheless, Enya had to press her today. "It's important. I need just two minutes of her time."

Collette sighed, then pressed a button on her intercom. "Tessa, Enya is here to see you."

"Enya?" came Tessa's reply, then the door was ripped open and Tessa stood in the doorframe. "Where on earth have you been? Everybody is looking for you."

Enya walked toward her. "Tell you later, but I need a favor now."

Tessa was already pulling Enya into the office. "No calls or visitors, Collette, thanks." Then she shut the door and hugged Enya. "The guys are beside themselves. You didn't come home. They couldn't reach you on your cell. Have you spoken to them? What's going on?"

"I'll tell you everything later, but there's something more important right now. Remember the day you were drugged by the demon?"

During the election for mayor, the demons had tried to harm Tessa and help another candidate who would have divided the racially-charged city even more. The demons had gone as far as painting Tessa as a drug addict to get her to bow out of the race. But Hamish, who'd been assigned to protect her, had saved her just in time after the demons had administered an overdose of heroin.

Tessa furrowed her forehead. "I don't like to think back to it, but I do remember it. Why?"

"Would you recognize the demon who drugged you?"

"I'll never forget his face."

"Good." Enya whipped out her phone and navigated to her photo app. "I'll show you several photos. If the demon who drugged you is among them, point him out, okay?"

"But—"

Enya turned the display to show Tessa the first photo.

Tessa gasped. "Oh my God, you photographed demons?"

"Is it this one?"

Tessa shook her head, and Enya swiped left and continued, until Tessa suddenly grabbed the phone. "That's him. That's the demon who came to my apartment and drugged me." She stared right into Enya's eyes. "Where did you find him?"

"You'd better pack up here. We're going back to the compound. I don't wanna have to explain everything twice. Okay?"

"This had better be good."

"Trust me, it is." When Tessa grabbed her handbag, Enya added, "Call Hamish that he doesn't need to come and pick you up."

"Oh, Hamish is already here. He just went to wash his hands."

Enya's heart started to beat out of control. "Oh shit!"

~ ~ ~

Zoltan knew he wasn't alone in the men's restroom. One of the five cubicle doors was closed, and somebody flushed the toilet. Zoltan turned to the row of sinks and turned on the faucet. To look inconspicuous, he pumped soap into his hand and foamed up under the water, then the cubicle door opened and a man came out. Zoltan glanced at his image in the mirror, then lowered his gaze back to his hands.

Fuck!

None other than Hamish, the Stealth Guardian married to the mayor, and one Zoltan had fought several times before, walked toward the sink. Zoltan felt his heartbeat accelerate. He wore his sunglasses to disguise his eyes, but the accessory was hardly inconspicuous when worn indoors. And Hamish wasn't stupid. Once he noticed them, he might take a closer look at Zoltan's face and realize that they'd met before.

It was high time to get the fuck out of here.

Zoltan turned away, shook off the excess water from his hands, and took a couple of steps.

"Have they still not fixed that damn hand dryer?" Hamish asked from the sink, and looked into the mirror.

From the corner of his right eye, Zoltan noticed Hamish fix his gaze on Zoltan's reflection. He paused, staring at the sunglasses.

If he didn't reply to Hamish's question, he would look even more suspicious, so Zoltan mumbled, "Guess not," and continued toward the door, passing by the hand dryer, when the damn thing suddenly came on—activated by motion sensor.

Zoltan hesitated for a fraction of a second. Drying his hands under the hand dryer would mean turning his face and giving Hamish another good look at it in the mirror. He couldn't risk it. But apparently the Stealth Guardian didn't need another look.

"Fucking demon," Hamish grunted.

Zoltan spun around. Hamish already held a dagger in his hand and had taken a fighting stance. But Zoltan knew he couldn't draw his weapon. If he injured—or worse, killed—Hamish, Enya would never forgive him.

"It's the sunglasses, isn't it?"

Hamish motioned to the large window behind him. "Been overcast all day. And I'd never forget a mug like yours." He paused. "Zoltan."

Zoltan lifted his hands. "Listen, Stealth Guardian, I don't want any trouble. I'm just gonna walk out of here and nobody gets hurt."

"I'm not gonna make it that easy for you." Hamish narrowed his eyes. "Guess you're not quite as brave when you don't have a bunch of demons to back you up."

The insult stung. "When I said I'm gonna walk out of here and nobody gets hurt, I was talking about you. I don't wanna have to hurt you. Take the out."

Hamish scoffed. Of course the idiot wouldn't accept what Zoltan was offering. He could tell from the way the Stealth Guardian looked at him. He wanted this fight. He wanted a chance at killing the Great One. And had he never gotten to know Enya, Zoltan would have given him the chance. But things were different now. Hamish was part of Enya's family.

"Hamish—that's your name, isn't it?" Zoltan didn't need a confirmation, nor did he get one. "If you attack me, I'm gonna have to defend myself."

"Oh, I hope you will defend yourself. It'll make your death so much sweeter. I've been waiting for this moment ever since you left Tessa to die."

Zoltan shook his head. "Wasn't me."

Hamish snorted. "So you don't do your own dirty work. What else is new?"

"I didn't sanction the overdose on your mate."

"A liar and a murderer. No surprise there."

"And the insults keep coming. You're making it increasingly difficult for me not to hurt you."

"Stop stalling."

"Fine." Zoltan pulled his dagger from his pocket and readied himself.

Hamish pounced first, charging toward Zoltan with a ferocity fed by his belief that Zoltan had harmed Tessa. His hatred for Zoltan was evident in the way he glared at his enemy. But Zoltan couldn't allow Hamish to take his revenge. Nobody would die today. Not if he could help it.

Zoltan jumped to the side, out of Hamish's path. But the Stealth Guardian seemed to have expected the move and swerved at the last second, his dagger grazing the hand Zoltan had raised in defense. The wound wasn't deep, but it bled. Green drops rained onto the tile floor.

Hamish grunted angrily, pounced again, and forced Zoltan into another defensive sidestep. As he spun on his heel, Zoltan slammed his elbow into Hamish's side, knocking him off his feet. But the bastard was agile and regained his balance inside a second.

"Fucking demon!" Hamish growled, and kicked out, slamming his foot into the back of Zoltan's knees.

The impact made him crash to the floor, but he immediately rolled to the side then jumped up, before Hamish could catch him in this vulnerable position. But Hamish didn't give up. He kept coming, kept stabbing with his blade, kept kicking and punching, while Zoltan only defended himself, only held Hamish back as best he could. It made Hamish even bolder, and seemingly more ferocious. When Hamish's dagger sliced into Zoltan's thigh, leaving a deep gash, Zoltan had had enough.

"You're fucking asking for it," he growled, and fought back.

Zoltan punched Hamish in the neck, then kicked him sideways so he crashed against the sink so hard that the old thing cracked. The faucet was still running, and water seeped through the crack onto the floor. Hamish didn't let the cracking sink distract him and pushed himself away, kicking

Zoltan in the gut, while behind him, the sink's anchoring to the wall snapped and porcelain pieces fell to the ground.

Zoltan tumbled backward and bounced against the bathroom stall. He saved himself from falling into the toilet by gripping the edges of the stall and catapulting himself toward his aggressor, losing his dagger in the process. It didn't matter. He wasn't going to use the blade on Hamish.

Hamish grinned, casting a triumphant look at the dagger that had slithered out of reach. Big mistake. It gave Zoltan a fraction of a second in which to knock Hamish backward, making him land on his ass. Together they slid on the now wet floor, until stopped by the wall. Despite being on his back with Zoltan on top of him, Hamish was able to aim his dagger at Zoltan's neck. Zoltan blocked it not a moment too soon. In the same motion, he slammed Hamish's elbow back and pinned his arm to the ground amidst pieces of broken porcelain.

With his left arm, Zoltan prevented Hamish from delivering a blow to Zoltan's temple. "Stop fighting, you idiot!"

But Hamish wouldn't have any of it. He kept struggling. But Zoltan had him pinned and was now slamming his fist on Hamish's wrist so he released the dagger. Zoltan snatched it, then whipped his face back to Hamish.

The Stealth Guardian stared at him. For a moment, neither of them moved.

"I'm sorry for what I'm gonna have to do," Zoltan said, and knocked the back of the dagger's handle against Hamish's pinned arm, slamming it against the jagged edge of the porcelain.

Hamish screamed in pain.

Zoltan jumped up, dagger still in hand, and moved a few steps away. "You gave me no choice."

Hamish stared up at him, sitting up with the help of his good arm, while the other hung limply, the bone broken.

"Next time, take the out when it's offered." Zoltan ran toward the half-open window.

"Why didn't you kill me?" Hamish called after him, while Zoltan pushed the window wide open and heaved himself onto the ledge.

He looked over his shoulder. "Ask Enya. She's the reason you're still alive." He heard the sound of a door being ripped open, but he couldn't stay any longer. He had to escape now.

Zoltan jumped.

22

Enya stormed into the men's room, Tessa a few paces behind her. The moment she came around the bend from where she could see the entire room, Enya almost slipped. Hamish was on the wet floor next to broken bits from a sink, his clothes disheveled and drenched in water, one arm hanging by his side as he rose. Enya cast a glance around the room, but there was no sign of Zoltan. When she looked back toward Hamish, her eyes caught a green streak on the floor. Demon blood.

"Where is he? Did you hurt him? Did you kill him?" She rushed toward Hamish. "What the fuck happened?"

Hamish glared at her, but he didn't get to answer, because Tessa finally charged into the men's room and threw her arms around her husband.

"Are you okay?" Tessa asked. "Did you get hurt?"

"I'm okay. Just a broken arm," he said to Tessa, his voice calm and reassuring. But his tone changed when he said, "Enya, I'd like you to explain to me why Zoltan didn't kill me even though he had the chance, and instead just broke my arm to stop me from chasing him."

Enya swallowed. Zoltan had made the decision to spare Hamish's life? Relief washed through her. Zoltan had good in him. And he'd gotten away, albeit with an injury—one that, judging by the small amount of blood on the floor, was minor.

"Enya!" Hamish snatched her bicep and shook her. "He mentioned you by name. He said to ask you why he spared my life. So you've a hell of a lot of explaining to do."

"Yeah, I guess." She sighed. "I'd say you might wanna sit down for that, but…" She motioned to the wet floor, then shrugged and decided to start with the good news. "I was kidnapped by demons and imprisoned in an Underworld cell. Zoltan helped me escape."

Hamish and Tessa stared at her.

"He what? Why the fuck would Zoltan help you escape?" Hamish asked.

Enya let out a breath. There was no good way to impart the bad news, or what Hamish would perceive as bad news. "Because he's my boyfriend. He's Eric Vaughn, and I think he loves me." At least, that was what she had to assume, even though he hadn't said the words. But why else would he have risked so much for her?

Only the continuing running of the faucet nobody had bothered to turn off could be heard in the men's room for the next few seconds. Nobody breathed. Nobody moved. And Enya could have sworn that Tessa and Hamish's hearts had stopped at the unexpected news.

"Fuck me!" Hamish said.

"Ditto," Tessa added.

"There's a lot more you need to know," Enya said. "But we should discuss it back home. Together with the others. I don't wanna have to tell the story twice."

At first it looked like Hamish would insist on hearing the full story right now, but then he motioned to his arm. "I'd better get this healed fast. I have the feeling I might need my arm again to punch somebody for their stupidity."

Enya took the jab in stride. Once Hamish knew the whole truth, he would change his tune.

To her relief, Hamish didn't press her for any explanations during their ride home. As soon as Leila had patched him up in the compound's state-of-the-art medical suite, and Ryder had given Hamish vampire blood to speed up the healing process, every resident of the compound— except the twins, who were doing their homework— assembled in the command center. The news that Enya had been kidnapped by demons and owed her escape to Zoltan had already spread. As had the fact that she was dating a demon.

When the door to the command center fell shut behind her, she felt as if she'd entered a courtroom where the jury had already decided her fate. She couldn't even blame them: in the eyes of their people, Enya had committed treason by fraternizing with a demon, by not killing him when she'd had the chance.

All eyes were on her. She opened her mouth, but no sound came out. Fuck, this was harder than she'd envisioned.

She cleared her throat. "When I started seeing Eric, I assumed he was human. I had no reason to believe otherwise, particularly since I was the one who made a move on him. Even when he helped me defeat the demons that attacked me the other night, he was still playing an ordinary man who knew nothing about demons."

She tipped her chin toward Pearce. "But when Pearce found Eric Vaughn's LinkedIn account and I saw the photo, I knew something was up. Still—call me stupid; I know in your minds you already do—I didn't suspect him to be a demon. I thought he was involved in identity fraud. So I confronted him the same night. That's when I found out. I should have killed him right there and then."

"Yeah, why didn't you?" Logan asked, and pointed to Winter. "Or have you forgotten what he did to Winter?"

Enya shook her head. "No, I haven't forgotten anything. I know about all his evil deeds. I just couldn't do it. And now I'm glad I didn't kill him, because the next day, when I took Winter to Cinead, I found out the truth about Zoltan."

"What fucking truth?" Logan cursed. "He's the leader of the demons."

"He's bad through and through!" Hamish added. Anger rolled off him. "He shot Tessa up with heroin to kill her, and you're glad you didn't kill him? Who the fuck are you? What happened to you?"

"Zoltan didn't try to kill Tessa. He never sent anybody to Tessa's place." Enya nodded to Tessa. "I showed Tessa photos of Zoltan and his cadre of lieutenants. And she identified one of them as the demon who drugged her. It wasn't Zoltan. He didn't do this."

"So he didn't do it personally. Big deal. Why are you still defending him?" Hamish almost yelled.

"Is he that good in bed?" Manus asked.

Enya braced her hands at her hips. "Yeah, he fucking is. But that's not why I'm defending him. Zoltan is one of us."

Confused rumblings went through the room.

"And what would that be?" Aiden asked, turning out to be the calmest of all her colleagues today.

Enya took a deep breath. "Zoltan is Cinead's lost son, Angus." She let the news sink in.

"You're making this shit up," Pearce said.

Winter shook her head. "I don't think she is."

Everybody looked at her.

"When Enya accompanied me to see Cinead, I had to tell him that I know what happened to his baby son. He's not dead. He's a demon."

Enya nodded. "Thanks, Winter. At least one person here is supporting me."

"Oh, I'm not supporting you. I'm just presenting the facts."

"Whatever," Enya said.

"Even if Winter is correct that Cinead's son is a demon, that doesn't mean Zoltan is that demon," Pearce said.

"I have proof." Enya pulled out her phone and navigated to her pictures. With her wireless connection, she sent a picture to the main screen in the command center.

Everybody stared at the photo.

Hamish stretched out his good arm. "That's Zoltan. I fought him just an hour ago. So what's his portrait gonna prove?"

Enya turned to him. "That's not Zoltan. That's Cinead when he was a young man."

Gasps echoed in the room and bounced off the bare walls.

She sent two more photos to the screen to show side by side. "On the left, you see the birthmark Angus carries on his butt; on the right is Zoltan's birthmark. They're identical. Zoltan is Angus."

Silence fell over the assembled. They exchanged looks and shook their heads, but from the expressions on their faces, Enya knew they believed the evidence she'd presented.

"Enya, I don't know how to say this," Pearce said, "but even though we now know what happened to Cinead's son, it doesn't change who Zoltan is. He's still a demon, no matter his origin. Cinead will be the first to tell you to kill him, even though he was once his son."

Enya shook her head. "No. You don't understand. Zoltan has some good in him. He's not all evil. He can be redeemed."

Kim put her hand on Enya's arm. "I'm sorry, Enya. I know you want to believe that he's good. But I've been at the other end. His demons killed my mother. And he nearly killed me for the book he was after." She motioned to Leila, Winter, Daphne, and Tessa. "We all suffered because of him. You can't just expect us to forget what we've been through because of him. You're blinded by whatever you think you feel for him."

Enya ripped her arm from Kim's touch. "It's not about what I feel. He can be saved." She looked at the assembled, desperate to find an ally. Her gaze settled on Hamish. "Hamish! You fought with him today. You said yourself that Zoltan had a chance to kill you. Instead, he spared your life. Doesn't that mean anything?"

Hamish hesitated. "I admit he could have killed me. I even admit that he didn't want to fight me in the first place. But does that really prove that there's still some good in him? Enya, he did it only for you. Because he needs you to be his advocate. What if it's still part of his plan?"

"No, no." She couldn't allow her brethren to plant doubt in her. "He confessed everything to me. He told me about his original plan, but he's changed. He won't do anything to hurt us. He risked everything for me. His own people are chasing him now, because he betrayed them—for me."

"Maybe that's what he wants you to believe," Aiden said.

"You're wrong. You're all wrong."

"Fine," Logan said. "Then tell us where he is. Let us bring him in and interrogate him. Then we'll see whether he can convince us too."

Enya glared at Logan. "How stupid do you think I am? The moment I tell you where he is, you'll kill him." Not that she knew where Zoltan was hiding out at present. However, before leaving the Underworld, she'd asked him to keep his burner switched on, so she could get a message to him should they get separated.

"Damn it, Enya," Manus said. "Don't you see that Zoltan's been manipulating you? Wake up!"

"I'm awake. And I know I can save him. I can give Cinead his son back. I'll find a way."

"There is no way," Manus replied. "Once a demon, always a demon."

"Yeah," Pearce added. "You can't just say sim-sala-bim, touch him with a wand, and suddenly he's a Stealth Guardian again. Doesn't work that way."

Enya spun her head to stare at Pearce. "What did you just say?"

"You heard me."

Yes, she did. "A spell," she murmured to herself, and remembered the morning just before she was kidnapped. In the shower, she'd thought about who to talk to about a cure for Zoltan.

Kim, who was standing closest to her, said, "You think a witch can turn Zoltan into a Stealth Guardian?"

Enya met Kim's eyes. "Not just any witch." She turned toward the door.

"Where do you think you're going?" Hamish called after her.

She looked over her shoulder. "To get help."

"You're not leaving!" Hamish said.

"I do what I damn well please." She marched toward the door.

"Let her go, Hamish," Pearce said. "It's no use…"

Enya passed through the door into the hallway and quickly typed a message on her phone, then sent it to Zoltan, telling him to stay put and wait for her to contact him again. The moment he replied in the affirmative, she switched off her phone and headed for the portal.

23

It took Enya less than half an hour to reach Scanguards headquarters in the Mission District of San Francisco. It was still daytime and would be so for a few more hours, which meant that many of the vampires employed by Scanguards wouldn't be present. She was glad for it. While she loved the Stealth Guardians' vampire allies, she didn't have time for extended chats today.

In the glass lobby, she walked to the reception desk, where a bright-eyed human woman greeted her.

"How may I help you?"

"I need to see Wesley Montgomery. It's urgent. Tell him Enya is here."

"Please look into this camera," she instructed Enya, and pointed to a small camera mounted on the reception desk. Enya complied, and the woman nodded and typed something on her keyboard. It appeared that Scanguards had a new system to announce visitors.

Within seconds, there was an audible ping, and the printer spat out a visitor pass. She looked at it, then handed it to Enya.

"Here you go, ma'am. Go straight down the hall. Wesley will meet you outside the V lounge."

"Thanks." Enya snatched the visitor pass and shoved it in her pocket, then turned to the corridor.

"Ma'am, you have to put it on your jacket…" the receptionist called after her.

But Enya didn't care and kept walking. She didn't have time for formalities. Zoltan's future was on the line. And so was hers. She wasn't stupid: if she couldn't convince her colleagues that Zoltan could be saved and turned back into a

Stealth Guardian, they would have to turn her in to stand trial before the council. It was their duty.

Wesley was just coming around a corner when Enya arrived at the entrance to the V lounge, an area reserved for vampires and other preternatural creatures. It was strictly off-limits to humans.

"Hey, Enya, what a nice surprise."

"It's good to see you, Wes. Can we talk?"

"Something wrong?"

She motioned to the door. "In private?"

Wes swiped his access card and ushered her into the large room that resembled an executive lounge at a five-diamond hotel. Enya glanced around. Apart from a bartender, nobody was around. Wes motioned to the seating arrangement closest to them, and they both sat down.

Wesley had been the first and only outsider who'd ever managed to access a Stealth Guardian portal, an action that had teleported him to Baltimore, where he'd subsequently brokered an alliance between the vampires and the Stealth Guardians—but only after an adventure that included a trip to the Underworld and winning the heart of a member of the Council of Nine, Virginia.

"What do you need?" he asked, all business.

That was what she liked about Wesley. Even though he was a goofball and happy-go-lucky kind of guy, he immediately recognized when something was serious.

"In a nutshell: your help."

"Okay? Give me the short version."

"I'm sure that at some point Virginia must have mentioned to you that her fellow council member Cinead had a baby son who was believed to be killed by the demons."

Wes nodded. "I'm aware of it. But according to Winter, the baby was kidnapped."

"Correct. And I found him."

"Wow! Something to celebrate. Knowing Cinead, he'll be over the moon."

Enya cringed. "Not exactly. I dread telling him."

"But why?"

"Because his son is now a demon. And not just any demon. He's Zoltan."

Wes slouched back in the seat cushions and blew out a breath. "Zoltan? We're talking about *the* Zoltan? Ruler of the Underworld, the Great One, yada, yada, yada."

She nodded.

"Oh, that blows."

"Yeah, you could say that."

"So you want Virginia to talk to Cinead, is that it?"

"No. I need your help, not Virginia's. I have no intention of telling Cinead that I found his son, if I can't at the same time tell him that he can be saved."

"Saved?" Wes's forehead furrowed. "Are you saying what I think you're saying? That you want to turn him back into what he was before?" He began to shake his head.

"I grew up with believing in the mantra 'once a demon, always a demon.' But I don't want to believe that anymore. That's why I need you. You and Charles. You are powerful witches. Between the two of you, you know every spell there is. I need you to find something that will turn Zoltan back into what he once was."

Wes let out a mirthless laugh. "How come you never ask me for something easy, like a simple spell to turn somebody into a piglet or a rat? I'm really good at that."

Enya shrugged. "I'm not in need of a piglet or a rat right now. Come on, you're my only hope."

"Okay, then, let's talk to Charles, see what he says." He rose. "He's downstairs in his new lab. We call it the cauldron."

"He's got a lab here now?" Enya followed him to the door.

"Yeah, after he nearly burned down the house twice, Roxanne suggested he move his potions somewhere else."

"Suggested?"

Wes winked at her. "Well, that's the story he's sticking to, anyway." He led her to the elevators and pressed a button. "Maybe better if you don't mention it." He grinned.

"Whatever you say."

The elevator doors opened, and they got in.

"So, what else is new?"

Enya shrugged. "I got dragged to the Underworld by a few overeager demons."

"Oh my God! How did that happen?"

"Long story. Tell you some other time. Creepy place. Stinks like rotten eggs everywhere."

Wes nodded. As one of the very few people who'd ever been to the Underworld, he could relate. "Sulfur. So, how did you make it back out?"

"Hitched a ride from a demon, like you and Virginia did." Not exactly like Wes and his mate had done, since the demon whose vortex they'd used to get back into the human world hadn't known about the stowaways he'd had onboard.

"Cool! Hope you got the chance to kill a few of those bastards."

The elevator doors opened, giving Enya a moment to decide whether she wanted to answer. She decided to remain noncommittal. "You know me."

She followed Wesley down another corridor, then he used his access card again and opened a door. He stepped into the room ahead of her, then looked over his shoulder. "Okay, the coast is clear. No imminent explosions."

"Very funny," a man said from farther inside the room.

"Welcome to the lab," Wesley said.

Enya entered and let the door snap in behind her. The place didn't look like a laboratory at all. Yes, the walls, floor, and ceiling were white, but that was where the similarities ended. Everything else looked more like it belonged in a hut in an ancient forest. Hansel and Gretel came to mind. The large cauldron that hung over a gas fire in a large stone fireplace was the first indication that this was no conventional laboratory. The glass jars lining shelves and cluttering any available surface were another clue, as were the many ancient-looking books, some of which predated the printing press.

"You guys have met, right?" Wes asked.

Charles, dressed in casual clothes and wearing an apron, came toward her and stretched out his hand. "Once or twice," he said. "Must have been at a Scanguards party. Nice to see you again, Enya."

Enya shook his hand. "Likewise."

"Did Wes talk you into a tour of the lab?"

"Actually, no. I'm here of my own free will," she joked.

"Okay, that's what I like to hear. I guess you need a spell or something. How can I help?"

"Actually," Wes interjected, "she needs both our help. We've gotta figure out if there's a way of turning a demon back into what he was born as."

Charles stared at her. "What the hell for? Just kill the damn bastards."

"I can't kill him," Enya said. "He's the son of one of our council members." *And I love him.* But that part wasn't relevant.

"You mean he was a Stealth Guardian and turned bad? Wow!"

"Worse," Enya said. "He doesn't remember that he was once a Stealth Guardian. He was kidnapped by the demons when he wasn't even a year old."

Charles ran a hand through his hair and blew out a breath. Then he looked at Wesley. "Guess it's time to hit the books. Let's divide and conquer."

"Agreed," Wes said. Then he looked at Enya. "This may take a while. Wanna go back up to the lounge while we work?"

She shook her head. "I'll stay here. Maybe I can help."

"All right, then," Wes said. "Let's get started."

24

Zoltan checked his phone again. Still no news from Enya. After the text message she'd sent him several hours earlier, he'd taken refuge in an apartment with a *For rent* sign in the window. As luck would have it, the place was fully furnished, so he'd made himself at home and waited. His superficial wounds were already healing.

Sick of waiting, he called Enya's number. It went straight to voicemail. He waited for the beep.

"Enya, where are you? Is everything okay? Call me."

He disconnected, then walked into the kitchen and turned on the faucet. He splashed cold water on his face and ran his hands through his hair.

The creaking of a floorboard behind him made him whirl around and reach for his dagger.

"I wouldn't do that," a male coming from right in front of him said.

"Definitely not a good idea," another added.

Shit! The jig was up. He'd trusted Enya, but it appeared she'd let her people convince her that he wasn't worth saving. Or had she given him up easily when she saw how he'd hurt Hamish? It didn't matter now. Without her trust, it was over.

Zoltan slowly raised his hands. An invisible hand disarmed him.

"That's really brave," he said. "Two invisible Stealth Guardians against one demon."

"Three," a third male corrected him, before all three men became visible, their daggers ready to kill Zoltan should he make a wrong move.

Hamish—probably still nursing his broken arm—wasn't among them, but Zoltan recognized the other three, though he wasn't quite sure about their names.

"Let me guess, the Baltimore compound is having an outing today. Oh goodie!" He'd be damned if he showed them that he knew he'd lost.

"Didn't know that Zoltan had a sense of humor," one of the Stealth Guardians said to his colleague.

Zoltan gave him a mock grin. "How long did it take you to convince Enya to give me up?"

"You think Enya gave you up?"

"How else would you have found me? She's the only one who knows my number."

"Sure, but we cloned her phone and traced your calls and text messages back to here. Took a while, since we had to search an entire block, but it was worth it, wasn't it, guys?"

The others looked at him triumphantly, but Zoltan didn't care. His heart skipped a beat. "She didn't rat me out…" Enya was still true to him. She was keeping her promise.

"Well, sometimes Enya needs saving from herself. That's what we're here for."

The other two nodded in agreement.

"So she won't be branded a traitor to her race," Zoltan said.

"Not if we can help it."

"Okay, fair enough. As long as nothing happens to her." It would be one consolation. Enya was back in the bosom of her race, and with Zoltan dead, the demon traitor would have no reason to go after her. But he had to make sure the demons knew he was dead, or the traitor would continue to hunt Enya.

"Let's go," one of the men said, and gripped Zoltan's bicep.

Another grabbed him from the other side, and together, they started to drag him toward the door.

"I have one request," Zoltan said.

"Demons don't get requests."

"It's not for me. It's for Enya's safety."

Three pairs of eyebrows went up.

"Make sure my subjects get wind of my demise. They need to see my body to believe it."

The three exchanged curious looks.

"And how does that have anything to do with Enya's safety?" one asked.

"There's a traitor in my ranks, a demon who wants my throne. As long as I'm alive, he'll do anything to destroy me, which includes hurting Enya. Because he knows hurting her means hurting me. He'll only leave her alone once he's convinced I'm dead."

For a moment there was silence, then one of the three said, "We'll think about it."

"Now let's get moving," the second one said. "Manus, you'll drive."

"Whatever you say," Manus replied. "Logan, cuffs."

Logan pulled heavy cuffs from his pocket. Zoltan didn't see any point in resisting. His life was already forfeited. "Guess you don't wanna do it here." He shrugged. "Doesn't matter to me where you kill me."

"Yeah, shut up," Manus snapped. "You've been talking entirely too much for a fucking demon."

"Last words, and all. I thought you'd understand," Zoltan replied. "It's not as if I were asking for a last meal."

"I don't know what she sees in him," Logan said, and put the cuffs around Zoltan's wrists. "Aiden, you've got the hoodie?"

Aiden handed him a black cloth, and Logan reached for it.

"Blindfolding? Really? Who am I gonna tell where you took me when I'm dead?" Zoltan asked. Dying was one thing; not seeing the blade coming was an entirely different one.

Logan pulled the hoodie over Zoltan's head, robbing him of his vision.

"Where are you taking me?"

But none of the three answered. They dragged him out of the apartment. Outside, they shoved him into the back of a vehicle. Two of them, presumably Logan and Aiden, got in the back with Zoltan, while Manus jumped into the front and drove off. Not being able to see anything, and with his hands cuffed behind his back, Zoltan was jostled around whenever Manus made a turn, sped up, or slowed down. And judging by how often this happened, he had the feeling that the Stealth Guardian did it on purpose just to piss him off. No matter. He wouldn't give the bastard the satisfaction of complaining.

When the vehicle finally came to a stop after what felt like an eternity, and Logan and Aiden dragged him out and put him on his feet, Zoltan prepared himself. He heard traffic sounds in the distance, but where they had stopped was relatively quiet. Through the hoodie, he saw only shadows, but he couldn't make out where he was. Probably somewhere where the Stealth Guardians wouldn't be observed killing him, and where washing away his green blood would be easy.

He took a breath and steeled himself for what was to come. His only regret was that he hadn't told Enya that he loved her.

"This is it, huh?" he asked.

"Yep," Aiden said.

"Let's get him inside," Logan said.

Two Stealth Guardians grabbed Zoltan and ushered him into another direction. It was only a few steps until the ground beneath his boots changed. The cobblestones he'd felt upon getting out of the vehicle were gone. Then he heard a heavy door shut behind him, and all traffic noise vanished. It was as quiet as a mausoleum. How fitting to kill him in a tomb.

They continued walking.

"Stairs, watch out," Manus said, and Logan and Aiden helped Zoltan navigate down the flight of stairs.

He knew what it meant. They weren't gonna grant his final wish to leave his body for the demons to find, so his death could be confirmed.

"Bastards," he cursed. "So you'll kill me in some dark hole where nobody will ever find me?"

One of the men kicked him, and Zoltan nearly lost his balance.

"Just get him inside the fucking cell," Logan said, "before I beat the shit out of him for what he did to Winter."

A heavy door creaked, then somebody lifted the hoodie off Zoltan's head. He quickly assessed his surroundings. A cellar, but no ordinary one. The runes along the walls told him immediately where he was. "You brought me to your compound? Why?"

"'Cause that's where we keep prisoners," Aiden replied, and shoved Zoltan to the entrance of the cell door, which stood open. "Turn around."

Zoltan complied, still stunned that they hadn't killed him yet, and seemed to feel no urgency to do so.

Aiden unlocked the cuffs and took them. "Inside the cell, now!"

Zoltan walked into the dark space and turned around. Aiden closed the door in his face. He heard the key being turned in the lock, imprisoning him.

Zoltan kicked his boot against the door. "What the fuck are you up to? Are you too chicken to just kill me? Are you?"

But there was no answer, only the sound of retreating footsteps that echoed against the thick stone walls.

25

Enya closed the heavy book she'd been studying. The knowledge base that Charles and Wesley had accumulated in their little vault underneath Scanguards headquarters was quite impressive, and included books detailing the history of the Stealth Guardians and tidbits of what was known about the Demons of Fear. She had found nothing in the volumes she'd been perusing that gave any indication that a demon could be turned back into his original form.

"Okay," Charles said, and rose from his chair, pointing to an entry in the book he was reading. "This could be something."

Enya eagerly looked at the paragraph. "Sorry, but my Romanian is pretty much nonexistent. Can you translate?"

Wesley joined them. "Nothing in any of the books I looked at. What's this?" He leaned over the entry. "Hmm. Something about a demon and the heartbeat of blood tears? What?"

"No, no," Charles said. "You're translating it wrong. Here: *When the demon swallowed the life*, or it could also mean heartbeat, *of his own innocent blood, his soul shed tears,* or wept, *and gave him back his true…* uh… *identity…* or maybe self. Yeah, I think that's it." Charles looked up.

"What does it mean?" Enya asked.

"Not sure. This is a gypsy tale from the eleventh century. And those stories are notoriously vague in their retelling. So it could mean that somehow the demon has to take an innocent's blood to wash himself of his sins and turn back into what he was before."

Wes shook his head. "Sacrificing an innocent? That doesn't sound right." He bent over the book again and pointed to a word. "That's not just blood. It's flesh and blood, which means a descendant."

"What if it doesn't mean descendant? What if it means ancestor? Like his father?" Enya asked. What if Zoltan's father could somehow redeem him?

"Hmm," Wes said, and glanced at Charles. "But it says innocent here, and let's face it, anybody over the age of five is hardly without sin."

"I agree," Charles said. "So let's assume it means descendant, then the translation would read: *When the demon swallowed the life*, or heartbeat, *of his innocent descendant, his soul wept and gave him back his true self.*"

"That's not much to go by," Enya said, deflated. "How can a demon swallow somebody's heartbeat? That doesn't sound right."

Charles sighed. "I'm sorry. I wish I could be of more help." He motioned to all the books they'd pulled off the shelves. "But I've got nothing else. This is the closest we've gotten to any reference about a demon being redeemed."

Enya nodded. Had she really expected that Wes and Charles would find something in such a short time frame? Not expected, but hoped. "What about spells?"

Wes shook his head. "Already thought about spells, but any transformation spell that I could do would only be temporary—you know, like making a person appear like another preternatural creature to fool somebody. But those spells only work for a very short time. We're talking minutes or hours. So that's of no use."

"I heard you did turn somebody into a rat once," Charles said.

Wesley grimaced. "Don't remind me. But seriously, no spell can permanently alter a person's self. Not the way you want to."

"I understand," Enya said. "Thanks anyway. I'm sorry I wasted your time."

"It wasn't a waste," Charles assured her, "and if I can figure out what that gypsy story really means, I'll let you know."

"Thanks, both of you." She turned to the door.

"I'll see you out," Wesley offered.

"Thanks, I know the way." She turned the handle and left the laboratory.

Outside in the bright corridor, she walked in the direction of the elevators, wanting to get as far away from where people knew her as possible. But she didn't get far. Halfway down the corridor, she had to snatch a breath of air, and with it, a sob tore from her chest. Another worked its way up her throat before she could force it back down. Tears were filling her eyes, and it was no use to try to stop them.

"Enya?"

She spun around and recognized Maya, a vampire physician dressed in a white doctor's coat, standing in the door to a room. Enya hadn't even heard the door open.

She tried to wipe away the tears that had already stolen down her cheeks, but it was futile. Maya was already pulling her into her arms.

"Honey, what's wrong?"

Enya tried to pull away, but the arms of the compassionate vampire felt too comforting to retreat from. "It's nothing." Because how could she explain what she was going through? How could she confess that she was in love with a demon who couldn't be saved?

"Come on into the medical suite. My patient is already gone. We'll be alone there."

She allowed herself to be guided to the medical suite, where she sat down on a bench and took a few deep breaths.

Maya took a seat next to her and put her hand over Enya's.

"I'm sorry, I don't know why I cried just now. It's really nothing," Enya lied. "Just stress, I guess."

Maya looked at her with the expression of a woman who had all the answers. "Don't worry. I was a bit of a watering pot myself when I was pregnant."

Enya shot up. "What?"

Maya slowly rose. "Yes, in the first few months, I was very emotional. I'm sure that's all it is. But just to make sure, why don't I quickly check you out?"

Enya stood there, frozen. "Check me out? But I'm fine. And I can't be pregnant. I'm not bonded." Stealth Guardians were only fertile when bonded.

Maya raised an eyebrow. "Honey, I sense two heartbeats coming from you. So unless you have a heart condition, which I doubt, or a second heart, which I also doubt, then the heartbeat belongs to another being."

"But… It's not possible…" Enya stopped herself, remembering the queasy feeling she had every time she traveled in a portal. Or the time she'd puked after finding out that Zoltan was a demon.

She felt Maya's hand on her arm. "Do you mind if I lay my hands on your stomach?" Maya asked.

"Don't you use a stethoscope for that?"

"Vampire senses, you know." She smiled.

Enya nodded, and Maya put one hand on her stomach, moving it up and down, then side to side, then resting it again. A warm smile appeared on her lips. "I can feel your baby's heartbeat. It's strong. You're definitely pregnant. And if you're not bonded, then I'm not sure how it happened, but trust me, it happened. Who's the father?"

Enya stared at Maya. There was only one man who could be the father, even though she couldn't explain how it had happened. Well, they'd had sex, of course, and without protection. But no Stealth Guardian female had ever gotten pregnant unless she was bonded to a man.

"Enya?" Maya's voice called Enya back to reality. "You looked like you were going to faint."

And why not? Wasn't the fact that she'd gotten knocked up by a demon enough reason for anybody to faint?

"I need to tell him."

To tell Zoltan, the ruler of the Underworld, that she was carrying his child.

~ ~ ~

Less than half an hour after leaving San Francisco via the portal located in a BART tunnel in the Mission neighborhood, Enya was back in her private quarters in the Baltimore compound. She'd made sure that nobody had seen her return, because she wasn't in the mood for twenty questions. She had too many questions herself. How it was possible at all. How Zoltan would react. But most of all, one question loomed over all others. Would the child be a demon?

After pacing for a good hour, she finally decided that there was no use in delaying any longer. Zoltan had a right to know. She called his burner phone and let it ring. Once, twice, then a click in the line.

"Hey, Enya."

Her heart stopped. The voice wasn't Zoltan's.

"Logan? What the fuck?" she said. "Why do you have his phone? Where is he?"

"Come to the command center, and we'll talk."

She disconnected and shoved the phone into her pants pocket, already charging out of the room and heading for the compound's command center. If her brethren had hurt Zoltan, they would pay for it.

Enya stormed into the room without bothering to open the door. Apparently, Logan hadn't expected her so quickly, because he was talking to Hamish, whose arm was in a sling. Pearce and Ryder were sitting in front of the computers, and Aiden was hovering over a desk.

"Fucking bastard!" She charged at Logan and catapulted him against the wall. "What did you do with him?"

When she lunged after Logan, who was already getting up and dusting himself off, Pearce and Aiden pounced and held her, pulling her back. She struggled against their grip and glared at them.

"Don't worry, you two will get a beating too when I'm done with him." She tipped her chin at Logan.

"You're not gonna beat anybody up, you hothead," Logan said calmly. "And we didn't harm your fucking demon boyfriend, so pipe down."

"Where is he?" She let her gaze roam and noticed the absence of Manus and Grayson. "What are Manus and Grayson doing with him?"

"Just watching him," Logan said.

Enya scoffed.

"He's telling the truth," Aiden said, still holding her in a tight grip.

She whipped her head to him. "Then where is Zoltan? Where is he?" She kicked Aiden in the shin, and he let go of her.

"Damn it, Enya!" Aiden said. "That wasn't necessary."

"Yeah, but it felt good." She snapped her head to Pearce as a warning. He heeded it and let go of her too.

When her eyes fell on Hamish, who'd been watching patiently with Ryder by his side, Hamish lifted his injured arm. "Your boyfriend already hurt me, so you can lay off me."

"So where are Manus and Grayson? Did they take Zoltan to the council?"

Logan rolled his eyes. "You think we're stupid? If we bring Zoltan to the council, they'll find out that you're sleeping with him. And you know what that means. You'll be marked as a traitor."

The word cut deep into her. Yes, she was a traitor to her race in more ways than her colleagues could even imagine.

"Give us some credit, Enya," Logan continued. "We're not gonna betray you just because Zoltan managed to trick you into trusting him. We'll sort this out our way, without the involvement of the council."

"Yeah," Hamish added. "Nobody will ever need to know that you made a mistake."

"A mistake?" she growled. "I made no fucking mistake. You are the ones who made a mistake."

"Be reasonable, Enya," Logan said. "In a few days, when you've calmed down, you'll understand that there is only one solution to this problem. You'll come to the same conclusion: even though Zoltan is Cinead's son, he can't be saved. He's locked up downstairs."

A ray of hope rose in her. Even Logan seemed to notice it.

"Manus and Grayson are watching him, so don't even think of trying to free him. None of your tricks will work. If you think of approaching them invisibly, don't. Grayson will smell you the moment you enter the corridor."

"Bastards!" she cursed. "I want to see him. I want to talk to him."

"No!" Aiden replied. "You won't get to see him until we are convinced that you're ready to kill him."

She glared at her colleagues. How dare they decide her life for her? Kill Zoltan? She hadn't been able to do it when she'd first discovered that he was a demon. How could she kill him now that she was carrying his child?

"That'll never happen!"

With a grunt, Enya turned around and charged out of the command center. She didn't bother running down to the lead cell to see if Manus and Grayson were really guarding Zoltan. She knew Logan had told her the truth. Instead, she retreated to her private quarters. She had to free Zoltan. He'd done the same for her.

Enya snatched her computer, plopped on the couch, and booted it up.

"Brothers, you're not the only ones playing dirty," she said. "I've got an ace up my sleeve too."

26

An alarm blaring outside his cell ripped Zoltan from his dozing. He instantly jumped up and rushed to the door, trying to hear what was going on in the compound.

"Perimeter breach," a female machine voice repeated over and over again, interlaced with the sound of a high-pitched horn. Then a male voice interrupted, "Demon attack! Everybody to the west entrance. I repeat: demon attack!"

Fuck! The demons had found them. How, Zoltan had no idea. They would attack Enya, and he was sitting in this damn lead cell and couldn't help her. Frustrated, he hammered against the door.

"Let me out! Damn it! Open the fucking door and let me out! I can help you against the demons!"

But nobody answered his cry for help. The two men who'd stood guard in front of his cell were probably already gone, racing to help their brethren. And he stood here, helpless. Again he slammed his fist against the heavy door, and it suddenly opened outward.

Light streamed into the cell, and for a moment he was blinded.

"Quickly, let's get out of here."

"Enya?" He blinked.

Enya reached for him, grabbing his arm. "Do exactly as I say."

He exited the cell. "Give me a weapon, so I can defend us from the demons." He let his gaze roam, looking for the intruders, but so far the corridors were clear.

"There are no demons," Enya said, and ushered him along a corridor.

"What?"

"It's a diversion. I tricked the computer system into thinking that demons are attacking us." She pointed to a flight of stairs. "Down that way."

He ran next to her, taking two steps at a time. "To save me?"

She cast him a sideways glance. "They posted Grayson, one of the vampire hybrids, and Manus as your guards. I would have never gotten past them."

"Smart girl." He looked down the corridor Enya was leading him to and noticed that it was a dead end. "Where are we going?"

"The portal." A moment later, she stopped dead in front of a stone wall and looked up.

Zoltan followed her gaze and looked straight into a camera. "Are we invisible?"

"Not yet." She pressed her palm against the stone, and Zoltan noticed a glow beneath it.

An instant later, the stone was gone. The portal was open. Instead of immediately entering the dark space, Enya looked up at the camera again, then lifted her fist and extended her middle finger. He had to hand it to her: Enya wasn't somebody who kept her opinions to herself.

"Get inside," she ordered him, shoved him in, and followed. Inside, she took his arm. "Okay, do exactly as I say. We're both invisible now, and we're gonna march back out. Silence from here on out."

He didn't ask any questions, but followed her instructions. The moment they were back in the corridor, the portal closed. Enya held his hand, and again they rushed through several corridors, up a different set of stairs. Meanwhile, the alarm still blared, yet Zoltan didn't talk, didn't express his gratitude or the pride he felt for Enya. She was fooling her colleagues into thinking that they'd left the compound via the portal. They wouldn't know where to start looking for them. And she'd done it all for him. His heart swelled with love. Nobody had ever shown him such loyalty, such devotion.

The alarm stopped. He looked at Enya. They were both thinking the same: her brethren had caught on to her diversion and realized that there was no demon attack. Another flight of stairs higher and Enya dragged him to the end of another corridor. There, she stopped and took a breath, then opened the door ahead of her. Finally, an exit.

They walked through the door, and Enya pulled it shut behind them.

Zoltan froze. They weren't outside; they were still in the compound. He spun around.

"These are my private quarters," she said. "They'll never suspect that I'm hiding you here. They'll be too busy figuring out where we went via the portal."

He shook his head and pulled her into his arms. He lifted her off her feet, then captured her mouth in a searing kiss. For the moment they were both safe, and that was something to be grateful for.

With a sigh, he released her and looked into her eyes. "You keep saving me. You keep risking everything you've ever worked for. Why?"

She took a deep breath, and instinctively he knew that her answer was going to be more than just a casual remark. "Because I want my child to know its father."

For a few seconds, the words made no sense, as if she'd spoken them in the wrong order, as if they'd gotten jumbled up on the way from her brain to her lips. But then they finally reached his brain, and he made sense of them.

"You're pregnant? By me?"

"No, I'm joking." She rolled her eyes. "Of course I'm fucking pregnant. And it's yours. I haven't slept with anybody else in months, so unless it was the holy spirit—"

Zoltan pressed his lips to her mouth and kissed away her curses. He wrapped his arms around her and pulled her into an embrace so tight that it left them both breathless. When she shoved her hands into his hair and held him, he knew she understood what this kiss meant. But just to be sure, he took his lips off hers to say what he should have said earlier.

"I love you, Enya, I love you with every fiber of my being. With every ounce of whatever miserable heart I have. And I'm gonna love our baby just as much."

A sob tore from Enya's throat, and her eyes filled with tears.

"Oh my God," he murmured. "Did I say something wrong? I'm so sorry, my love—tell me what I did wrong. Please."

She sniffled. "Nothing. You did nothing wrong." She smiled through the tears that ran down her cheeks in small rivulets. "You said all the right things. I just didn't expect it. I didn't dare hope that you…"

He used his thumb and forefinger to tip her chin up. "That I what? Want this baby? That I welcome it?" He ran his hand over her hair, caressing the soft tresses.

"That you love me," she said.

He moved his head to the left, then the right. "Do you really think I would have risked my life and my kingdom for you if I didn't love you? You're more important to me than anything else. For you, and for our child, I'd sacrifice my life. Anything to keep both of you safe."

Enya pulled his head to her. "I love you, Zoltan. But I don't want you to die for me. I want you to live for me. For me and our child. Because this child is a miracle."

Zoltan chuckled. "A miracle? Don't get me wrong, I welcome this child. But a miracle? Hardly. Babe, we had unprotected sex. And not just once. Sooner or later, it had to happen."

She shook her head. "No, you don't understand. Stealth Guardians aren't fertile, not until they've bonded. I should have never gotten pregnant."

Stunned, he stared at her. This was something he hadn't known about Stealth Guardians. "If that's true, then I don't understand. I mean, I'd like to think that I'm… uh, you know, a stud…" He winked at her and got an eye-roll in response. "But maybe you should see a doctor, make sure you're not mistaken. After all, it's only been a month since we first had sex. Isn't that a little early to confirm that you're pregnant?"

"Normally, I'd say yes, but I already saw a doctor earlier today. A vampire doctor in San Francisco."

"A vampire? One of your allies?"

Enya nodded. "I went to see her colleagues about some advice and ran into her while I was there. She heard the baby's heartbeat. That's how I found out. It's certain."

Zoltan pulled her back into his arms. "I'm happy it happened. Now the chance of you dumping me is decreasing."

"That's your concern? Me dumping you?"

"Can't blame me for wondering about that. I've got a few strikes against me, you know, being a demon and all." He motioned to the door. "Your people don't exactly like me. They were debating when to kill me. Not sure why they didn't do it right when they captured me. Almost as if they had scruples. As if they were worried how you'd react."

For a moment, Enya said nothing, but behind her blue eyes, the wheels in her mind were working overtime. "I think we can use that."

"Use what?"

"They don't want to piss me off."

"I hate to point out the obvious," Zoltan said slowly, "but you breaking me out of the lead cell kinda means you just tossed that card out the window. You betrayed your people—it can't really get any worse than that."

"There's one thing worse I could do…"

He lifted an eyebrow. What was his sexy warrior cooking up now? "Why would you wanna do something even worse?"

"To make it better."

"I don't follow. How would doing something worse make it better?"

A smile curved Enya's lips. "Because it would mean that they can't touch you. Nobody would dare hurt the mate of a Stealth Guardian."

For what seemed like an eternity, Zoltan's heart stood still. Enya was offering him the ultimate proof of love. And what could he give her in exchange? A whole world of unhappiness, because if she was bonded to him, her people would cast her out. They would never accept a demon among their midst. If he accepted her offer, he would be condemning her to a life in exile, a life away from the people she loved. She would never be safe: the moment the demons discovered that she was carrying his child, they would hunt her down, and without friends, without allies, it wouldn't take long until the demons would kill them both and cut the child from her womb.

"We can't do that," he said. When their eyes met, he saw the hurt. The disappointment. But before she could free herself from his arms, he added, "Because it means you'll lose your people's protection. They'll never accept me. They'll cast you out. All you'll have is me to protect you. It won't be enough against the hordes of demons who'll be on our ass. You can't possibly want that." He released her and looked down to her flat stomach. He reached out and touched her there. "I want our child to live, even if I can never see it, never touch it, never feel its life force. This child is innocent. Don't let us drag it into this war."

Enya, whose gaze had followed his hand, now looked up at him, a strange expression on her face. "It's not the heartbeat. That's the wrong translation." She appeared as if she was talking to herself. "Charles and Wesley were wrong. It's not the heartbeat."

"What are you talking about?" Zoltan said, concern for Enya's wellbeing crawling up his spine.

She gripped his biceps. "Charles and Wesley, the two witches I consulted in San Francisco to find a way to turn you back into a Stealth Guardian, found something. A story told by the gypsies. A story about a demon who was redeemed."

"A story? Oh, Enya, there are lots of fairy tales going around." And he didn't want to get his hopes up, nor did he want to crush hers, so he added, "Tell me what the story said."

"*When the demon felt the heartbeat of his own innocent flesh and blood,*" she recited, "*his soul wept and gave him back his true self.*" She squeezed his arms. "But they translated it wrong. It's not the heartbeat. It's the child's life force. It's its virta. And the only way you feel your child's virta is during the bonding, because only then will you not only receive my virta, but also that of our child. Your own innocent flesh and blood."

Zoltan ran a shaky hand through his hair. "This is crazy." But what if it was true? What if it worked? He suddenly realized that the question he'd had before, whether he could give up the power of the Great One, didn't even figure into his calculation. All that mattered now was one thing: "And if it doesn't work, if I remain a demon, what will happen to you and the child?"

Enya smiled. "You'll be my mate. And we'll deal with whatever we're up against."

Zoltan took a strand of her blond locks and brushed it out of her face. "I've never met a woman braver than you." He pulled her to him. "Nor sexier."

"Is that a yes?"

Zoltan smirked. "Is that a proposal?"

"Yes."

"What took you so long?"

Enya rolled her eyes. "It's traditionally the man's job."

"Enya, babe, I doubt our relationship will ever be a traditional one. But I'm good with that. As long as I can call you mine, I'm good with anything." He paused for a moment. "I'd also be good with a shower right now—the stink of the Underworld is still clinging to me."

She smirked. "Under one condition: I get to join you."

"That can be arranged."

27

Enya ran her eyes over Zoltan's back when he walked into the shower tiled with pebbles in all shades of green and blue to resemble a rain forest. He turned on the water, allowing it to run down his body in rivulets that caressed the ridges and grooves of his muscular physique. The scene reminded her of the night she'd snuck into his condo and watched him pleasure himself, awakening her desire for him which never stayed far beneath the surface.

"Are you just gonna ogle me, or are you gonna join me?"

"There's nothing wrong with ogling."

He looked over his shoulder, his eyes a bright green, reminding her of the forbidden fruit she was craving. Yet she regretted nothing. Not a single moment. Not a single touch.

She followed him into the shower, put her hands on his back, and slid them down over his smooth skin to the firm muscles of his buttocks. He was more than just well proportioned. It was as if a higher power had sculpted him, made him perfect in every way.

Zoltan braced his hands against the wall and dipped his head to let the water run down his hair and face. "I love feeling your hands on me."

"Then let me wash you." She reached for the soap, squeezed a generous amount into her palm, and began to wash him.

She felt him relax into her touch with such ease that she wondered what luxuries he'd enjoyed as the Great One. "In the Underworld, did you have your demon females do this for you? Wash you? Please you?" She reached around him and put her soapy hand around his cock. "Pleasure you?"

He sucked in a breath and bucked his hips so her hand slid down to the root of his hardening cock. "I never wanted that kind of intimacy. Letting somebody take care of me like that would have meant to give up control. To let down my guard. It was never like that. It was only fucking." He turned around to face her. "I could never trust anybody before."

Enya ran her hands over his front, soaping him up and washing the dirt of the Underworld off him, then took particular care with his cock and balls. She felt him hold his breath when she rubbed his cock between her palms, caressing him gently. When she looked up at him, she noticed how his gaze was focused on her breasts.

"You excite me more than any other woman ever could."

Zoltan moved so the water could wash away the soap. Then he reached out with both hands and cupped her breasts, squeezing them in his palms. A moan rushed over her lips.

"I think it's my turn to wash you."

He turned her, then pulled her against his chest. A moment later, his hands were on her chest, lathering her breasts with soft foam, massaging them, while she leaned back against him, his cock pressing against her bottom. Again and again, he rhythmically worked her breasts, before he slid one hand down between her legs and gently washed her there too. Before she knew what he was planning, he'd already taken the handheld shower attachment and was using it to wash away the foam from her pussy. But he didn't seem to be done with it, even when no foam was left. Instead, he changed the setting, allowing the water to spray from it with more force. He directed it to her pussy and moved it up and down, side to side, until Enya let out a yelp of pleasure.

"Ah, right here," he murmured into her ear, while his free hand still squeezed one breast. "Tell me, have you ever made yourself come like this?"

Enya leaned her head against his chest, her legs turning weak from the strong stream of the water targeting her clit and igniting it. "Yes."

A hoarse chuckle sounded in her ear. "You're a wicked woman, Enya. You're gonna keep me on my toes, making sure you'll never get bored of me." He brought the shower attachment closer to her flesh, increasing the water pressure.

She gasped at the intensity of the pleasure. Another few seconds, and she would come.

"You'll always tell me how you want me to pleasure you, won't you?"

His deep voice catapulted her over the edge. Her orgasm charged through her like a tornado, making her knees buckle. But she didn't fall. Zoltan was holding her pressed against him with both arms now, having dropped the shower attachment. He placed his palm over her pussy, cupping it gently, until the waves of pleasure subsided.

"I think you're the wicked one," Enya murmured, and turned her head to him.

"Why's that?" He grinned the shameless grin of a man who knew exactly what he'd done. "I'm not the one whose knees just buckled."

"Your fault."

"Can you stand on your own again?"

"Yes, why?"

"So I can do this."

He captured both her breasts and resumed kneading them, while he rubbed his cock against her butt, making her realize how big and hard he'd gotten. Her nipples felt tender to the touch, and her pussy was still sensitive, yet ready for more. And she knew Zoltan could give her exactly what she needed.

"Zoltan?"

"Hmm?"

"Dry me off. And then please don't make me wait any longer and make love to me."

~ ~ ~

At Enya's words, Zoltan smiled. "I'm good with that."

He dried her and himself with a large, fluffy towel that was softer than anything he'd ever had in the Underworld. Enya's long hair was down and wet in places, though not soaked. She didn't bother with a comb or a brush, just took his hand and led him into her bedroom. From the back she looked like Lady Godiva, beautiful and strong at the same time. He was one lucky son of a bitch to have earned her heart and her trust. He just hoped that he wouldn't disappoint her, because there was no guarantee that he could ever shake the shackles of being a demon.

Enya pulled back the sheets of the king-sized bed and lay down, immediately turning her gaze to him. Her eyes swept over his body, making no secret out of the fact that she liked what she saw. He felt her desire physically, sensed how the mere knowledge of it sent blood rushing south to make his cock swell even more. When her eyes rested on the engorged organ, a growl rose from deep within his chest. Damn, deep down he was a beast, an animal waiting to claim his mate. Everything else was just a mask, a disguise so as not to frighten the fairer sex.

He almost chuckled at that thought. Enya could hardly be described as the fairer sex. She was anything but weak or docile. In fact, she was perfect for him.

Zoltan slid onto the bed and rolled over Enya. She was already spreading her legs to welcome him, and without a word, without a preamble, he thrust into her wet pussy. Months ago, he had never imagined that Enya would give herself to him so freely. He'd expected her to fight him all the way, and that with time, he would tame her to accept him. But even then, he would have never even dreamed of getting what she was offering him tonight: a bond that could never be broken.

Enya put one hand on his chest, the other on his neck. "I love the way you feel inside me."

He withdrew a few inches, then plunged deeper. "That's good, because I'll never leave this place again—not for long, anyway." He began to move back and forth, rocking his hips, supporting his weight on his knees and elbows, while he locked eyes with her. "From the moment I first saw you, I knew we were meant to be together. I just never dreamed it would be this good."

Enya caressed his nape, sending an erotic shiver down his spine and into his tailbone. "It'll get even better." Her smile was sinful and promising at the same time, while she forced her interior muscles to squeeze him tightly.

"Vixen," he murmured, and thrust harder, though his tempo remained slow and steady. He wasn't going to rush this. Taking Enya as his mate was an event he wanted to savor for as long as he could.

Enya pulled his head down to her and captured his lips. Their tongues mated, and he tasted the depth of her devotion to him, the truth of her love, the vastness of her trust. And one other thing: the enormity of her hope. Those same attributes filled him now too, as if he'd been given permission to love, trust, and hope. He didn't question those feelings any longer, didn't try to analyze them. Instead, he accepted the changes Enya had brought about in him.

Without a conscious thought on his part, their lovemaking took on a different tempo, a more urgent pace as they writhed against each other, connected not only by his cock in her pussy, but by their lips fused, their tongues dancing, their hands touching. It was as if they moved entirely in sync with each other, their bodies moving as one, their breaths combined, their hearts beating as one. He felt it then: a stream of energy, of power that seemed limitless, infusing him, spreading in his cells, engulfing him, until he felt it, felt her. Before his mind's eye, he saw her: without a wall around her, without anything to protect her. Her true self, the warrior woman who loved him. The woman who offered herself to him so he could be free.

He felt his chest tighten with heavy emotion, as if he was going to burst, and ripped his lips from her. His orgasm hit him out of nowhere, sending more pleasure through his body than he'd ever experienced before.

"Send the virta back to me. Complete the bond," she demanded. "Show yourself to me."

Even though he didn't know what exactly he was supposed to do, his body seemed to. He laid one hand on Enya's left breast and willed the virta she'd shared with him to travel back to her. To his astonishment, he felt something akin to a flame charge down his arm, into his hand, before tiny fireworks seemed to explode underneath his palm and penetrate Enya's skin.

She arched her back, her chest bucking toward him as if she'd received an electrical shock. Stunned, he almost jerked back, afraid of hurting her, but his body refused to break the bond. Then a second wave hit him, a different one. This wasn't Enya's virta but the child's. It traveled through him at a different speed, but with no less intensity, until it streamed back down his arm and merged with Enya once more.

Only now he noticed that the color of his skin had changed. He was shimmering golden. Zoltan lifted his hand from Enya's breast and examined it in wonder, then looked at the other arm and found the same color.

"We're bonded," Enya said with a smile.

He looked into her eyes and wanted to respond, but a spasm went through his torso. The first spasm was followed by a second, before he managed to roll off Enya, clamping his hand over his heart in an attempt to stop the feeling of a vise squeezing all blood from his heart.

"No!" he yelled out in agony.

Enya was on her knees next to him on the bed, trying to help him, but there was nothing she could do. The waves of pain kept coming; the spasms didn't subside, didn't give him the chance to even say goodbye to her. Because he knew this was the end. He felt it.

"Zoltan! Oh no, please!" Enya sobbed.

I'm sorry, he tried to say, but he had no breath to form the words. His vision was blurring now, his head near exploding. Through his pain, he reached for Enya, for the mate whose virta was killing him. It was poetic justice, wasn't it? The last defense of a Stealth Guardian, should a demon ever manage to win a guardian's heart: their bond would be their downfall.

"Enya," he managed to say. He swallowed, trying to wet his hoarse throat, and with it, he tasted his own tears. Or were they Enya's? They had to be, because a demon couldn't cry.

He suddenly felt her lips on his, kissing his face, soothing him. Their tears mingled, and in his heart he felt only one thing now: Enya's love. With a start, he realized that the vise around his heart was gone. His lungs were filling with air. The pain vanished. He jerked up to sit and wrapped his arms around Enya.

She squeezed him. "I thought I'd lost you." She pulled back to look at him. Her eyes widened in shock.

"What?" he asked, alarmed.

A loud sound reached his ears.

"I thought I smelled demon."

Zoltan whipped his head to the menacing male voice and saw a vampire standing in the open door. "Fuck!"

28

Enya spun her head to the intruder, and simultaneously snatched the duvet to cover herself and Zoltan. The intruder was no other than Grayson, a triumphant expression on his face, as if he'd just won a competition with his colleagues. And he probably had—he'd used his superior vampire sense of smell to find Zoltan.

Behind him, Hamish rushed into the room, his arm no longer in a sling, having fully healed in the time since Zoltan had broken it.

"How could you?" he said, looking past her to Zoltan. "You shared your virta with a fucking demon?"

It was plain for all to see, so she didn't deny it. "We're bonded. You can't touch him now."

Hamish looked at Grayson. "Call the others. Tell them the search is off. And have them come back to the compound immediately."

Grayson pulled out his cell and pressed a number, then talked quietly.

When Hamish made a few more steps into the room, Enya lifted her hand. "Stay the fuck where you are, Hamish."

Zoltan pulled her toward him, shielding her naked body even further. "How about some privacy? As you can see, Enya isn't dressed."

The sound of his protective demand sent a shiver down her spine.

"Yeah, neither are you," Hamish snapped, and narrowed his eyes. "So was that the plan, to seduce her, make her bond with you so you could destroy us from within? Do you have any idea what you've done?" He pointed to Enya. "Do you have any idea what punishment is waiting for Enya for bonding with a fucking demon?"

"He's not a demon anymore," Enya interrupted. "Look at his eyes. They're brown now. They've turned."

"They are?" Zoltan asked, looking at her.

"Oh, big deal. So he's wearing colored contacts. I'm not falling for crap like that," Hamish said.

"But it's true. He's not wearing contacts. His eyes turned after we bonded. He's a Stealth Guardian again. It worked. What Wesley and Charles figured out worked. Don't you see?"

"Wes and Charles know about this?" Hamish's voice turned increasingly angry. "They advised you to bond with Zoltan? Well, let me just add them to my list of people to beat the shit out of."

"They don't know about the bonding. And they know nothing about Zoltan," Enya said. "So pipe down. If you would just shut up for a moment, I can explain."

"Yeah, right. He's not a Stealth Guardian. Don't you see that? He's got no aura. So whatever you two are playing at, I'm not buying it."

Zoltan grunted and glared at Hamish. "So you wanted her for yourself, is that it? Is that why you're so pissed? Well, you can't have her. Enya is mine." He put his arms around her to underscore his statement.

Hamish shook his head. "Enya and I? What the fuck gives you that idea? Enya is like a sister to me. And I don't take it lightly when somebody hurts her."

"And you're implying that I'll hurt her?" Zoltan's chest seemed to expand. "I'd give my life for her and our child if it means they'll be safe. So don't—"

"Child?" Hamish gasped.

Grayson, his phone still pressed to his ear, said to the person he was talking to, "Hold on." Then he stared at Enya. "You got knocked up by a demon? Oh fuck!"

"A little respect, if I may?" Enya snapped, then took Zoltan's hand. "And if you must know, yes, I'm pregnant."

"That's bullshit. Just another trick so we won't hurt him," Hamish said. "You just bonded. You can't be pregnant yet."

Enya shrugged. "Maya confirmed it. She heard the baby's heartbeat."

Hamish motioned to Grayson.

"Well, in that case," Grayson said, "I can confirm it too." He started to walk closer. "My vampire hearing—"

"Not another step!" Zoltan growled. "Or it'll be your last. Enya is still not dressed. And I'll be damned if I let another man get any closer. Do I make myself clear?"

Grayson's fangs extended, and his lips peeled back from his teeth.

"Put your fucking fangs away," Enya ordered him. "Or I'll put them away for you."

With a growl, Grayson slowly allowed his fangs to recede.

"Now give us a few minutes to get dressed. Then we can talk. We'll meet you in the great room."

"Not a chance," Hamish said. "We'll be right outside this door. We'll escort you." He motioned to Grayson. "Grayson, out, now."

Both men left the room and closed the door behind them.

"And hurry up," Hamish yelled through the closed door. "Or we'll help you get dressed."

"Shut up, Hamish!" Enya yelled back.

Zoltan let out a breath. "I have the feeling Hamish isn't convinced that I'm on your side."

Enya shrugged and jumped out of bed. "He'll change his tune once we can show him how you've changed." She walked to her closet and opened it, then took out a clean pair of jeans and a long-sleeved shirt. "You'd better get dressed, so we can change his mind before the whole gang comes down on us like a ton of bricks."

She started pulling on her clothes, and saw from the corner of her eye how Zoltan looked down at his cock, which was still rock hard.

"Uhm, yeah, about that," she said, and pointed to his erection. "It won't come down as long as your skin shimmers golden."

"And how long will I shimmer?"

"A few hours."

"You're kidding, right?"

She smirked for the first time since they'd gotten interrupted. "Nope. It's the virta that's still running through you. It makes sure a man can satisfy his mate."

Zoltan's chin dropped. "I never heard you complain before that I couldn't satisfy you."

"And I haven't had anything to complain about. But unfortunately, I can't turn this off. Every time I give you my virta, you'll get hard."

Zoltan pulled on his pants and shoved his massive appendage into it, before zipping up. "So you're saying this won't be the last time you'll give me your virta?"

She fastened the buttons of her shirt and continued watching him get dressed. "No. And if everything goes well, then you'll give me yours, and I'll shimmer golden."

"And what'll do that to you?" he asked, grinning and approaching.

"It'll give me an orgasm every time you touch me."

He pulled her into his arms. "I think I like this."

"Good." She kissed him quickly, then wound herself out of his arms, not wanting to succumb to the temptation of making use of his erection. "Now let's see what else besides the brown eyes our child's virta has done. That can't have been the entire transformation."

"Maybe we'll have to do it a few more times."

Enya rolled her eyes. "As much as I would like to do that, I'm not gonna risk it until I've spoken to Wes and Charles about this. You almost died in my arms. What if the next time kills you?"

"What if it doesn't?"

She ignored the question. "Let's test what else you can do, whether you've gotten any of the Stealth Guardian powers and what demon attributes you might have lost."

"How do you wanna do that?"

Enya pointed to the wall that separated the bedroom from the bathroom. "Walk through that wall."

Zoltan raised an eyebrow. "And how am I supposed to do that?"

"Just think it. See yourself walking through that wall, and it will happen."

He hesitated, then slowly walked toward the wall. Before reaching it, he turned his head to her. "You sure?"

"Just try it."

He took another step and bumped his head against the wall. He jerked back and held his hand to his forehead. "Ouch!"

Enya hid her disappointment. "Maybe it'll take a little while. How about you try to make yourself invisible?"

"Let me guess: I think it, and it will happen?"

She smiled. "See, you're catching on."

He grimaced. "Yeah, right."

Suddenly, he disappeared before her eyes. Her heart skipped a beat, and excitement charged through her veins. It was working! Their baby's virta was turning him back into a Stealth Guardian. She was choking up, and tears welled up in her eyes.

"I'm sorry, babe. I'm sorry it's not working. Maybe we got it all wrong."

She felt Zoltan's hands on her upper arms, pulling her to him.

Amidst the tears, she shook her head. "That's not why I'm crying. Zoltan, you're invisible. You did it."

"What?" The moment he spoke, he appeared before her, a confused look on his face. "But I still saw myself."

"A Stealth Guardian always sees himself, even if he's invisible to all others."

"But then how will I know that I'm invisible?"

"You'll sense it. Don't worry, you'll be able to distinguish between being visible and being invisible."

"I hope you're right."

"Let's go." She motioned to the door. "I think Hamish will get impatient. And Grayson is just looking for a reason to get his fangs into a demon."

"I'll punch his lights out if he even tries," Zoltan said.

Enya took a deep breath and walked to the door. She opened it and saw Hamish and Grayson waiting for them. The moment Zoltan walked into the corridor, they ran their eyes over him.

"I hope you didn't give him a weapon," Hamish said.

"I'm unarmed," Zoltan said tightly, and looked at the dagger in Hamish's hand. "So ease up. I'm not here to harm anybody."

"That's yet to be seen," Hamish said.

Enya walked ahead. "I'll see you in the great room once you two are done comparing the size of your dicks." She smiled to herself, because she knew exactly who would win that competition at the moment. And she knew that Hamish was aware of that fact.

She heard Hamish grumble as the three men followed her

"Zoltan, you should teach your mate some respect," Hamish said.

To her surprise, Zoltan laughed. "Waste of time. This woman will never be tamed. And that's just how I like her."

"I stand corrected," Hamish replied. "You didn't manipulate her. *She* manipulated *you*. Man, you're totally pussy-whipped, and you're not even aware of it."

Enya suppressed a chuckle. Hamish was in the bag. And the others would fall like dominoes.

29

By the time the remaining Stealth Guardians had assembled in the great room, Zoltan had figured out who was who. He'd encountered most of them before, not only when they'd captured him, but also during the various battles they'd fought. There were two vampires among them—Grayson, the jerk who hadn't been able to keep his eyes off Enya's half-naked body, and Ryder, equally young, but somewhat calmer and politer than his vampire friend.

Except for Hamish, the Stealth Guardians gave Zoltan hostile looks. And one other thing was noticeable: none of the women were here. Perhaps they'd been locked away for fear that Zoltan might do them harm. Well, he had no such plans, but it would take some effort to convince these warriors of it.

Enya had given them the short version of who he really was, not just Zoltan, the Great One, but Angus, Cinead's son. She'd also explained to them that their bonding had changed him. But the guardians didn't look convinced.

"Brown eyes don't mean he's a Stealth Guardian now," Logan said. "I mean, look at him: he has no aura."

"But he can make himself invisible," Enya protested, and motioned to Zoltan. "Show them."

Zoltan concentrated, willing himself to become invisible. But the guys still stared at him, looking directly into his eyes, which meant they could still see him. It had worked earlier. So why wasn't it working now?

"Relax, Zoltan," Enya said. "Just wish that nobody could see you, not even I."

He looked into her eyes and saw that she believed in him. He wasn't going to disappoint her.

"Fuck!" Manus said.

The others let out similar curses and gasps.

"Show yourself, Zoltan!" Pearce ordered him.

Zoltan felt an odd sense of security inside. Was that how his body was telling him that he was using his powers of invisibility? He ordered his body to become visible again, and by the looks the guys gave him, it worked. They could see him again.

Enya smiled. "See? He's got our powers. He's not a demon anymore."

"Okay," Logan said slowly. "Let's assume you're right. Let's assume he's really changed—does that mean all his demon attributes are gone?"

Enya hesitated.

"So, they're not all gone," Logan said. "Well, maybe we should check." He motioned to Manus, and both approached Zoltan, while Aiden stepped to Zoltan's side as if to prevent him from escaping. "If you're really one of ours now, I'm sure you won't mind a little cut, will you?"

Logan drew his dagger, and instinctively Zoltan wanted to shrink back, but he forced himself not to move.

"Fine." He stretched out his arm. If his eyes had changed color, for certain his blood would have too.

Logan made a thin cut across the top of Zoltan's forearm. Instantly, green blood dripped from the wound. Logan and Manus gasped. Zoltan's heart sank. Had he hoped for too much? Would he remain in this state of limbo?

"Still a demon," Logan announced, and held up the bloodstained dagger.

"That means nothing!" Enya said. "He's still transforming. Just like his powers are still ramping up, it will take some time to turn him fully."

Zoltan glanced at Enya. He knew she was lying; she didn't know why he hadn't transformed fully. She was only guessing to appease her brethren.

"You can't know that," Logan said. He pointed to Zoltan. "He's the first demon who's going through this so-called transformation. This could just as easily be the effects of your virta. The fact that he's still got demon blood just shows us that it's only temporary."

Enya braced her hands at her hips and glared at Logan. "Well, you can't know that either. It's not just my virta. It's like Wes and Charles said: the life force of Zoltan's unborn child has transformed him."

Logan tilted his head. "His unborn child? What the fuck are you talking about?"

When Enya didn't immediately answer, and Grayson and Hamish exchanged a knowing look, Zoltan stepped in. "Enya is pregnant. By me."

Outraged gasps filled the room.

Grayson held up his hand. "He's speaking the truth. I can hear the baby's heartbeat." He was standing only a few paces away from Enya. "Ryder?"

Ryder, the other vampire hybrid, approached and looked at Enya, who nodded. He stopped in front of her but didn't touch her. A moment later, he turned around to the assembled and nodded. "Yep, I can hear it too."

Manus sighed and shook his head. "I'm not even gonna ask how that could have happened in the first place. Let's just deal with that issue later." He nodded at Logan. "I'm with Logan. We don't know whether this is temporary and whether Zoltan will just change back in a few hours. We have to be certain."

Zoltan ran a hand through his hair, frustrated. "There's no way to be certain. Hell, when it first happened, I thought I was dying. Maybe I was. Maybe a part of my demon self died." He glanced at Enya. "It's true: nobody here knows what'll happen. Hell, I only have one Stealth Guardian power so far. I have no idea if I'll ever be able to walk through a wall, or if I'll develop an aura. How is anybody here supposed to know? This is new for all of us. We're all just guessing."

The men didn't contradict him.

"All I know is that I feel different. And I know I won't hurt any of you."

"That's what you say now," Pearce said. "But we can't just take your word for it."

"Let's talk to Wes and Charles. Maybe they can help," Enya suggested anxiously. When nobody said a word, she added, "It can't hurt to just ask them."

Pearce looked at his colleagues, then nodded. "Fine. I'm gonna get them on the speaker." He reached for a tablet on the sideboard, pulled up an app, and selected a number. It rang loud enough for everybody in the room to hear.

"Hey, what's going on?"

"Yeah, Wes, it's Pearce. We've got some questions for you and Charles. Let me just patch him in."

"Oh, Charles is right here with me. We're in the lab."

"Hey, Pearce."

"Hey, Charles. Okay, then. I'm here with the whole gang."

A collective "hey" went through the room. Then Pearce nodded to Enya.

"So, Wes, Charles, it's about the gypsy story you found. I figured out what it means," Enya said, leaning over the tablet.

"Were we right?" Wes asked.

"Basically, yeah. Though it wasn't the life or the heartbeat—it was the life force, the virta."

"Huh?" Wes said.

"What's that supposed to mean?" Charles asked. "If the demon feels the virta of his child, he gets transformed? But that can't happen, Enya. I mean, the child of a demon wouldn't have virta."

"It would," Enya said, then cleared her throat. "It does. But that's beside the point. There's something else."

"Okay, shoot," Wes said.

"Is it possible that the transformation is only partial or that it takes a while to be fully complete?" Enya asked.

"Funny you should ask," Charles said. "Wes and I dug a little deeper after you left, and there was more to the story."

"Like what?" Enya asked, and locked eyes with Zoltan.

"Apparently a demon's soul is a split soul."

Several of the guys in the room said, "What?"

"Well, let me explain that," Charles continued. "When a person turns demon, his soul is split into multiple parts and scattered. So, when a demon is redeemed, it makes sense that not all parts of his soul come back at the same time. In that story, there's a reference about a night and a day, or something like that. Wes?"

"Yeah," Wes said, "it was something like a full cycle of the sun. Which makes me believe it can take up to twenty-four hours before the entire soul is restored."

Zoltan felt the tightness of his chest ease and took a breath. So there was a chance that soon he'd transform fully. There was hope.

"Thanks, Wes. Thanks, Charles," Enya said.

"Anytime," both replied.

"Bye, guys," Pearce said, then disconnected the call.

"See," Enya said triumphantly, and looked at Logan and Manus. "It'll just take time."

The five men exchanged contemplative looks.

Logan finally spoke. "So if that's correct, and we're gonna give it the benefit of doubt, that leaves one thing."

Zoltan watched Logan's expression. It was clear that even once he fully turned Stealth Guardian, he still had an uphill struggle to get accepted.

"Spit it out, Logan," Enya said tightly.

"Zoltan committed unspeakable atrocities against humans and against us. That can't just be wiped away. And even if we might believe that he'll be good from now on, that doesn't mean the council will believe it, or forgive what he's done when he was a demon." Logan turned to look directly at Zoltan. "You threatened our mates."

"You had Nancy Britton killed. She was Kim's mother," Manus said. "She's still grieving for her."

Aiden cleared his throat. "Leila had to go into hiding because of you. You almost dragged her into the Underworld with you."

Zoltan lifted his hands. "I know what I've done. And I know what I'm not responsible for." He motioned to Manus. "I never gave the order to have Kim's mother murdered. When I found out about it, I killed the demon responsible for it. I know that doesn't bring Nancy Britton back, but rest assured that the killer paid for it. And Hamish already knows that I never overdosed Tessa. There's a traitor who wants my throne, and he's responsible for Tessa's overdose." He looked at Hamish.

Hamish nodded. "I believe him. Enya had photos of various demons, and Tessa identified one of them. It wasn't Zoltan."

Zoltan nodded to the Stealth Guardian. "I don't expect any of you to just forgive and forget as if none of this ever happened. I'm willing to earn your forgiveness and that of your people."

"How?" Aiden asked.

Zoltan took a breath. He didn't know when he'd made the decision. But he knew it was the right one, the only one that would keep Enya and his unborn child safe. "By helping you destroy the entire Underworld and making sure the demons will never rise again."

30

For a few seconds, silence filled the large room. None of the assembled talked; nobody even breathed. If Zoltan had the sensitive hearing of a vampire, he would've heard his child's heartbeat. Wide-eyed, they stared at him. Myriad facial expressions showing mixed emotions prepared him for an onslaught of questions. It was evident that disbelief was the predominant emotion in the room.

Even Enya seemed surprised. However, she didn't mirror her brethren's feelings. Instead, love and gratitude shone from her eyes that were now covered with a wet sheen.

Finally, Aiden cleared his throat. "Are you serious?"

Zoltan nodded.

"And why would you do that?" Logan asked. "Why destroy your own kingdom and kill your subjects? What's your motivation?"

Manus grunted. "Yeah, same question here. Plus another one: why should we believe you?"

Zoltan let his gaze wander over the men, contemplating where to start. He knew he had to win them over, because he needed their help for this endeavor. Without help, his plan was dead in the water.

"I know you still have doubts about me. I don't blame you. Hell, I'd have doubts if I were in your shoes. And all I can say to dispel them is this: I love Enya, and I love my unborn child. To make sure they're safe, I will do anything. And if you love your women the same way, then you know that I'm not lying. You risked everything to save them, your very lives." He pointed to Logan. "You even invaded the Underworld for the woman you love, not knowing if you would ever make it out alive. That's the kind of love I'm talking about when I tell you that I love Enya."

Again, there was silence in the room. The men dropped their gazes, suddenly studying their shoes as if they were of paramount importance. Almost as if Zoltan's declaration had embarrassed them. Only one person looked straight at him: Enya.

She said nothing, but her lips formed silent words. *I love you too.*

"Okay," Aiden said, glancing at his brethren. "I believe you."

The others nodded in agreement, but didn't go so far as putting it into words. It was good enough for Zoltan.

"Thank you," he said.

"So tell us how you think of destroying the demons," Aiden said. "We've sure tried for centuries and haven't gotten anywhere."

"It's rather simple. We won't have to kill them all. We won't even have to engage them in a battle."

Several eyebrows rose.

"We only have to make sure they can't leave the Underworld anymore."

Manus scoffed. "And how do you suggest we do that?"

"I assume you're aware of the vortex circles in the Underworld?" When the men nodded, Zoltan continued, "There are only three of them. No demon can cast a vortex in the Underworld unless he's standing in one of the vortex circles. If we destroy them, the Underworld will become their tomb. They wouldn't have a way out. And the few demons that are currently topside won't be too hard to annihilate. It might take us a few months, but one by one, we'll kill them."

"Interesting idea," Aiden said, "but what if they build more vortex circles? What then?"

Zoltan shook his head. "They don't know how." When several of the Stealth Guardians grumbled in disbelief, Zoltan lifted his hand. "Yeah, I didn't believe it either at first, but I put my best men on the task. See, my plan, once I'd destroyed your race, was to invade the human world, and to do that, I needed more than just three vortex circles. We looked at everything we could get our hands on—old scriptures, magic, anything that would give us a hint at how the vortex circles were created in the first place. We came up with exactly zilch." He paused and let the news sink in. "There isn't a single demon alive who knows who or what created the vortex circles and how. Which means if we destroy them permanently, the demons have no way out."

"And how do we destroy the vortex circles?" Manus asked.

"We flood them with lava."

"Where exactly is the Underworld?" Aiden asked.

Zoltan sighed. "I wish I could tell you."

"I see," Aiden said tightly. "Still keeping things from us. That's not tipping the scales in your favor, just so you know."

"I'm not keeping things from you. The truth is, nobody knows where the Underworld is located. It could be under Antarctica, Russia, Australia, or the U.S. For all I know, it moves constantly. Nobody knows. That's why the demons need the vortex circles. They are the only things that can anchor them to their home. The only way to find their way back."

When he saw the skeptical faces of the Stealth Guardians, Zoltan added, "But we don't need to know where it's located. All I need to do is open a vortex topside and travel down to one of the three vortex circles in the Underworld. Once I'm down there, I can set the plan in motion. But I need help."

"What do you need?" Aiden asked.

"Explosives. I know where the largest magma chambers are in relation to the vortex circles. If I blow up the right chambers, the lava inside will flood the vortex circles and destroy them. The lava will remain liquid for centuries, and even if it cools one day, whatever created the vortex circles in the first place will have been stripped away."

"That's a suicide mission," Enya said, her voice shaking, her eyes boring into him. "If you destroy the vortex circles, you can't get back."

"I'll set a timer and transport out just before." Of course, there was always a risk, but he was willing to take that.

Enya shook her head. "That would assume that you can still cast a vortex by then. What if you can't?"

"Enya, I—"

"Don't Enya me," she interrupted, bracing her hands at her hips. He recognized that gesture. She was ready for a fight. "If Wes and Charles are correct, then you'll turn fully back into a Stealth Guardian within twenty-four hours and will lose all your demon powers, including the power to cast a vortex. You'll be stuck there. It'll be your tomb too, and I'll be damned if I allow that to happen."

"But it's the only way," Zoltan said. "We have to destroy the Underworld, otherwise you'll never be safe, and neither will our child. And if that means that I won't ever see my child, I'm good with that, because I know that the two of you will be safe."

"There has to be another way." Tears welled up in Enya's eyes, and he wanted to pull her into his arms, but he couldn't, didn't dare, or he would break down himself. He had to be strong, for both of them.

"There is none. The only way out of the Underworld is by casting a vortex in one of the circles." He let out a bitter laugh. "Just like you need your portals, the demons need their vortexes."

Enya sniffled, then wiped her face with the back of her hand, her eyes widening. "That's it. A portal."

"What?" Zoltan asked, not understanding, while several of the Stealth Guardians started shaking their heads as if they knew what Enya was alluding to.

"That's crazy," Logan said.

"And it won't work, not for him," Manus said, pointing at Zoltan. "He hasn't got all his powers."

"The council will never approve it," Aiden said. "And without their approval—"

"Would somebody fucking tell me what you're talking about?" Zoltan interrupted, raising his voice.

Everybody fell silent for a moment.

"It's not even an option," Pearce grumbled.

"Too risky," Logan agreed.

But Enya lifted her hand to silence her brethren. "Sure it's risky, but we signed up for risky when we became warriors." She looked at Zoltan. "If we carve a portal somewhere in the Underworld, we could make it out even if you lose your ability to cast a vortex, or if the circles are destroyed before we can teleport out."

Zoltan let the statement sink in. It made sense, though there was one thing he needed to clarify. "Who are you referring to when you say *we*?"

"You and me, of course."

"Out of the question!" he snapped.

"You have no choice. To carve a portal requires the blood of a Stealth Guardian, and your blood is still green. And I'm the only one here who's seen a portal carved. I know how it's done."

"Then teach somebody else." He pointed to her brethren. "Any of them."

She shook her head. "No. If something goes wrong, I'm not going to be responsible for having sent one of my brothers to his death. Not happening. It's gonna be you and me."

Pearce cleared his throat, making everybody look at him. "Has somebody else here forgotten one of the most important things?"

Everybody stared at him.

"The dagger. The council will never hand us the source dagger so we can send you both down to the Underworld.

Even if we try to convince them of this plan, they'll never go for it."

"Then we won't tell them," Enya said.

Grayson raised his hand. "Uhm…"

"Yes?" Enya snapped.

"How are you gonna get the dagger? My understanding is that it's locked up in the council compound and very well guarded. You said so yourself."

"Yes, it's guarded, but against outsiders. There is a way for a Stealth Guardian to retrieve the dagger," Enya said.

Aiden raised an eyebrow. "How?"

Enya smiled. "Did you know that the door to the council's archive where the dagger is kept isn't made of lead?"

Hamish blew out a breath. "Son of a gun. You're just gonna march in there invisibly and steal it, aren't you?"

Enya shrugged. "I was hoping one of you will, because I need to shore up support from Scanguards."

"What's Scanguards got to do with it?" Grayson asked.

"We need their help with the explosives."

"You're missing something here," Hamish said.

Enya turned her head to him. "What am I missing?"

"You need three teams to work on the vortex circles simultaneously, otherwise the chance of the demons discovering the explosives is too high."

Aiden nodded. "Hamish is right. Three teams means three Stealth Guardians to make those who plant the explosives invisible. Plus protection."

"But I can't ask for that," Enya said. "I can't make you do that."

Aiden looked at his brethren. "No, you can't. But we can volunteer."

"But the risk—"

"The risk is much smaller if you and Zoltan go down using a vortex, then carve the portal somewhere where it's hidden away, then come get us," Hamish said. "What do you say, guys? Are you up for kicking some demon butt?"

Grunts of agreement bounced off the walls.

"Guys," Enya said, choking up.

"I think what Enya wants to say is thank you," Zoltan said, and squeezed her hand. "And so do I. You won't regret it."

Logan nodded. "Make sure of that, because if you betray us…" He didn't need to complete the sentence. Zoltan understood.

"By the life of my unborn child, I promise to be true to my word."

31

Enya gave Grayson a long look. "You'd better be okay with lying to your father, or you might as well turn back now."

She, Zoltan, and Grayson had traveled to San Francisco via the portal and were approaching the Scanguards headquarters in the Mission District. Simultaneously, Pearce and Aiden were traveling to the council compound to retrieve the source dagger. An invisible Pearce was following Enya's instructions on how to remove the dagger from its hiding place, while Aiden was visible at all times to provide a cover for Pearce. Had Pearce traveled alone and exited the portal invisibly, suspicion would have arisen. But by Aiden exiting the portal visibly, nobody would blink or question what Aiden was doing at the council compound. He would visit with his father under a pretense, then return with a still-invisible Pearce and the source dagger.

"Don't worry," Grayson assured Enya. "It won't be the first time I don't tell my father the whole truth. Though I really don't know why you can't tell him—"

"If he knows that the council didn't sanction this, he'll feel obligated to inform them. You of all people should know his high moral ethics."

Grayson shrugged. "His ethics never stopped him from doing the right thing. And the right thing is defeating the fucking demons, no matter how." He glanced at Zoltan. "No offense, man."

"None taken." Zoltan motioned to the large building on the next block. "That it?"

Grayson nodded. "Yeah."

Enya heard the pride in his voice. As the son of Scanguards' owner and founder, it was his destiny to take over the business one day—if Samson ever decided to retire, which was questionable.

"Uhm, so the building is full of vampires. Is that right?" Zoltan asked.

"Yep, and humans and witches," Grayson said.

Zoltan stopped walking and looked up to the top floor. "I'm assuming your father has his office on the top floor."

"Yeah, so?"

"Then I think we have a problem."

Enya turned to him. "What do you mean?"

Zoltan pointed to the building. "The moment we encounter a vampire, he'll take one sniff of me and identify me as a demon. Remember? I still have green blood. I still have no aura. They'll attack me faster than you can explain to them that I'm not a threat."

Enya looked at Grayson. With everything that had happened in the last hour, she hadn't even thought of this issue. "Grayson, I'm assuming you have the highest clearance?"

"You bet." Grayson seemed to understand her unspoken question immediately. "If we enter through the garage and take the elevator from there to the executive floor, we have the best chance of not encountering anybody." He pulled out his phone. "I'll text Blake to clear the executive corridor for us." He typed a message on his phone and sent it. A moment later, his device pinged. "Okay, let's go."

As they walked around the corner to the entrance of the parking garage underneath the east side of the building, Enya asked, "What did you tell him?"

Grayson smirked. "That I'm bringing a high-value prisoner in and need an escort to my father's office."

Zoltan stopped. "Are you shitting me? Why don't you stab me in the back while you're at it?"

"Calm down," Grayson said. "It's the only way to assure that nobody attacks you. I know what I'm doing."

"I hope you do," Enya said. And she hoped that Blake would keep a cool head once he realized who exactly they were bringing in. "Let's do this."

Grayson used his access card and thumbprint to open the gate for the parking garage, and they walked inside. By the time the gate closed behind them, they'd already reached the elevator. Moments later the doors opened, and Grayson ushered them inside. He used his access card again to select the executive floor, then pressed a second button.

"What's that for?" Enya asked, pointing at it.

"To make sure the elevator won't stop at any of the other floors."

"Good." It appeared Grayson was much smarter than she'd given him credit for.

The elevator slowed, and a soft ping sounded.

"Here we are," Grayson said.

Enya's hand instinctively went to the dagger hidden inside her jacket pocket. She was prepared to defend Zoltan should Blake make a wrong move.

The elevator doors slid open, revealing Blake already waiting for them. He wasn't armed, but vampires were strong and fast, and lethal even without weapons. Their fangs and claws could tear flesh apart more efficiently than a butcher knife.

Blake's nostrils flared. No doubt he recognized Zoltan's scent. Grayson stepped out of the elevator and raised his hand.

"Yes, he's a demon. And no, he won't hurt anybody."

Still, Blake looked past Grayson, his eyes finally focusing on Enya and Zoltan's intertwined hands. His eyebrows went up. He looked at Enya. "I wish I could say it's nice to see you again, Enya, but maybe I'll reserve my comment for once I know what's going on here."

Enya nodded and let go of Zoltan's hand. "We need to see Samson. It's urgent."

Slowly Blake stepped aside and motioned them to enter the hallway. "Amaury is with him right now. I'll escort you."

Grayson marched ahead and knocked on Samson's door, then opened it without waiting for an answer. "Dad, Amaury, I need you to remain calm. I brought somebody."

"Grayson, what—"

Enya entered with Zoltan by her side. Two pairs of vampire eyes fell on them—Samson's and Amaury's. Immediately their nostrils flared like Blake's earlier.

"He doesn't mean you any harm," Enya said quickly. "He's on our side." She made a point not to mention Zoltan's name yet, suspecting that once Samson and Amaury knew that the ruler of the demons had just walked into Scanguards, they wouldn't be willing to listen to her. She needed to buy time to explain the situation to them.

Behind her, Blake closed the door and blocked it from the inside.

Samson glanced back at Blake, then at his son. "A little advance notice would have been nice."

Grayson took the reprimand in stride. "There was no time." He motioned to Enya. "Enya will explain."

Samson glanced at Amaury, who shrugged. "We might as well hear what she's got to say." Then Amaury tipped his chin toward Zoltan. "We can always kill the demon later."

His expression unreadable, Samson told Enya, "Go ahead."

As concisely as possible, Enya laid out the situation, telling their vampire allies that the demon she'd brought was in fact Cinead's kidnapped son, and that he was transforming back into a Stealth Guardian. She divulged Wesley and Charles's involvement, as well as their belief that Zoltan would completely lose his demon powers within the next twenty-four hours, making it paramount for them to mount an attack on the Underworld immediately. For obvious reasons, she left out his name and instead called him Angus, the name Cinead and his wife had given their baby son.

When she finished, Samson ran a hand through his dark hair and Amaury blew out a breath.

"That's one heck of a story," Samson said.

"You believe us, don't you?" Enya said.

"Oddly enough, I do. You can't really make this shit up, can you?" He gave a bitter laugh. "So, this is Angus?" He shook his head. "You do actually resemble your father quite a bit."

Zoltan nodded. "I know." But he didn't say more. Mentioning that he hadn't actually met his father yet would raise too many questions and reveal that the council knew nothing of this situation. "Enya said you could help us destroy the demons."

"What do you need?" Samson asked, all business now.

"Explosives, and a couple of people who know how to handle them," Zoltan said.

Samson looked at Amaury.

"Quinn," Amaury said, then looked at Enya. "Ryder is trained too."

"We need a third person, if you can spare somebody," Enya said. "There are three vortex circles in the Underworld. We'll have to blow them up simultaneously."

"I can handle it," Amaury said.

"You sure?" Samson asked him with a sideways glance.

Amaury rolled his eyes. "Do you have any idea how long it's been since I've done anything fun, like blowing up demons?"

Samson chuckled. "You've got a point. Maybe I should join you."

"Delilah is gonna kill you," Amaury said.

"She doesn't need to know." Samson looked at his son. "Right?"

Grayson lifted his hands. "I'm not gonna tell Mom anything."

"Then it's settled."

Relief washed over Enya. They'd cleared another hurdle.

Zoltan held out his hand, and after a moment of hesitation, Samson shook it. "We'll need a little time to plan things. Do you have a layout of the tunnel system and the vortex circles?"

Zoltan shook his head. "No. But I can draw it from memory."

"We'll have to hurry," Enya interjected. "We have no idea how long Z…Angus can still conjure a vortex to get us down there."

"It won't take long," Samson assured her. "We have everything we need in-house."

32

Zoltan was impressed, to say the least. Seeing the vampires and the Stealth Guardians work together in preparing the destruction of the demons was a thing of beauty.

He and Enya had traveled back to the compound in Baltimore, bringing with them three vampires, Samson, Amaury, and Quinn, and a whole lot of supplies that looked sufficient to blow up a whole continent. Now, everybody was assembled in the command center of the compound, an air-conditioned, windowless room with multiple computers and monitors and an assortment of electronic gadgets. No wonder he'd never been able to destroy the Stealth Guardians: when it came to technology, they were superior to the demons in every way.

Enya was taking charge, assigning each vortex circle to a team comprised of three people: one person with explosives experience, and two others for protection, one of which had to be a Stealth Guardian to render the team invisible.

"You've each got a map showing the location of the three vortex circles. Don't lose it. The three explosions have to be timed exactly." She looked up. "With thirty-second intervals."

"Why thirty seconds?" Grayson asked.

"So we'll be able to hear all three explosions and can be certain that the demons didn't find and defuse them in time. We can't leave any of the vortex circles operational."

Everybody nodded in agreement.

"Quinn, you're with Aiden and Logan. You're taking circle one. Ryder, you'll rig the explosives at circle two. Hamish and Manus will be with you. Samson and Amaury, you two are with me. Pearce and Grayson are staying at the compound."

"You've gotta be kidding me," Grayson said. "Why don't I get to go?"

"Because Ryder has explosives expertise, and somebody has to stay here to protect the compound should we be so unlucky as to have demons on our ass on the way back."

Grayson grunted. "Yeah, like that's gonna happen."

"Grayson," Samson said in a sharp voice.

Grayson snapped his head to his father.

"Shut up!" Samson said. "Enya is right. Ryder has to do this. After Quinn, he has the most experience with explosives. And between Amaury and me, we've got enough expertise to rig a vortex circle too. But you're needed here. There are women and children in this compound. If the demons manage to follow us back via the portal, you need to defend them." He put a hand on his son's shoulder. "Can I count on you, son?"

Grayson straightened. "Of course, Dad."

"Good. Now, Angus, where will the new portal be located in relation to the three vortex circles?"

Zoltan didn't react. He'd been studying the map while Samson reprimanded his son, weighing up the pros and cons between two different locations.

"Angus?"

"Zol—" Grayson stopped himself, swallowing the second syllable before it could come over his lips.

But everybody's eyes were already on him.

"What?" Samson asked, his eyes narrowing.

"Nothing."

But Samson wasn't stupid. Nor was he born yesterday. His heightened senses must have picked up Enya's tiny gasp and the acceleration of her heart rate at hearing Grayson's misstep. Samson's gaze snapped to Zoltan. "Your name isn't Angus, is it?"

Zoltan knew there was no sense in lying. "No, it's not. It was when I was born. But now everybody knows me as Zoltan." He let a second tick by. "Or the Great One."

For a long moment, Samson gave no indication whether this piece of information changed his willingness to help them. Then he looked at Enya.

"You didn't find it necessary to tell me who he really is?"

"Would you have agreed if you knew?" Enya countered.

"You trust him?"

"He's my mate. I trust him with my life."

Samson nodded slowly. "And that of your child, too, I presume."

"Who told you?" Enya's gaze wandered to Grayson.

"For a change, it's not Grayson's fault. He told me nothing. But my hearing is as good as his. I heard the baby's heartbeat when we traveled here in the portal. I had to hold your arm, remember?"

Enya nodded. "The baby is Zoltan's." She reached for Zoltan's hand and squeezed it.

Samson ran a hand through his raven-black hair. "Well, I guess if the Council of Nine approved this undertaking, who am I to contradict them?"

There was a silence that lasted just a second too long.

"Yeah, sure, of course," Manus said. "We should get this show on the road."

But Samson had already caught on. "Are you guys shitting me? You didn't run this by the council?"

Enya gave a one-shouldered shrug. "They would never go for it. It was hard enough to convince my compound mates. So if you want to blame somebody, blame me. But I would do it again. What are you gonna do now?"

Samson sighed and looked at Amaury and Quinn. Both nodded. "We do what we came here to do: destroy the vortex circles. We'll deal with the fallout later." Then he looked straight at Zoltan. "And don't think I'll hesitate to kill you should you betray us."

"I wouldn't expect anything else," Zoltan said. And for some reason, that threat made him respect Samson.

~ ~ ~

Shortly later, everything was ready. Zoltan and Enya stood outside in the alley in front of the invisible compound—a revelation that Zoltan didn't really have time to appreciate—while several of the others stood farther afield.

Enya looked up at him. "The moment of truth."

Zoltan nodded and made a circular movement with his free hand. When he felt the draw of the vortex he was casting, a sigh of relief left his chest. "I've still got it," he murmured to Enya.

She looked over her shoulder. "I'll come and get you as soon as I can. Be ready."

He took her hand. "Time to go." Their eyes met. Trust shone in Enya's blue eyes, even though he could feel her trepidation about returning to the Underworld.

He pulled her close to him and stepped into the swirling mass of the vortex. Enya gripped him tightly, and he understood. The pregnancy caused her to feel dizzy. "Almost there."

She didn't answer, only held on to him.

We're here, he thought, knowing Enya could read his thoughts while inside the vortex. *Showtime.*

Zoltan stepped out of the vortex, Enya still holding on to his arm, but now she was invisible. Which was a good thing, because two demons were standing guard at the vortex circle. Both cast him a stunned look, their mouths dropping open.

"Oh Great One," the shorter of the two managed to say. "We were told you, uh…"

"You were told what?" Zoltan growled, immediately assuming his usual role, so his subjects wouldn't think that anything was amiss.

Shorty didn't answer. His companion, a demon with a full head of blond hair, cleared his throat. "Uhm, what Jeff is saying… uhm, is that after the prisoner escaped, we should assume you were killed."

Zoltan went toe to toe with the man. "Is that right?"

The demon began to tremble. "He said—"

"Who? Who spread lies about my supposed demise, huh?" Zoltan pulled his dagger. "Whoever answers first gets to live."

"Oh Great One." This came from the entrance to one of the tunnels.

Zoltan snapped his head to the approaching demon. It was just his bad luck that Yannick was showing up now. Somehow Zoltan had to distract Yannick so he and Enya could get away. Zoltan couldn't afford Yannick asking any questions. "Yannick? What is going on here?"

Yannick approached and motioned to the two demon guards. "Get back to work. You know what to do." Then he addressed Zoltan. "Oh Great One, we thought you were lost. We found the dog Silvana said was with you when the prisoner escaped. We assumed…" He shook his head. "Vintoq said…"

"Vintoq? Where is he?"

Yannick motioned to one of the corridors. "In your study."

So the traitor had told everybody to assume Zoltan was dead and made himself the Great One? Zoltan made a few steps toward the tunnel heading to his study, but he had no intention of going there. There was no time, as much as he wanted to drive his dagger into the traitor.

"Thank you, Yannick. You may go."

"I'll show you to him," Yannick said, to Zoltan's annoyance. Before Zoltan could protest, Yannick added, "For your protection."

"Lead the way, then," Zoltan said. Damn it, there was no time for this now, but Yannick was in the tunnel already, and Zoltan could feel the eyes of the two demon guards on his back, watching him for as long as they could from their position at the vortex circle.

Yannick's footfalls as well as Zoltan's own disguised Enya's much lighter ones. She pulled on his shoulder, and he felt her warm breath ghost over his neck.

"Yannick, he's the one Tessa identified," she whispered.

Yannick turned. "Did you say something, oh Great One?"

Fuck, Yannick was the traitor. It all made sense now. As the demon in charge of the vortex circles, he kept track of everybody's comings and goings—and had falsified records to make Vintoq look like the traitor. Why hadn't Zoltan seen this before? It was so clear now. Vintoq had been set up to take the fall.

"No. Now go. I want to speak to Vintoq."

But Yannick didn't want to comply. He glanced past Zoltan, inclining his head a fraction, as if giving a sign to somebody, before he said, "I'm afraid your loyal servant can't help you anymore." Yannick pulled his dagger, his grin triumphant. "He had a little accident."

Behind him, Zoltan heard heavy footsteps. The demons guarding the vortex circle were approaching, no doubt following Yannick's unspoken command.

"Lower your weapon," Zoltan said calmly, and pulled his dagger from his pocket.

Yannick didn't comply with his command. He snorted. "You can't give me any orders anymore. I'm the leader now. You were weak. Soft." He spat on the ground. "You showed mercy far too many times. Like a fucking human. No more. You don't deserve to be the Great One. Hell, you don't deserve to be a demon. But you'll be dead soon enough. I'll make sure of that."

"I doubt that very much." After all, Zoltan had an ace or two up his sleeve.

Yannick glanced around. "She's with you, isn't she?"

Zoltan didn't blink.

But Yannick looked undeterred. "Fine, have it your way." He glanced past Zoltan. "Do it!"

Enya let out an audible gasp for everybody to hear.

Zoltan whipped around and saw the two approaching demons. Each held a spray bottle with green liquid in one hand, a dagger in the other.

Knowing he didn't have much time, Zoltan made himself invisible and pivoted. He charged toward the unsuspecting Yannick, who'd probably expected him to attack the two approaching demons first, so Enya wouldn't be sprayed with green demon blood, revealing her position. But Zoltan knew Enya could take care of herself. He slammed into Yannick, who lost his balance and tumbled backward, but held on to his dagger. A split second later, he'd regained his balance and flicked his wrist, releasing the dagger, but without a clear visual, Yannick's aim was off. Zoltan had already jumped to the side and was now crashing down on Yannick, slamming his dagger into the traitor's throat. Gurgling sounds rolled over his lips, together with green blood.

Zoltan made himself visible, wanting the dying Yannick to see him. "You know what the problem is with traitors like you? You talk too much. And act too late. Should have killed me when you had the chance."

But Yannick didn't hear the last words. He was already dead.

Zoltan jumped up and whirled around. One of the demons attacking Enya was dead on the ground, but the other had pinned her to the tunnel wall. Her clothes were stained with demon blood, robbing her of her advantage. Zoltan raced to her, grabbed her attacker from behind, pulled his head back by the hair, and sliced his neck open. More blood spurted onto Enya, but that couldn't be helped now.

"Thanks. That was tight," she said, and took a deep breath. "Sorry I didn't tell you about Yannick earlier. I totally forgot."

"Doesn't matter now. He's dead." He pointed to Yannick's body. "We've gotta stash the bodies quickly, before somebody comes."

"Where?"

"There's a little alcove around the corner that should be big enough for three bodies."

They went to work, carrying each body about fifty yards, where they dumped them behind a large rock outcrop. Then they covered any of the blood spatter with dirt.

"You've gotta get rid of your clothes," Zoltan said, but Enya was already ridding herself of her shirt and pants and tossing them on the heap of dead bodies. Within seconds, she stood in front of him only wearing panties and a camisole, the source dagger strapped to her torso by a holster.

"Can you see any green blood on me now?" she asked, and made a full turn.

"No. And on me?" He also made a turn.

"No."

"Good." He unbuttoned his shirt. "You're taking my shirt."

She didn't protest and put on his shirt, which reached almost to mid-thigh. "Ready."

Invisibly, Zoltan took her hand and led her in the direction they'd chosen for the new portal. "We won't have much time. Once somebody notices that the vortex circle isn't guarded, they'll get suspicious and raise an alarm."

"How far from here?" Enya asked.

"Just a few minutes."

They ran the entire way, encountering nobody, until they reached a small, unused cave the size of a gas station bathroom.

"This is it," Zoltan said.

Enya didn't waste time. She pulled the source dagger from the holster beneath the shirt and set the blade against the rock wall. Zoltan watched in fascination how the dagger, seemingly under its own steam, etched the symbol of a dagger into the rock.

"It's like magic," he said.

She smiled. "Yes, ancient magic."

Moments later, the symbol was complete. Enya took a step back and looked at it.

"That's it?" he asked.

She shook her head, and before he knew what she was about to do, she sliced her palm with the source dagger, then pressed her bleeding hand over the symbol in the wall. Instantly, the spot beneath her palm began to glow, and a few seconds later, a portion of the rock wall was gone. Behind it was a dark cave smaller than the elevator in Zoltan's condo building.

He gasped in awe.

Enya turned to him. "I'll bring the others back. Most likely in two trips. There isn't enough space for all of them and the equipment."

He nodded. "I'll stay here to make sure nobody ambushes you when you and the others come back. But hurry. We don't have much time."

Zoltan pulled her into his arms and kissed her. Then she turned around and stepped into the portal. The opening closed a moment later, and she was gone.

33

Enya concentrated on her destination and arrived in the portal in the Baltimore compound without incident. Nevertheless, her waiting comrades, fully armed and combat-ready, gave her odd looks.

Manus pointed to her clothes. "What happened? Too hot down there and you decided to strip?"

Enya rolled her eyes. "A word of advice: avoid any demons carrying spray bottles with green blood." She handed the source dagger to Pearce. "Keep it safe, will you?"

Pearce nodded. "You bet."

"So, slight change of plans. The portal on the other end isn't big enough for all of us to go in one group with all that." She pointed to the bags with explosives and other electrical equipment. "We'll need to do it in two trips. So, I'll take one group now, then turn around immediately and get the second group. Good?"

All nodded. They knew that Enya had to be the one to guide them to the portal in the Underworld, since she was the only one whose mind was now anchored to it, because she'd been there. Once the other Stealth Guardians had been at the portal in the Underworld, they would have no problem returning to Baltimore on their own.

"Okay, Quinn, Logan, Aiden, Ryder, you're up."

The guys grabbed their bags and squeezed into the portal with her. She willed the door to close. It went pitch-black.

"Everybody holding on to me and each other?"

After everybody confirmed that they were connected, Enya concentrated on her destination and felt the subtle motion of the portal as they were transported. This was less jarring than how she'd felt while in the vortex, and her stomach didn't get a chance to rebel this time.

Arrived at their destination, Enya watched the four men leave the portal, but remained inside. The moment she was alone in the portal, she willed it to close again and was back in Baltimore within seconds.

Hamish, Manus, Samson, and Amaury piled into the portal, carrying more equipment. Grayson and Pearce waved them goodbye. Then darkness surrounded her once more. She felt like a chauffeur, having to shuttle everybody back and forth. Luckily, it was a short trip.

When Enya finally closed the portal at their destination behind her, she looked around.

Ryder said, "Quinn already left with Aiden and Logan. Their vortex circle is the farthest away."

Enya nodded. "Did you synchronize your watch with theirs?"

"Yep. No problem." Ryder lifted his stopwatch. "Set your timers." He gave them exact directions. "Okay, first circle to blow forty-four minutes from…now." Everybody confirmed their timer settings. "Second circle thirty seconds later, and third circle another thirty seconds later."

Enya nodded, "The portal will blow five minutes after the last circle. Make sure you don't miss the bus. There won't be another one."

Ryder, Hamish, and Manus grabbed their equipment and turned to leave, but Enya noticed something. "Where's Zoltan?"

Ryder looked over his shoulder. "He wasn't here when we arrived."

"What?" Panic rose in her. "He has to be here. I left him right here. He was going to watch so that nobody could ambush us."

Ryder shrugged. "Sorry, that's all I know. Gotta go."

"I'm sure he's not far," Manus said, but he didn't sound convinced.

Ryder's group moved out, leaving her alone with Samson and Amaury.

Enya didn't like the way Samson and Amaury now looked at each other.

"He didn't betray us," she snapped. "He would never." She looked around the small cave. No signs of a struggle. No blood.

Samson cleared his throat. "Maybe he had to draw somebody away from the portal." He put his hand on her shoulder. "He'll be back. Right, Amaury?"

Amaury nodded. "We can't wait around here. We've gotta rig that vortex circle. He knows the timeline. He'll show up."

Though she wanted to look for Zoltan, Enya knew her first duty: to destroy the vortex circles. Samson and Amaury needed her to make them invisible so they could reach their destination undetected and set up the explosives. People were counting on her, and the faster she could get this part of her job done, the earlier she could look for Zoltan. Because she wouldn't leave without him.

The vortex circle assigned to Enya's team was the one where Enya and Zoltan had arrived and whose guards they'd killed. When Enya saw from afar that new guards had been assigned to the circle, she turned to Samson and Amaury.

"They discovered that the guards were gone," she whispered. "Zoltan and I stashed their bodies behind some rocks. They might have found them, which means they'll be prepared."

Samson shrugged. "Can't help that. And it doesn't change the plan."

Amaury nodded and pulled his dagger from its sheath. "Yep, still the same plan." He looked at his stopwatch. "Gotta hurry."

Enya nodded and pulled her dagger too. "Do it cleanly." Then she motioned to the two vampires to follow her. They kept their footfalls light and approached in total silence. Only Enya could see them, Samson carrying the equipment,

Amaury ready to strike. Enya motioned to the guard standing near the first tunnel entrance to the left, then pointed to Amaury, while she approached the guard who stood at the fourth tunnel entrance, which was located directly opposite the first one. When she reached him, she cast a glance over her shoulder, and saw Amaury in position, looking back at her.

She mouthed, *One, two,* then whirled to the guard and stabbed her dagger into his heart, making sure to immediately sidestep him, so none of his blood stained the shirt Zoltan had lent her. The demon collapsed with a soft gurgling sound, and she heard a similar sound from behind her, attesting to the fact that Amaury had killed the other guard.

Enya rolled the guard over so she could retrieve her dagger. She wiped it clean before she slid it back into its sheath. Then she turned to look at Amaury. He was doing the same.

She walked over to him. "Let's hide the bodies," she said in a low voice, then added to Samson, "We'll only be gone about fifty yards, but I might not be able to keep you invisible while I'm that far away."

"Don't worry, my hearing is excellent. I'll hear anybody approach before they can possibly see me. Now go." He was already opening his bag of supplies and pulling out a hand-crank drill to make holes in a strategic rock that would cause the magma chamber below it to open up and fill the vortex circle with lava.

Together, Amaury and Enya carried the first body to the same spot where Zoltan and Enya had deposited the other three demons. When she reached the spot, only two of the demons were still there. One was gone: Yannick.

"Shit!" Enya cursed. "Yannick is gone. He was the traitor who worked against Zoltan."

"You think he wasn't dead?"

She shook her head. "Oh, he was dead. Zoltan and I made sure of it. I think somebody took his body."

"Why?"

"Because somebody cared about him." It was clear all of the sudden. "He had a partner. Yannick wasn't the only traitor."

"Well, soon it won't matter whether he had help or not." Amaury pointed his thumb over his shoulder to where Samson was working. "Let's get the second body."

They did just that. By the time they were done, Samson had made good progress, and Enya made sure that all three of them were invisible again. Amaury helped Samson place the explosives for maximum impact, then they attached the fuses and the timer. Samson was just setting the timer when both vampires froze. A second later, Enya could hear it too: dogs. The Underworld was on full alert.

A few more seconds, and Samson rose. Then he and Amaury grabbed several rocks the size of footballs and basketballs and piled them around the explosives, hiding them as well as the timer without crushing the latter.

"Done," Samson announced.

"Let's go," Enya said, and together they traced their way back to where they'd come from.

The direction they were heading was almost devoid of demons. Zoltan had chosen the space for the Stealth Guardian portal well. It was off the beaten track, yet close enough to the three vortex circles to reach within a reasonable time.

When Enya, Samson, and Amaury reached the portal, Quinn was already back with his team, Logan and Aiden, and was busy rigging the portal itself. For obvious reasons, it had to be destroyed. They couldn't leave a functional portal in the Underworld, potentially giving the demons a way out of their fiery grave.

"Almost done," Quinn said without looking at them.

"Good," Enya said, then told Aiden, "I have to find Zoltan."

Both he and Logan shook their head. "There's no time," Aiden said. "The first vortex circle will blow in"—he looked at his stopwatch—"thirteen minutes."

"That gives me nineteen minutes to find him and transport back."

"That's suicide," Aiden said, "and you know it." He sighed and ran his hand through his hair. "I admit I don't know Zoltan well, but I know one thing: he wouldn't want you and the baby to perish. He would want you to save yourself."

She knew that. But it didn't mean she had to agree with it. "Well, he'll just have to suck it up, won't he? Because I'm gonna find him and bring his ass back."

"That's if he wants to be found," Logan said.

Enya glared at him. "You're wrong. I need to find him. Save him."

"Save him? From what? From himself?" Logan asked.

"Zoltan and I killed Yannick, the traitor. But his body is gone, even though I know he was dead. Which leaves only one conclusion: he had a partner. And that person is now hunting down Zoltan. Probably already has him in his claws. I have to help him. He would do the same for me."

Just then, Manus stepped into the cave, followed by Ryder and Hamish. For a split second she hoped that Zoltan would be right behind them, but he wasn't.

"Our circle is rigged," Manus announced.

"I'm done here, too," Quinn added.

"Then let's get the hell out of here," Manus said, and laid his hand on the portal's symbol, opening it.

"Thanks all of you," Enya said, and turned away, but she felt a hand on her shoulder, making her turn her head.

Aiden looked at her. "Let me help, at least."

She shook her head, her heart filling with gratitude. "I can't let you do that. You have to get back to your family." Then she cast a look over the rest of the group, all of whom were looking at her. "With a bit of luck, you'll see me soon."

Before anybody else could protest, she walked out into the tunnel and made herself invisible. One glance at her stopwatch and she took off running.

Eighteen minutes until the portal home would blow.

Eighteen minutes to find out what fate was in store for her.

Eighteen minutes to find Zoltan.

34

Zoltan had made a mistake. He'd heard voices and dogs in the tunnel and wanted to ascertain that the demons they belonged to weren't entering the small cave where the Stealth Guardian portal was located. He'd stepped into the tunnel, but hadn't concentrated hard enough to make himself invisible—after all, it was still new to him—and promptly been spotted by Tamara and two male demons she had in tow, and the dog they'd brought. There was no going back, or Zoltan would have risked them following him and running straight into the arms of the arriving Stealth Guardians and vampires.

He'd had to draw them away from the portal, or the dog would sniff out the invaders. In theory, it should have worked.

Zoltan was still the Great One, and all demons followed his orders. When he ordered the three demons to head toward his study under the pretense that he needed to show Tamara something he'd discovered, they walked with him, the two men behind him, the woman in front. But they never made it as far as his study.

After walking for five minutes, turning several times until they reached the throne room, which they needed to traverse, the two demons behind him kicked him in the back of his knees, making him stumble and fall forward. He managed to brace his fall and whirl around, pulling his dagger from its sheath as he jumped up.

"The fuck!" he said, and jumped toward the two demons, who clearly were in Yannick's camp and didn't know yet that their leader had been killed. "Tamara, help me kill these bastards." He was already exchanging blows and kicks with the two assailants. He managed to drive one of them back, cutting into the demon's arm, making him lose his dagger. The dog, no doubt smelling the blood, jumped onto the injured man.

"Tamara, damn it, a little help here!" he thundered, and chanced a look over his shoulder.

Tamara stood there, her dagger in her hand and a sneer on her face. "And why would I? You killed Yannick."

Continuing to fight against the other demon, Zoltan gave denial a shot. "What? Yannick is dead? What happened?"

But Tamara didn't fall for it. "As if you didn't know. You fucking bastard!"

It was clear: she was part of the conspiracy.

Zoltan kicked his opponent, slammed him against the rock wall, then dove after him to ram the dagger into his heart. But there was no time to celebrate this victory, because the injured demon had managed to recover his dagger, and stabbed the dog, killing the poor animal. He jumped up and wielded the blade in his good hand. However, he wasn't quite as coordinated with the left. Tamara seemed to see it too, because she charged toward them.

Zoltan lunged sideways to get out of her path. "Fucking uppity bitch!"

She whirled around, snarling at him. "Yeah, well, that's for dumping me after using me." She motioned to the other demon to attack from the opposite side, then barreled toward him again.

Zoltan pivoted, managed to grab the attacking male demon, and used him to block Tamara. Her blade drove into the demon's chest, killing him instantly.

Tamara growled, utterly pissed off now. As she shoved the dead demon out of her way so he wouldn't take her down with him, she snapped, "And just so you know: you're not that great in bed!"

Zoltan let the insult roll off his back like water off Teflon. She wouldn't be able to distract him. "Wish I'd never fucked you. That's ten minutes of my life I'll never get back."

They circled each other like prize fighters. It was one against one. Yet it wasn't an even fight. Zoltan was bigger, stronger, tougher. However, he had to hand it to her: Tamara didn't give up, showing neither fear nor respect for her ruler.

"I enjoyed killing Yannick," Zoltan admitted, knowing it would rile her up. "I admit I didn't suspect him, nor you. I thought Vintoq was the traitor. All clues led to him. Kudos. You had me fooled. But all good things come to an end, don't they?"

Tamara glared at him. "Yeah, like your life."

"Then let's get this over with," Zoltan said, waving her closer.

She pounced, but he'd anticipated her move—he'd seen her in battle training often enough and knew her preferred moves—and sidestepped her, then spun around to get behind her. It would only take one quick swipe with his dagger, and her throat would be slit, but he never got to execute the move.

Searing pain shot through him and spasms followed, crippling him. It wasn't Tamara, nor was it another demon surprising him. "Not now," he said through a clenched jaw, but there was no use. This was the second wave, the one Wesley and Charles had predicted would happen within twenty-four hours, of Zoltan's turning back into a Stealth Guardian. And it was more debilitating than the first.

He stumbled and fell backward, barely able to see. But what he saw was sufficient to make him realize that he wouldn't survive this event: Tamara was staring at him, first stunned, then grinning in that conniving way he'd always hated about her.

She laughed, and the sound echoed in his ears as if she was in a different cave.

As he landed with his back on the ground, Tamara towered over him, her eyes roaming his body. Something she saw seemed to surprise her. She shook her head and jumped onto him, landing on his chest, causing air to rush from his lungs. With her dagger she scratched his neck with a curiosity usually reserved for kids dissecting their first frog in biology class. "You're bleeding red! You're not even a demon. You're one of them."

He tried to lift his arms, but felt paralyzed, unable to move, to even lift a finger or turn his head. Pain clawed at him, wrung him out and spat him out. He'd never felt so helpless.

Tamara realized it too. She threw back her head, laughing like a cartoon villain. "Killing you will be the sweetest feeling." She pressed her dagger to his throat, ready to drive it through his flesh. "I'm gonna take it slow, so you'll savor your own death."

Tamara was suddenly pulled back, her body lifting off him.

"Over my dead body!" It was Enya. Her voice. Or was he hallucinating already?

"Bitch!"

No, definitely Enya. She was here, saving him.

Relief and the knowledge that he would survive flooded him. With it, the pain dissipated, and movement was reanimating his limbs.

He heard a body slump to the ground and saw Enya's face appear in his field of vision. She crouched down next to him. "She's dead." She gripped his arm. "Can you move?"

"Yes." With Enya's help, Zoltan rose. By the time he was standing on his own two feet again, his strength had returned. Yet he felt different. He touched the spot where Tamara had broken his skin and felt the blood there. He looked at his fingers. "She told the truth. It's red. I'm bleeding red blood."

Enya nodded. "And you have a Stealth Guardian's aura. But we've gotta get outta here now." She looked at her stopwatch. "Shit."

An explosion rocked the Underworld, nearly swallowing Enya's last word.

"The first circle," Zoltan said, and took Enya's hand. "We've got six minutes."

They hurried out of the hall and into the next tunnel. He didn't know how he knew, but he was certain that he and Enya were invisible, which could only mean that Enya was making them both invisible so they could escape.

"What happened?" she asked.

"Bad luck. I collapsed just when I had the upper hand. If you hadn't come in time, I would be dead." Knowing how little time they had left to make it back to the portal, he added, "You shouldn't have risked looking for me."

A second explosion echoed through the tunnels, making the ground beneath their feet vibrate.

Enya shot him a glance. "If you think you can shirk your duties as a father, think again. I'm not gonna let you off the hook that easily."

"That's what I love about you: you speak your mind." He grinned. "And there's no way I'll be an absent father. I'm afraid you'll have to deal with me, whether you're getting sick of me or not."

Another boom, indicating the explosion of the third vortex circle, blasted through the tunnel. This time, Zoltan felt the shock wave physically, as it sent a strong gust of air through the tunnel system.

"Five minutes," Enya said.

"We'll make it," Zoltan said, his words more a wish than certainty.

They ran faster, Zoltan choosing the shortest way to the portal, which was equidistant from circle two and three and a little farther from circle one, which had been the first to blow. As they ran, they encountered panicked demons, all running in different directions, some charging toward danger without knowing it. Every time Enya and Zoltan had to squeeze close to the tunnel walls so as not to collide with them. Yet there was no need to remain quiet—demons were shouting and screaming in the confusion, nobody realizing that they were already doomed. Even the dogs seemed perplexed at the goings-on, whining and barking nervously. Nobody was paying them any attention.

For a moment, Zoltan thought of the animals' lot. They were innocent, yet they would pay the same price as their demon masters. He wished he could free them and bring them to the human world, but it was impossible.

"How much farther?" Enya asked. "I'm all turned around."

"Just a minute more. We're almost there."

He caught her looking at her stopwatch, a ray of hope illuminating her face. Yes, they would make it.

At the next intersection, Zoltan turned right—and came to a rocking halt. He spread his arms wide so Enya couldn't race past him.

"What?"

But he didn't have to tell her what had made him stop, because she saw it too now.

"Oh God!"

But God had nothing to do with what lay before them: a river of lava, cutting them off from the tunnel that led directly to the portal. The portal that was only two hundred yards from their position—so close, yet so far.

"It's too wide to jump over it," Zoltan said, looking at Enya, whose eyes were wide. For the first time, he saw real fear in them.

"This is it," she murmured, and slung her arms around him.

He put his hands on her shoulders. "No, it's not. There's another way." There had to be. "We have to reach the tunnel that connects to the portal from the other side."

"But how? How are we gonna reach it? We can't just pass through who knows how many yards of stone wall."

Zoltan blinked. "No, not through here. But parallel to this tunnel, there's an older one. Its entrance collapsed years ago. But the exit on the other side is open." He took her hand in his and pulled her back in the direction they'd come from. "This way."

He let his eyes roam over the tunnel walls, looking for the spot where, years earlier, a parallel tunnel had caved in after an earthquake. The demons had never bothered excavating it, since they'd had another path to reach the caves that lay behind it.

Finally, he saw the formation of rocks that indicated the collapsed tunnel. He pointed to it. "Here." They stopped in front of it.

"How thick is the rock here?" Enya asked.

"Three to four yards max."

She nodded. "You're fully Stealth Guardian now." Her voice trembled, telling him that she knew the risk he was taking, not having tried going through walls before. "You can do it. Just think it, and it will happen."

He nodded. If something went wrong, and he didn't make it through the wall and into the tunnel behind, at least Enya would make it. "The tunnel is maybe a hundred and fifty yards long. At the end of it, turn right and you'll see the entrance to the cave with the portal. If I don't make it through, don't wait for me. Just leave."

She shook her head. "Not gonna happen." She clutched his hand. "Let's go."

Together they walked into the wall, and to Zoltan's relief, he didn't feel any resistance. He didn't bounce back, didn't hit his head. He felt nothing pushing against him. A moment later, they were through. The tunnel before them was clear of any obstruction, clear of any lava.

Still holding hands, they sprinted toward the end of the tunnel, turned right, then ran into the small cave ahead of them. Enya slammed her hand onto the portal's symbol, and a second later, it opened.

They jumped inside. Zoltan glanced over his shoulder and noticed the floor at the entrance to the cave giving way, falling into the ever-expanding stream of lava. Then everything went black. The door to the portal had closed.

He put both arms around Enya, then felt a faint vibration—the bomb to blow up the portal was exploding.

But they were already teleporting. Zoltan felt Enya let out a sigh of relief.

"You did it," Enya said.

"*We* did it." He kissed her.

Moments later, he released Enya from his embrace.

The portal opened, and she stepped out ahead of him. Zoltan heard her gasp before he saw why. Two men and a woman Zoltan had never seen before were part of their welcoming committee comprising vampires and Stealth Guardians. Nevertheless, he recognized one of the newcomers immediately. Their gazes locked on to each other. The man visibly shook before his knees buckled.

35

Cinead didn't collapse. Virginia was by his side, steadying him just in time, and he seemed to regain his strength quickly.

"I should have the whole lot of you locked up in a lead cell," Barclay thundered. He glared at the entire contingent of the Baltimore compound, then pointed to the vampires. "And to drag our allies into this behind the council's back... despicable! You'll all have to answer for this."

That one of the men he was accusing was his own son, Aiden, didn't seem to matter much to primus, the head of the Council of Nine. Clearly, Aiden knew it, because he kept his mouth shut.

"So I guess somebody blabbed," Enya said, tipping her chin up. She wasn't afraid of anything right now. She'd just escaped certain death. Whatever Barclay and the council could do to her now was a slap on the wrist in comparison.

Barclay narrowed his eyes—by the looks of it, ready to douse her in a barrage of insults—but Virginia put a hand on his shoulder.

"Allow me." As a member of the council, she had the same voting rights as Barclay and Cinead. "Yes, somebody blabbed, as you call it." She motioned to Samson and Amaury. "As you know, Blake is good friends with Wes. He couldn't wait to tell him what you all were planning. In fact, he sounded a bit jealous that you didn't need him to join you. And since you, Enya, had asked Wes and Charles about a miracle cure for a demon named Zoltan, well, it wasn't hard for him to put two and two together. So, when he got home and I asked him about his day, he told me about your idiotic plan, even saying he was surprised the council authorized it."

Barclay huffed. "Yes, imagine our surprise, since we never got to vote on this."

"I take full responsibility," Enya said. "I talked the others into it. It's not their fault. I made them do it."

Before Barclay could respond, Zoltan stepped forward. "It was my idea. Therefore, I take the blame. Do with me what you want. But spare Enya and the others. They did what they thought was right."

Barclay looked at Cinead.

For the first time, Cinead spoke up. "And was it right?"

Zoltan turned his head to look at him. He nodded. "It was. We defeated them. All three vortex circles flooded with lava. They're destroyed. And the portal we carved and which brought us back was rigged to explode behind us. I heard the explosion. The demons are imprisoned in the Underworld. There's no way out for them. And no way for the demons currently topside to return. They'll be easy pickings. We'll chase them down and kill them, until none is left."

"We?" Cinead asked, and looked Zoltan up and down, scrutinizing him as if seeing him for the first time. "So you have no regrets having destroyed your own kingdom? It is your kingdom, Zoltan, isn't it?"

Zoltan nodded. "Yes, and I had no choice but to destroy the Underworld. I did it for Enya and our unborn child."

Gasps came from the three council members, and Enya instinctively took Zoltan's hand. They were in this together, and whatever punishment they would receive, she would take her share to lighten his.

"Is that true?" Barclay asked, looking at Enya.

"Yes, Primus, I carry Zoltan's child." She turned to Cinead. "Your grandchild. You must have guessed it already. I saw the way you stared at Zoltan when we arrived. You saw yourself in him, didn't you? You already know that he's your son. He's Angus."

Cinead's lips quivered, and it took a few seconds before he had the strength to speak. "I didn't dare hope." He looked at Zoltan. "Not after Winter told me that he was a demon. In my mind, I buried him then." He shook his head. "I buried you because I saw no hope. No way of redemption for you." He lifted his hands as if wanting to reach for Zoltan. "Yet you stand before me, the aura of a Stealth Guardian surrounding you. And I don't understand how it happened. How you were able to cast out the demon."

Zoltan leaned toward Enya and put his hand on her flat belly. "My child saved me. My child's virta gave me back my real self."

Enya smiled at him. "He has all his Stealth Guardian powers back, and his blood is red now. There's no demon left in him."

Cinead nodded to Barclay and Virginia. "A word."

While the three stepped aside to talk quietly to each other, Enya's brethren came closer.

"We thought we'd lost you," Hamish said, and pulled her into a quick embrace. Then he looked to Zoltan and squeezed his shoulder. "Both of you."

"Yeah, what happened down there?" Aiden asked.

"Enya saved my life," Zoltan said. "I got cornered by the traitor's partner, Tamara. She attacked me just as I went into another convulsion."

When the others stared at him, confused, Enya explained, "Zoltan turning back into a Stealth Guardian came with spasms so bad that I thought he was dying. The second wave hit him down in the Underworld, gave him all his powers, but practically incapacitated him while it happened."

Zoltan took her hand and squeezed it. "You came just in time."

Behind them, Quinn piped up, "And the vortex circles and our portal? You sure they all blew up and were destroyed?"

Zoltan chuckled. "Yeah, about that. Do you think you were overdoing it a little on the explosives?"

Quinn shrugged. "Maybe I added a little extra just to make sure."

"Yeah, you did," Zoltan replied.

Enya smiled. "In fact, the explosions were so powerful that the tunnels started flooding with lava. Cut off our route to the portal."

Hamish gasped. "Then how did you make it out?"

"There are advantages to having grown up in the Underworld," Zoltan said. "I knew every corner down there, and I knew of a tunnel entrance that had collapsed years ago, but I knew the tunnel behind it was still intact and led to the portal…"

"And with Zoltan's powers intact, we just passed through the stone wall and got out on the other side. We reached the portal with only seconds to spare."

Manus and Logan shook their heads.

"Gotta hand it to you," Manus said, and looked at Enya, "when you want something bad enough, you do whatever it takes."

"Don't we all?" Logan asked.

Everybody laughed. Then Enya looked at the vampires. "Samson, Amaury, Quinn, Ryder, I don't know how to thank you guys. You risked so much for me, for us."

"That's what friends do," Samson said.

"Thank you," Zoltan said. "One day, I hope to be able to repay you for what you did."

Samson shook his head. "Friends don't have to repay friends. We're just glad we could help." He motioned to where the three council members were talking quietly. "But I'm not the boss here."

Moments later, Barclay, Cinead, and Virginia rejoined them.

"For today, I suggest you all get cleaned up and get some rest," Barclay said. "But this isn't over. That goes for all of you. Do we understand each other?"

All members of the Baltimore compound nodded.

"Good," Barclay said. "Well, I guess that concludes the official portion of our visit." His expression relaxed, and a grin spread on his face. "You guys did it, you really did it! I don't know what to say."

"How about congratulations?" Virginia suggested.

Cinead nodded. "Well done, all of you." Then he took a few steps closer until he stood in front of Zoltan. "Well done, my son." His eyes were filled with myriad emotions. "I don't know whether I'll ever get used to your name, but maybe you'll allow an old man to call you by the name he gave you when you were but a wee bairn."

Enya noticed Zoltan swallow hard. "Nothing would give me greater joy…" He hesitated for a second. "Father."

36

There was an inquiry before the Council of Nine, but in the end, Zoltan destroying the Underworld for good and risking his life doing so outweighed all bad deeds he'd committed as a demon. The members of the Baltimore compound were scolded for acting on their own and without the council's approval, yet no punishment was levied on any of them. The vampires who'd been crucial in the destruction of the Underworld returned home after a talk behind closed doors. Their alliance remained intact and was stronger than ever. For once, things had worked out for everybody.

Another thing had also come to light: the reason why Enya had gotten pregnant even though she wasn't bonded and therefore considered infertile. In the council's archives, Cinead had found old scriptures warning Stealth Guardians never to copulate with demons. According to the writings, a demon's semen initiated the same chemical response in a Stealth Guardian as a bonding: the Stealth Guardian became fertile instantly. Enya conceiving had been inevitable.

Zoltan opened the door to Enya's private quarters and entered. He wasn't used to simply walking through it yet. It would take a while until he'd be comfortable with all the changes his body had gone through in the last few days. At the same time, he finally felt whole. There were no more migraine attacks, no more lingering doubts. He was a Stealth Guardian, and virta was coursing through his veins now, making him yearn for his mate more than ever before.

"You're back." Enya rose from the sofa, stifling a yawn. She wore nothing but a pink see-through negligée. "How is Cinead?"

He approached, never taking his eyes off her lovely form. "He's happy, I think. Though when he showed me a portrait of my mother, I noticed tears in his eyes. I didn't call him on it. Didn't want to embarrass him. I still don't really know him." He shrugged. "I put my hand on his shoulder, and I think he appreciated the gesture."

Enya smiled. "Over time, you'll get to know him better. He's a good man."

"I can feel it when I look at him. I hope I can live up to his expectations." Zoltan sighed. "I was evil for so long. I hope I can be good for even longer."

Enya reached for his hands and pulled him to her. "I'll make sure of it. You'll never have to worry about slipping back into evil. I'll always have your back."

Zoltan put his arms around her and lifted her up, bringing her head level with his. "I'm counting on it." He walked toward the bed. "Are you very tired?"

She chuckled. "Never too tired for that."

"Am I that transparent?"

"I can feel your hard-on. It's a dead giveaway."

"Can't blame a man for reacting like that when his wife greets him dressed in nothing but a flimsy negligée that leaves nothing to the imagination."

"Would you rather I greet you dressed in battle uniform?"

"I'm not complaining, just explaining." He gently laid her on the bed, then began to undress, until he stood in front of her without a stitch.

He noticed Enya run her eyes over his naked body and lick her lips.

Zoltan grinned. "I'm glad you're not a woman who plays coy. With you I always know where I stand."

"Playing coy is for amateurs."

Without another word, he lowered himself over her, pushing her legs apart in the process to make space for himself. With one hand he shoved her negligée up to her waist, while he balanced his weight on the other.

Enya put her hands on his hips, drawing him closer, until his cock nudged at the entrance to her body.

"Hmm," she said. "I've been thinking of this all day."

"Of this?" He plunged deep and hard into her.

"Yesssss!"

"That makes two." Whenever he was away from her, even if it was only for a few hours, he longed for her. Longed for this special connection, for the way they shared their life force, their souls with each other.

Sex had taken on another dimension. It was more intense, gave him more satisfaction, more joy, and more happiness. Being with Enya was fulfillment he could have never dreamed of. Every touch was magic, every movement part of a sensual dance that they only danced with each other. A dance that was theirs, and theirs alone. They had no secrets from each other any longer. Because they were one.

Overwhelmed by his love for Enya, Zoltan called to his virta and allowed it to pour into her, to fill her body, her every cell, until her skin shimmered golden, and waves of orgasm after orgasm shook her body.

"I love you," she murmured between moans. "Zoltan, you're mine, all mine."

"I'll always be yours. Your master and your subject. You're my queen and my slave, my mistress, the only woman who'll ever rule my heart."

And nothing would ever change that.

37

Seven months later

Zoltan rushed into the mini medical center at the Baltimore compound just in time to see Leila press a tiny bundle into Enya's arms.

"It's a boy," Leila announced, and looked over her shoulder. She smiled. "What took you so long?"

"Killing a few stragglers," Zoltan said, and rushed toward the hospital bed Enya was in. Over the last few months, he and the other Stealth Guardians at the compound had made sure the demons who'd been topside when the vortex circles were destroyed were taken care of. His dagger was stained with their green blood, and soon the day would come when every last one of them was dead.

"My son was early, huh?" he said with pride as he reached the bed.

Enya's long hair was sweat-dampened, her face glistening, yet she wore a smile. "He's got brown eyes."

She met his gaze, and Zoltan kissed her. "I'm sorry I wasn't here, babe. I'm sorry you had to do this alone."

She chuckled. "I'm glad you missed this. It was kind of messy, and Leila handled it much better than you would have." She looked to where Leila was drying her hands. "Thanks, Leila, for everything."

"I'll leave you guys alone."

A moment later, Zoltan heard the double doors close behind her, but he was already looking at his son. His healthy baby boy. He exhibited the aura of a Stealth Guardian, and already had a full head of dark hair.

"We'll name him Angus, if you're all right with that," Zoltan said.

"Your father will like that."

Zoltan brushed his knuckle over the baby's rosy cheek. "He's perfect."

"He looks like you."

"Maybe the next one will be a girl and look like you."

The baby suddenly gripped his finger and pulled it to its mouth, trying to suckle on it.

"Looks like he's hungry," Enya said. She tucked on her gown to free one breast, but the baby turned impatient and started crying.

"Hey, Angus," Zoltan cooed, "you'll get fed in a second." He reached for him so Enya could open her gown in the front. But the baby kept crying. Zoltan stared at his son. "Oh my God."

"What? What's wrong?" Enya asked, alarm creeping into her voice as she reached for the baby. Then she saw it too. "His aura. It's…"

"Gone." And one other thing had changed when the baby had started crying. "His eyes. They've turned demon-green."

Enya met his gaze. "He's still our son." She pulled Angus into her arms and led her nipple to the baby's mouth. Immediately, Angus's cries subsided and he began to suckle.

Before Zoltan's eyes, the baby's Stealth Guardian aura returned, and when his son opened his eyes again as he suckled contentedly, they'd changed back to brown. All signs of the demon were gone.

"What is happening?" Enya asked.

"He was conceived when I was still a demon. I think he inherited that part of me." He bent to Enya and kissed her softly. "I think he was angry because he was hungry. And now, look—he's a perfect Stealth Guardian baby again."

"Zoltan," Enya murmured. "Will he be in danger because he's part demon?"

He shook his head. "Every person has a little bit of demon inside him or her. We'll teach him to control it, just like we all control that side of ourselves. He will learn to listen only to the good inside him."

"You sound so sure."

Zoltan smiled. "That's because he's inherited something that's stronger than evil: he's inherited your goodness. You believed in me when nobody did. You trusted me when I didn't trust myself. You've made me good. And you've given this goodness to our son. Good will trump evil. I believe in that."

"Good will trump evil," Enya repeated, and pulled his head to her to kiss him.

"I love you," he murmured against her lips, before he captured them and showed her how much.

ABOUT THE AUTHOR

Tina Folsom was born in Germany and has been living in English speaking countries for over 25 years, since 2001 in California, where she's married to an American.

Tina has always been a bit of a globe trotter: after living in Lausanne, Switzerland, she briefly worked on a cruise ship in the Mediterranean, then lived in Munich, before moving to London. After 8 years she decided to move overseas.

In New York she studied drama at the American Academy of Dramatic Arts, then moved to Los Angeles a year later to pursue studies in screenwriting. In 2008 she wrote her first romance and never looked back.

She now has over 43 novels in English and dozens in other languages (Spanish, German, and French) and continues to write, as well as have her existing novels translated.

For more about Tina Folsom:

www.tinawritesromance.com
http://www.facebook.com/TinaFolsomFans
Instagram: @authortinafolsom
Email: tina@tinawritesromance.com

Printed in Great Britain
by Amazon